CELTIC CIRCLE

for Better, for Worse

a novel by

Sherry Schubert

Published by Sunway Press
P.O. Box 5825
Twin Falls, Idaho 83303-5825
mcallistersh@yahoo.com

This novel is a work of fiction. Any references to real people, events, establishments, organizations, or locales are intended only to give the fiction a sense of reality and authenticity, and are used fictitiously. All other names, characters, places and incidents portrayed in this work are the product of the author's imagination. Any resemblance to actual persons, living or dead, places or events is entirely coincidental.

Cover design by Sherry Schubert McAllister

ISBN 978-0-9829563-6-6   (pbk)
ISBN 978-0-9829563-7-3   (ebook)

Dedicated
to

Aunt Aggie

whose house on Quincy Street
was a true sanctuary

I wish to acknowledge the many supporters
who continue to encourage me.

Books by Sherry Schubert
Puffin Island
Celtic Compass, Part I
Celtic Compass, Part II
Celtic Circle~for Better, for Worse

Celtic Circle

for Better, for Worse

...to have and to hold from this day forward;
to love and to cherish,
for better or for worse...

What is the life span of unconditional commitment?

Chapter 1

Kirin Koyle O'Connell gazed up through the branches of her evergreen tree, Aurora. From her vantage point on the ground beneath it, she marveled at how firmly it had taken root in the last three years just as her marriage to Michael had. She counted numerous fresh branches, more than the previous year, promising new and exciting choices for them on this, their third anniversary. Since surviving near death in the Yemeni desert and the hasty secret wedding vows they exchanged, this early October date when they planted the Douglas fir in the back garden of their modest Dublin home was the one they agreed to celebrate for the life of their marriage.

No one in the family knew exactly when the young couple first made their vows. The others accepted the December day shared with their parents in a very unusual public ceremony. That allowed Kiri and Michael to spend their true anniversary alone together, exchanging pledges—symbolic gestures—promises for the year ahead. Until today. Her mother, Paula, scheduled one of her grandchildren outings for this Saturday and needed their help. With another overseas assignment looming on the horizon for BBC reporter Michael, the couple had no choice but to accept and make the most of the beginning and end of their day on the ground beneath their symbolic Christmas tree, Aurora.

Stiff from her night on the hard earth, Kiri wondered how many more years Michael would insist on the twenty-four-hour ritual. She loved her giant bed with the quilt of wildflowers and wished she could awaken there instead, but resigned to the day, she pulled their sleeping bag tight around her ears against the chill morning and closed her eyes for just a few more minutes. Those minutes did not last long enough. She cracked an eyelid and noticed Michael staring at her while tickling her nose with a black feather he unearthed from the duff beneath the tree.

She straightened her legs, curled up her toes and opened into a long cat-stretch. "Happy anniversary, oh husband of mine," she mocked with an affectionate smile.

His seriousness prevented his returning it. " 'Tis time, Kiri."

"Not today? I thought you had a couple more weeks before the mission."

"No, not that. 'Tis time… for us to start our family."

Kiri allowed his blunt assertion to settle on the air before she replied. "But…"

"No more buts. We've waited three years. If we're not recovered by now, we never will be. We're healthy. We're strong. Our financial house is in order. We rarely have nightmares anymore. 'Tis time for the next step, so I'm going to have my say. Then 'twill be your turn."

Kiri hid her smile now, awaiting Michael's launch into an appeal he had repeated many times. Over their three years as husband and wife—and prospective parents—two main points of contention dogged them: Michael's job and family planning. They agreed to disagree to maintain a provisional peace, so whenever one of them broached the forbidden, the other received equal time.

"I know you're frightened every time I leave on an extraction assignment. I appreciate that you don't like to worry at home alone. I felt the same when you left me behind for your water certifications and psychotherapy fieldwork. I hated wondering what you were doing. I get that you were a reluctant participant in the missions we served together last summer, but we do make a good team. I understand that you don't want to work for the agency anymore; you only do it to remain privy to information about my assignments. I accept that you don't want our children to be farmed out while they're growing up but that you do want to start your own aquatics business. We've taken steps toward resolving that one by finishing plans and acquiring permits for building a pool next door. Now 'tis time for this robust pair of thirty-four-year-olds to rethink our positions again. Questions?"

Michael took a deep breath and sat back for the onslaught. Kiri usually challenged every claim, so today he steeled himself to defend them. He registered surprise when she voiced only one. "If something should happen to me, will you forego your own aspirations to raise our children as you believe I… both of us… want them raised?"

With no hesitation, he blurted out, "Absolutely!" and removed his anniversary pledge from its hanger on a lower branch of the tree. "And here is proof."

Kiri accepted the proffered promise and, still masking her smile, opened and read it. *I promise to refuse all extraction missions after completing this next one, to limit reporting and networking assignments abroad to 3 – 4 days at a time, to focus on training new recruits… and to take at least half of the 2 a.m. feedings.*

Her expression changed immediately to one of disbelief. "Do you really mean this? You're cutting back on the part of your job you love the most?"

"Absolutely. One of us had to make the first move. I decided 'twas up to me to do it. My request for change of assignment is ready to submit as soon as I return. After this one, the network will owe me big time. What do you think?" His deep-set blue eyes twinkled. "Can we try to break this stalemate? I really want us to start our family soon."

"Your promise is very generous—especially the offer to help. I'll think about it." Again she pressed back her smile. "Your turn." She handed him her pledge.

He opened it with a similar look of disbelief. *I promise to make your dream a reality.* "Does this mean what I think it does? That you're ready to start our family too?"

The broad smile beneath her wide cheekbones revealed her answer.

"You little scamp! You planned for this all along, and you let me flounder through begging and pleading. Maybe I don't want such a trickster for the mother of my children after all," he joshed, pulling her down further into their sleeping bag.

"Too late now. I've given my pledge, and you're bound to accept it. Those are the rules."

Michael rolled the two of them over and over on the dewy lawn under the tree until dampness seeped through. He expressed his joy at finally convincing Kiri to trust in their future together with a passionate, hearty Irish thank you. His hand slipped down to her tummy.

"What are you doing?"

"I'm looking for that dratted patch you wear on your belly to remind me that you're the one in control of your reproductive future. I want to rip it off with my teeth and burn it with our pledges. Never again!" He dove deeper into the bag and poked his head back out with a huge grin of success. "You have made me the happiest man in Ireland today! Let's burn our promises right now to seal the deal." He reached out toward the tree for a lighter. The two held their pledges and watched the edges char and curl, smoke circling upward carrying their dream through the branches of Aurora. Michael ignited the patch, and when there was nothing left but ashes, the couple turned them under the soil beneath their tree with the remnants of past pledges.

Michael snuggled back into the bag and pulled Kiri close for a full-body Irish I love you. "I say we start on number one right now."

She held him off. "You mean there will be more than one?"

"You're lying next to a hot-blooded Catholic Irishman. What do you think?"

She cocked her head. "Maybe two—one for each hand?"

He shook his head. "At least three or four. Maybe even..." He expected her to respond with a wide-eyed "five!" But she teased him with "Dozens!"

"Dozens?" He shook his head again. "I don't know if I could stand dozens. I don't have enough arms and legs and shoulders to corral and carry that many. Plus, I don't want you forever pregnant, in a bad mood, and taking more than your half of the bed for the next fifteen years like my sisters. Besides, where would we store them all in this tiny house?"

"Build a sky-walk to next door? I don't know," she said with a shrug. "You'll come up with a plan, but don't even think of leaving this house. I love the way you remodeled this old place to suit us. And what would we do about Aurora?" she asked dramatically. "We couldn't leave our tree. We'd have no place to settle differences or to spend anniversaries plotting out our lives. No, we'll never leave our peaceful home where the sun shines all day on the flowers that cover our bed."

At that, Michael scrambled from the bag they shared, bunched the top together in his broad hands, and shook it until Kiri was a lump in the bottom. He swung the protesting load onto his back and started for the house.

"Michael! What are you doing?" She punched at his rear.

"Taking you to that bed of ours. If 'tis dozens you want, we'd better get started."

"But we have to meet up soon for the picnic with the nieces and nephews."

"They can wait. The long, proud line of Michael O'Connell begins now!"

*   *   *

Irish patriarch Thomas O'Connell labored up the three flights of stairs to the storage room in the Dublin four-story Georgian home he shared with American Paula Koyle, his wife of nearly three years now, but his love for more than forty. She allowed him to play the leader most of the time in the short while they lived together, but for grandchildren days, he was happy to be her servant. He wiped his brow at the end of his third trip up. First was for coolers; the second, for picnic baskets; and this last, for ground quilts. On his return to the kitchen, he would follow her orders explicitly.

When he first brought bohemian Paula home to meet his children, she devised a scheme of entertaining all of the grandchildren once a month as a means of doing something helpful to coy favor with his daughters and to help him grow closer to his ten grandchildren. Their ranks now swelled to fifteen. Shortly after their marriage in late December of 2009, Paula expressed a desire to cut back on such playdays. Maybe three or four a year would be as many as two mature adults in their late sixties could handle. But the downturn in the economy changed her heart. The parents grew testy, sullen and argumentative, and the little ones suffered for it. Thomas urged Paula to reconsider, not so much for the benefit of the parents, but for relief from tensions in their homes for the kiddies. Taking them away once a month for some carefree play was a way these two loving elders could help.

"Into the van?" Thomas asked as he scooted past Paula toward the back door. She nodded, all business in preparation for their grand undertaking. Renting vans for three or so trips per year allowed flexibility in numbers and a ready rental supply of car seats of varying sizes, depending on the need for the day. Today they needed two vans, for the younger kids would return early while the older went on to a water park with Michael and Kirin.

"Coolers?" Thomas asked when he returned.

Paula shook her head. "The drinks are ready to go, but you'd better wait for Michael's help." He checked the weight and decided she was right as usual. He shook his head in frustration at his increasing limitations. "What next then?"

"I'm about finished with the food, so why don't you pack the plastic ware? Plates, cups, a few bowls, and utensils."

He picked up a basket and headed for the pantry where plastic bought in bulk was stored. "How many?"

"This trip is for two-year-olds and up, so the three youngest will stay with their mothers today. Twelve children and four adults will go, making sixteen. Better pack twenty of everything, to be safe. Someone is sure to break, bend, lose or soil something. Oh, that reminds me," she said hurrying toward the bathroom. "We need damp cloths for washing up, and we better stick in some extra towels in case some of the big kids come without one."

Big kids and little kids were relative terms when it came to the grandchildren parties. For any activity that was not appropriate for all— now ranging from three months to twelve years—an age limit was preset to divide them. The need for such a device became evident when the oldest were preteens and the youngest were babies. Even though they were all cousins and devoted to their grandfather, they did have different interests and abilities, Paula pointed out. A Christmas cookie party was fun for all, but sometimes they needed an age-appropriate experience.

That issue came to a head when all the little ones wanted to go see the buffalo in Colorado when they heard the grandparents planning their annual July trip. The story of the white buffalo and the Ritual of Consumption were staples during many of their get-togethers. O'Connell offspring never begged, but they did know how to put on long faces and doleful eyes. Thomas and Paula consulted with Michael and Kiri who planned a camping trip to Yellowstone themselves, with a stop by Paula's house on the hill for a 4th of July celebration with Kurt and his girlfriend and any neighbors who dropped in for barbecue and fireworks.

Thomas recalled Michael asking, "Why not? There's plenty of room at Paula's. They could fly over with you and come back with us. Might be fun."

Kiri protested. "No way! There are twelve of them now, and even if we left the babies behind, that's still too many for one pair of adults to tend in an airport and on a plane.

An idea sprouted in Michael's cunning mind. "What if we take only a few of them?" he asked. "I'd like Brendan and Connor to come camping with us, especially now that their absent father started his second family. They're feeling pretty down and need a boost. A camping trip to Yellowstone would be perfect!"

"Where did that come from?" Kiri asked. "I thought we were talking about the 4th at Mom's, not spending our vacation taking care of other people's kids."

"They are *not* other people's kids. They are *family*, and right now this is something we can do to help them... since we don't have children of *our own* at present," Michael shot back.

Chastised, Kiri replied, "Why not any of the others? The rest of the cousins would be resentful of Meghan's boys. That wouldn't be conducive to family harmony."

Paula chimed in. "I agree. You can't seem to play favorites—one family over another. Think of a logical way of dividing them, or don't do it at all."

"We'll take Anne's Ronan. He and Connor are best buds."

"Boys only? That doesn't seem fair. You're favoring one gender over another," Kiri complained.

Michael set his jaw. "Fine! You think of an impartial solution."

"What about age?" she suggested. "If you want Brendan and Connor to go, then take Connor's age and up, since he's the younger, and establish that as your limit. We'll take Brendan, Connor, Ronan and Grace—unless you can't handle four at once, Mighty Mike."

Thus, age limits for outings were born, Thomas remembered as he put the last of the cups in the basket, added a handful of napkins, and returned to the kitchen. Those limits functioned well. No one questioned Uncle Michael. When he drew the line, the children accepted and obeyed. To be fair, sometimes they planned an outing for the younger and left the older behind, like when they went to the zoo and Michael drew the line at seven and under. The others stayed at the house with Paula for pizza and movies, each inviting a friend, and understood that complaints were not allowed. If they did not like the rules, they could stay home. Not a one did, of course.

To manage the age limit system, Paula held a calendar party each January. All the grandchildren found their birthdays on a brand new calendar, wrote their names and new ages on their special days and then discussed some of the things they would like to do for Paula's parties. If he and Kiri needed to help, Michael worked the final list around his assignments abroad and *he* set the age limits for those activities. So far, so good, Thomas thought as he and Paula put baskets and towels into the van. "Remind me. What's the age limit for today?" he asked her as they returned to the kitchen.

"Six and above go with Michael and Kiri to Clara Lara Fun Park after lunch, so that makes eight in their van and four in ours. Meggie is so excited. This will be her first trip there. She has called at least once a day for the last week to remind me that she is now six so she will be going with the older kids. Kiri reports the same. I hope Meggie can keep up with the rest of that rambunctious bunch."

"Do we have a special cupcake this time?" Thomas referred to another of Paula's attempts to cut back on family responsibilities. With fifteen grandchildren and the nine children and spouses who had birthdays annually, she refused to plan her life with Thomas around them. "We must

6

have our time alone together, too," she insisted. If they were in the city and available, they would happily attend whatever was planned; otherwise, they sent their good wishes in their stead.

As a concession to the grandchildren, Paula baked and decorated a special cupcake for anyone celebrating a birthday between the current activity and the next. That child—or children, since some interludes had more than one such day in them—basked in their five minutes of good wishes and a rousing chorus of "Happy Birthday" by the group—all except Uncle Michael who could carry three boys on his back at once but could not carry a tune. "Yes, we do. Aidan's birthday is at the end of the month. He will be five. Oh, that reminds me. We need to take the calendar to announce our next date and plan. Michael is likely to be gone, so no age limit. While we're waiting for everyone to arrive, why don't you quiz me again?"

Thomas turned to the back of the calendar on which she had written each set of parents together with their children. The first time Paula did that, he scoffed at her. "You can't remember the names of the little ones?" The following year it was his turn; he got them mixed up too. He wondered, did that happen to other grandparents when they neared seventy?

Paula began counting on her fingers. "Tommy and Margaret O'Connell have Caitlín, Fíonna, Breeda, Eileen and Nora, the baby. Daughter Anne and Charles Geary have Grace, Ronan, Gemma, Aidan, Erin and Niall, the baby. Daughter Meghan Daly has the two boys, Brendan and Connor. And daughter Emily and Stephen Flynn have Meggie and Liam who is one. That makes fifteen. How did I do?"

"Perfect." He handed her the calendar with a smile.

She dropped it into her bag and took a last look at her list for the day. "Sunscreen. I knew I forgot something." She rushed out and returned bearing a tube. "Lean over."

Thomas could not imagine why, but this was his day to follow orders so he sat down in the breakfast nook and bent forward. He jerked when he felt a cool squirt onto the top of his head.

"Don't you complain. There's not enough hair left up here to keep you from burning to a crisp on this beautiful sunny day. Be sure to take your cap," she said as she left to wash her hands and grab their wraps. When she returned, Thomas had not moved. His arms rested on his knees with his hands folded and his eyes focused on the floor tiles. "Why the long face? This trip to Glendalough is one of your favorite excursions."

Thomas shook his head. "All those names. All those beautiful grandchildren... and not a one of them will pass the name of O'Connell onto the next generation. The six boys come from my daughters and will not have sons called O'Connell. Tommy has produced five little girls, and Kirin and Michael, married for nearly three years now, show no sign of... Do you suppose there is something wrong with her?"

7

"How dare you suggest that their being childless at present is Kiri's fault!"

"My mistake. I didn't mean that. Michael is so dedicated to the well-being of his nieces and nephews that I know he wants nothing more than a family of his own. Can't I hope his family will include a son? I can't accept that my O'Connell branch will die out with my two boys. I want so much to hear the cry of one true O'Connell grandson."

"Thomas, stop it! We've been through this before. What you wish and what the future will bring are not the same. You cannot order gender-specific grandchildren any more than you can expect adult children to love one another. If Tommy should have a son, so be it. If Michael should have a son, so be it. If Michael should have no children or a dozen girls, so be it. You cannot demand that *your* will be done! Count your blessings, Thomas O'Connell. I think you'll find you have too many for those knobby toes and fingers of yours."

"Quite right as usual, my dear," he chuckled. He pulled her onto his lap, stripped her of her shoes and, amidst her girlish giggles, he began to tally all those blessings by name on her ticklish piggies.

Chapter 2

Glendalough glowed with the golden colors of early autumn. Nestled in a glacial valley in the Wicklow Mountains, its serene Upper Lake mirrored the colorful foliage and green hills surrounding the water. First stop for the group, the plunging waterfall, drew oohs and ahs from first-timers when they hit a hiking trail to visit Kevin's Bed and Cell where Michael began his story of the 6th Century Irish saint.

"An angel baptized Kevin, and a white cow appeared at his door every morning to feed him from her milk." Michael remarked on the similarity with the white buffalo story he frequently told the children. "He left home at the age of seven to study at a nearby monastery. As a measure of his merit, the young boy was sent to bring back hot coals from a small church. He had nothing to carry them in, so he turned up his tunic, placed the coals in it, and ran back to his master. He arrived with the hot coals, but not a singe or hole burned into his clothing—the first of many miracles surrounding his name. He left to live a solitary life right here where we stand." Michael pointed to the bed and cell.

"He spent seven years as a hermit, living in this cave with the stone slab for his bed and a rock for his pillow. He wore skins, ate nettles and herbs, and prayed a lot." He guided the children in examining various plants surrounding the site for those that might be edible. They decided Paula's sandwiches would taste better. He motioned toward blackbirds nesting in the bushes.

"But they aren't black. They're brown," a niece observed.

"Females. The mommies. Only males have iridescent black plumage showing a hint of blue in sunlight."

"They're quite small," another added.

"If four and twenty of them fit in a pie, they must be," their leader said with a wink. "Now, look here at his cell, the tiny space where he slept, prayed and studied, and where the blackbird we'll hear about after lunch visited him."

The little band of pilgrims hiked along the river to the Lower Lake while the vans inched along the road to pick up stragglers. "Kevin established a monastic settlement here—still an important destination for pilgrims today." The children explored the medieval stone buildings and wondered how the circular tower built 1,000 years ago could be so round and so tall with no apparent purpose for it. "St. Kevin asked that his body be laid to rest near the monastery he founded. 'Tis an Irish thing, to wish to be buried in sacred ground, an important and significant place in your life— the soil of your land—because that will be the place of your resurrection."

Rowdy playtime with lots of running followed—games of hide-and-seek and snatch Uncle Michael's handkerchief from the sleeping giant— while Paula and Kiri set out the food. Thomas laid out quilts, and when the lunch bell rang, the older children pulled theirs slightly away from the younger so they could "talk." For the first time, Michael positioned his far enough away for some privacy with Kiri.

After consuming enough food to satisfy that giant, he stretched out, then rolled to his side and perched his head on one hand while placing his other on Kiri's tummy. "Having fun?"

"This has been a great day. I thought poor Breeda would burst into tears when you grabbed her by the ankle and wouldn't let go," Kiri laughed.

"No harm. She survived. Next time she won't stand so close to me."

"Speaking of Breeda, where did she get her name?"

"From one family or the other. Probably her mother's because I don't remember it in mine. We should check our family histories for names we'll use for our own children."

"You mean, there are rules for naming children?"

"Not hard and fast ones anymore, but if you consider our bunch here, you'll find all the boys with a Thomas or their father or grandfather in there somewhere, as a first, second, or sometimes a third given name. Like Brendan Thomas. They're just called by the most unique one. Think of the girls. We have an Anne in every generation, and we have Meghan and Meggie, not her own daughter but both of which can be traced to a Margaret in our past, and a Kathryn in every family. Grace is really Kathryn Grace, and Caitlín is your Kathleen, a form of Kathryn. That's just how it's done."

"Well, no son of mine will be Michael or Thomas!"

"You don't like my name?"

"I love your name so much, I don't want you to share it. There can be absolutely only one Michael in my life, and that is you." She gave him a peck on the cheek and lay back to drink in the sun.

He looked hurt. "But I was counting on naming my first son Michael Thomas. 'Tis important to me."

"If we do, what will we call the poor tyke? You're my only Michael and I won't saddle him with Mikey. Thomas and Tommy are already taken. Don't even think of adding Killian."

"How about MT?"

"And have him grow up thinking he's hollow inside? No way!"

"Let's start on girl's names, then. We're bound to have some of those too. I planned on Ki…"

"No! There will be no other Kirin in the family. I'm pleading vanity here. I don't want to share my name either. I'm a unicorn, remember, standing alone on the fringe of the forest, faithful forever."

"Then Au…"

"No! No daughter of mine will be named after a fairy princess and a tree."

"And for a second name I want to use Kathryn after my mother."

She read his sentiment in his eyes. "But there are so many already."

"I've decided. Aurora Kathryn and we'll call her Katie. I'm the father, and I will name my first son and my first daughter."

"You sound just like your own father."

"He's not wrong every time he opens his mouth, you know. Tell you what. I'll name the first of each, and you can name the dozens that come after. Anything you want. Animals, mythical beasts, constellations, whatever. You can even call them by letters, B for Bertha, C for Christy, D...."

While their conversation continued through the alphabet, the nieces and nephews camped a few yards away offered observations of their own. "I think Aunt Kiri is pregnant," Grace revealed.

"What makes you say that?" Brendan asked.

"She's playing all coy and cute, and Uncle Michael doesn't take his hand off her belly. He just keeps rubbing it around in circles and nuzzling her behind the ear."

"Grace is right. None of our parents behave like that unless another brother or sister is near," Caitlín said.

"That's super! Uncle Michael will be a great father. Look at how much he does for us," Ronan chimed in.

"That's the problem," said Gemma. "As soon as they have kids of their own, they won't have time for us anymore. I vote for no babies... yet."

Kiri stopped Michael in mid-sentence suggesting a boy's name beginning with U. "I think we should table the rest of this discussion for later."

"Why's that? I'm just getting started."

"Because we have quite an audience." She nodded toward the nearby group.

Michael glared at the pairs of eyes staring at the young couple. "You lot, put your eyeballs back in your heads!" he shouted as he scrambled toward them.

Aidan saved them from the giant's clutches by running in between and announcing, "Paula says it's time for my cupcake, so you have to come *now!*"

The youngsters scattered, pulling quilts and rubbish with them—all except for Meggie who stood alone in tears. Michael swooped her up and tucked her head under his chin. "What has you looking so sad, Little Meg? You can tell your uncle."

"I'm afraid when you have babies, you won't play with us any more," she sniffled. "And... and... I'll never get to see the buffalo, and... and... I'm almost old enough to go."

"For heaven's sake, don't bother yourself a bit. We'll always have time to play with you. You must never worry that we won't. Growing up can be quite an unpleasant business, as I remember—scabby knees, sore throats, nightmares and disappointments—especially when your parents go through rough times. But Kiri and I, and your grandparents, and your

11

cousins will always be here to help you through the ugly times—to love you, to keep you safe and to help you enjoy life."

She rubbed her eye with a fist. "If you have babies, will you still take me to see the buffalo?"

"I promise."

He carried her over to the group where Aidan proudly displayed his cupcake—a bunny with chocolate ears and jellybean nose and eyes. All his cousins gave him good wishes for the coming year, and then they sang "Happy Birthday." During the brief celebration, Michael snooped in the bushes and along the hiking trail. The children knew what would come next to finish the outing—the game of St. Kevin and the Blackbird.

Their uncle continued the story of the solitary saint who, on awaking one morning in his narrow cell, stretched his arms so wide that one reached clear out the slit of a window. "Before he could draw it back in, a blackbird perched on his turned-up palm, built a nest and laid her eggs. Poor Kevin, a true lover of life and especially his friends the animals, was faced with a dilemma. If he pulled his arm back into the cell, his hand would be forced to turn, drop the nest, and the eggs would be crushed on the ground. He had no choice but to stand with his outstretched arm and hand stiff as a tree's branch until the eggs hatched. He remained thus for weeks and cradled the nest firmly through warm sun, cool rain and wind. His fingers tingled and his legs grew numb. He trusted the good Lord would not give him a burden he could not bear, so he remained steadfast until the eggs hatched, the little birds grew feathers and finally flew away."

Michael never varied the story or its message, but he frequently changed the rules of the game or how he applied them. He always arranged the group in a circle with an arm outstretched, and he built a nest in each palm, bit by bit, with each circuit he made around them. He usually started with a little grass, then added a twig or two, small stones for eggs, and a few surprises. Sometimes the last nest still in hand won, and sometimes a time limit was used to assure many winners.

The children understood that the oldest and strongest were not always victors when Michael put a heavy stone in Brendan's hand right off, forcing his nest down and out of the game. Paula's was sure to fall if he blew into her ear like wind to cause her to shrug her shoulder, and once he put a handful of crud from under a rock into Kiri's nest. A big bug crawled from it and crept along her arm, freaking out all the little kiddies. Determined not to let Michael get the best of her, she endured the creepies until the critter was almost to her armpit and she could not stand it any longer. Everyone screeched with delight when she finally shook her arm, the nest fell, and she stomped on the bug. One time Michael was in a hurry because inclement weather threatened, but the youngsters insisted on playing, so he plopped a handful of ice into each nest and the game ended quickly.

This day, Michael introduced a new rule and added a "but." Today it would not be each child for himself. Today they would work together as a family to de-nest Grandfather Thomas. If his nest fell first, everyone else would win, but if anyone's fell before his, they would lose together. Thomas grumbled, realizing he had no choice but to play along. He steadied his bulky frame and chunky legs, much like his son's. Michael put his hands on Kiri's shoulders and whispered in her ear. She nodded and whispered to Paula. Then the game began. "Everyone. Airplane arms. Palms up. Right hands in your pockets."

The first two rounds with grass and twigs proceeded as usual. For the third, Michael dropped nuts into each nest, and two-year old Eileen's began to quiver along with her lips. Kiri quickly left her place, and still holding her nest, ran around the circle to the little girl and slid her arm perpendicular to and underneath it as a brace. Everyone was surprised. That had not happened before. Next round was pine cones. When three-year-old Erin started to falter, Paula ran to her rescue without losing a blade of grass on the way and supported the little girl's arm from beneath with her own. Thomas saw where this game was headed and called "Foul!"

"Not so, Father," Michael smiled devilishly. "The rules are, 'Work together as family.'"

Thomas, who liked to win at games as much as his son, took a deep breath and planted his feet more firmly.

Next round, stone eggs. Everyone froze when Meggie's arm started to tremble. She pinched her eyes shut, lifter her chin and shouted, "He...e...lp!" A cousin ran to her rescue.

After a couple more rounds, the older cousins supported the younger, and still Thomas held out. Michael decided it was time to de-nest him. "The mother blackbird said, 'Christmas is not too far off. I think I'll decorate my nest. Red and gold and silver will look beautiful.'" He tucked a red or gold leaf gently into each cozy handful until he reached Thomas. When he held up a nettle, the grandfather protested. "That *is* foul."

Michael spun the stinging plant's stem between his fingertips, making sure the older man's attention was focused there. The cunning son admitted, "Perhaps you're right." Before Thomas noticed, Michael reached his free hand to the back of his father's head. "Perhaps this one needs a beautiful silver thread." He yanked a white hair from behind the aging man's ear. Thomas yowled and clapped his hand to the smart. His nest fell. The rest of the group collapsed in stitches. Game over.

"Now," the fun uncle continued when the laughter subsided, "what is the lesson we learn from St. Kevin?"

The family answered in unison, "The good Lord will never give you a burden greater than you can bear."

"But...." Michael coaxed a new additional phrase.

Meggie announced, "But sometimes you have to holler for help!"

*   *   *

"We're delighted to find your park open past September 1ˢᵗ this year. The children are anxious to go for a splash." Michael greeted the ticket agent at Clara Lara Fun Park.

"Yeah, so. With the weather still warm, folks seem to want a few last days in the water."

"We're eight children and two adults, please."

The man raised his eyebrows at such a large group of look-alikes of similar age. "All of 'em yours?"

Michael smiled, thinking *someday*. "Negative. We're the crazy aunt and uncle, the ones who don't know any better."

The man chuckled. "Well, have a good time, then." By the look on the children's faces, he knew they would.

Kiri selected a spot for base camp. The children stripped down to their swimsuits and waited anxiously for Uncle Michael's instructions. "Keep your shoes on for the time being. There are lots of things to do: tree houses to climb, Tarzan swings, rope bridges to cross, row boats, rafts and canoes, and of course, water slides. First-timers will go with Aunt Kiri for a walkabout to get the lay of the land; then, you can go on your own too. Holler if you need help. Meet back here in two hours, and we'll plan from there. Ready... Set..." He took off running and shouted over his shoulder, "I'm first on the Tarzan swing... Go!"

After the others disappeared in all directions, Kiri oriented Meggie and Fionna. "See that clock and the blue flag above the buildings? Our camp is right beneath. No matter where you are playing, you can see the flag, know where to find us, and never feel lost. If you become anxious or frightened, what will you do?"

"Holler for help!"

The trio explored. They found the tree house, crossed a bridge and Kiri took them out in a rowboat. The two little girls wanted to try a raft, so she did her best to keep them from going in circles until they ran into a couple of the cousins and got involved in a water fight. Everyone got wet, but she ended up in the water. After a time, and several checks for the blue flag and the clock nearby, the little girls took off on their own.

Kiri stumbled slowly back to camp, unaware that almost two hours disappeared. She found Michael spread out on a quilt for a snooze. The children straggled in. Thoughtfully, two of the older gathered in the little girls on the way. Michael took one look at the motley lot and decided, "We need food."

"Mom sent along drinks and extra eats."

"With all due respect to Paula, we've had enough nuts, twigs, leafy greens and seaweed snacks for one day. This bunch needs greasy fish and chips and messy sauce. I'll be right back." He returned within minutes, arms loaded, to the delight of the famished youngsters.

When he had his fill, Michael lay back on their quilt, enjoying the late afternoon sun in nothing but his swim shorts. "It takes way too long to grow a baby, Kiri. I want one now! I want to plant my seed deep in your belly and watch it grow plump with the spring. In summer you'll be as big as a pumpkin. My hands won't be able to cover it when they rest right here..." He placed one on her tummy and massaged it. "...to detect the beat of a heart or the kick of little feet. That heart and those feet will be the union of us both—a piece of you and a piece of me formed into something new and beautiful. Then harvest time, like today. What a blessed and bountiful harvest it will be. What do you suppose they'll look like—these urchins of ours?"

"Judging from this gangly, grubby group, I haven't a clue. None of them are dead ringers for their parents, except for Meggie, so probably not like either one of us. They can't, if they're the fusion of us both. I'd settle for your blue eyes."

Michael shook his head. "Yours are alluring—deep blue with hazel flecks, and your soft wavy hair is gorgeous. Of course, those might not go so well on a strapping young man such as my son will be."

"Strapping, for sure. You're built like a boxcar, solid and square. I imagine our sons tall and lean, like my brother Kurt."

Michael shook his head again. "Not going to happen. That would leave stocky with kinky curls for our daughters. Imagine a girl with my hairy chest!"

On the quilt not too far away, the nieces and nephews could not help but eavesdrop. "I told you they were expecting," Grace said.

"Guess there's nothing we can do to stop it now," Brendan added. "I wonder if we'll grow up to look like Uncle Michael?" The nephews self-consciously rubbed their smooth, flat chests just waiting to muscle out and tucked their skinny legs beneath them with eyes on their uncle's enormous calves. The nieces could not decide whether he looked sexy or weird, but they secretly wondered what he felt like.

"I wouldn't mind having a body like Aunt Kiri's," Caitlin said.

"Thin and bony?" Connor asked.

"She's not bony. She's toned," Grace explained.

"What's 'toned'?" Meggie's little voice asked.

"That's when you have strong muscles and no fat to cover them up. Uncle Michael's scars still show," Gemma observed.

"He let me touch them once." Brendan sat tall. "He said it didn't hurt. I wonder about Aunt Kiri's, though."

"She won't let anyone touch her arm except Michael. I like how he traces her scar with his finger, and then he kisses it gently. I think that's romantic." Caitlin batted her eyelashes.

"Yeah. Romantic enough to make a baby!" That remark from Ronan ended their conversation when Connor pointed at their uncle's glaring eyes.

"Twenty more minutes. Then ten to clean up. We move out in exactly thirty. Spend your time wisely. Now go!" He turned to Kiri. "What would you like to do to wind this up?"

"I'm taking a break. Do what you like."

"You're leaving me alone with all eight kids?" he hollered after her.

"Too many for you to manage, Mighty Mike?" she hollered back. "Better rethink your grand plan."

*   *   *

After a long, aromatic soak in the bathtub, Paula padded into the bedroom suite she shared with Thomas. He removed his reading glasses and set his book aside. "Who gets the first backrub tonight?" he asked his exhausted wife.

"You do. The minute you touch me, I'll be out."

"How disappointing." Thomas rolled onto his stomach. "My left shoulder is killing me. Give it a good go, will you?"

"Too much play today?"

"That dratted Blackbird game did it. I flexed my shoulder muscle too tight and held it too long. I should have let my nest go as soon as I realized what that rascal son of mine had in mind, but I do still like to win, Paula."

"I have to admit, I enjoyed watching you try to hold out. When he plucked that silvery thread of yours, it was such a surprise that I almost dropped my own nest first."

"What do you suppose brought on the change in the game?"

"Meggie, I think. I saw Michael try to comfort her when she had a little cry. I think he seized the opportunity to help her feel better. She's had a tough time of it this past year with a new baby in the house. An only child for five years, she struggled to welcome a new attention-getter into the family. A different perspective was good for all the grandchildren."

"The next time Michael wants to teach a lesson, he can use his own body. Ow!"

Paula lay down for her turn. "I have to admire Michael for the way he handles those kids. He may seem gruff when he barks orders, but he is as gentle as can be when the occasion calls for it. I had to laugh when he brought his group back to clean up after the water park. 'Twenty minutes. Not a speck of mud left on you or in the bathrooms. Dirty clothes and shoes in the laundry room. Get going!'" Paula mimicked. "And they did. At the appointed time, they were at the door looking as if they spent the entire afternoon sitting on the sofa watching out the windows, the only evidence of an active day outside being all those rosy cheeks and noses. They will sleep well tonight."

"I don't know how many more days of 'active aging' I can take—like minding a basket of kittens. Was this your idea or mine?"

"I think the guilt belongs to both of us."

"Do you think there will ever be a time they'll be satisfied to sit and talk with us, enjoy our company?"

"Not a chance. Kids are so plugged in today." She sighed and turned her head to the right. "Michael and Kiri are doing the best they can to combat glazed-eye syndrome. I love how he insists they leave all their pods and pads on the console table by the door before he'll let them get in the van. He tells them that if they want to talk to their friends, they can stay home and do that. No electronics allowed. Could be he wants to prevent them from taking pictures and sharing."

Thomas nodded. "Can't be too careful these days."

"Did you notice how well Anne has taught her children? They were as mannerly as ever. On the way out, Grace lined up her brothers and sisters—and the other families followed suit—and very properly thanked us. 'Thank you, Grandfather, for the lovely day. Thank you, Paula, for the lovely lunch. Thank you, Aunt Kiri, for the lovely time. Thank you, Uncle Michael, for the lovely visit to the water park.' I wonder what she was taught to say if the day is a disaster instead of 'lovely'?"

Thomas laughed out loud. "Did you watch Kirin and Michael today?"

"I watched the youngsters watch them. Your son was a little more familiar than he should have been with all the little ones around, I thought."

"I disagree. It's nice for the children to witness adults they admire showing affection for one another. They don't see enough of that at home, for sure. I mean, did you *really* watch Michael and Kirin? I think they are expecting. I think they'll have an announcement for us at Christmas. What a grand surprise that will be—a true O'Connell grandson for the New Year."

"Stop it!"

"Wha? Can't a man indulge in a little wishful thinking in his own bed?"

"You are indulging your enthusiasm a little too deeply in my muscle tissue. I'll thank you to temper both until your wishes become reality."

"I'll settle for the second wish on my list, then, for the near future. Come nearer, my 'lovely' future."

* * *

Kiri pulled herself from a warm soak in their tub, wrapped a robe around her exhausted body, and padded to their octagonal bedroom muraled in mountains at the head of a bed quilted with wildflowers. In search of Michael, she noted that his boots were not beside their bed as usual. She stepped to the wall of windows and peered down into the back garden. She saw him scurry about near Aurora and realized he did not forget. This anniversary night would be a replay of the last two, a ritual he intended to continue.

She remembered fondly how, on their first anniversary after awaking beneath the evergreen Aurora and spending a quiet day together, Michael surprised her with a fulfillment of his cryptic pledge from that morning: *I promise you a true wedding.* He explained that evening when they sat beneath their tree not ready to call an end to the day. "Our secret wedding was a surprise—no time for a plan—so I promised you a true one. Our second wedding was orchestrated by Father, unbeknown to him—no plan of

17

our choosing. Tonight, on the first anniversary of our first wedding, I devised a private ceremony—a true wedding of body and spirit—that I hope will be to your liking.

"You have borne the brunt of the major changes marriage brought to our lives, Kiri, not the least of which was your journey into a religious perspective different from your own. 'Twas you who gave up your job. 'Twas you who gave up your home. 'Tis up to me to try to make it right."

He attempted to explain his reasoning to his skeptical wife of one year. "The success of St. Patrick in Ireland was due in part to his ability to adapt Christianity to the realities of an Irish pagan kingdom society. Likewise, we must adapt our individual beliefs into a credo that satisfies us both." He removed some items from under a piece of Irish linen. "Here we have an earthenware jar that I begged from Paula, made from the clay of your land to signify the Koyle line, and a piece of Irish crockery made from my Killian soil. Next, a small bottle of Rocky Mountain spring water and another of water from a holy well in County Kerry where my families originated. These four items represent the elements from which life is created and the elements that sustain it. In the soil we maintain a connection with our lands, and in water we've found purification, healing and consummation."

Michael uncorked the bottles and poured from each into its respective vessel. "This is the simplest, most delicate glass bowl I could find. In it we'll combine the elements we hold in our hands with the pledges we make to one another taken from an old Celtic wedding vow. As each of us recites a pledge, we'll pour from our own vessel into the bowl. When we're finished, that bowl will be filled with clear, sparkling water—our 'spirit' water—containing both of our beliefs and vows combined—*our* O'Connell creed."

Kiri was overcome with emotion that first anniversary, when they repeated it on the second, and now she faced their third. She so hoped that repetition would not dull the ritual's significance. She pulled on her own boots, turned out the lights and went outside to join Michael.

"Finally! I was afraid you might skip out on me tonight. Too tired?"

Kiri shook her head. "I wouldn't miss this for the world. You can wait on me hand and foot tomorrow," she smiled.

He pulled her close and buried his face in her long hazelnut brown curls. "You smell like heaven." He took her hand and led her to peek over the fence that separated their yard from the one to the west. "Let's have another look at last year's pledge. As soon as you say the word, I have a crew ready to begin digging there between the patio and that oak tree to the south. By February, weather permitting, the water lines, drainage and pumps and heating should be installed and the concrete for your pool, poured. By March you should be able to take your first plunge and start plans for your business.

"By summer, when you are as round and fat as a pig filled with the first of our many, you'll just float there all day long, you lazy mother. And by the following summer, you'll have a little one learning to paddle in the water while riding around on his mummy's tummy—the fulfillment of all of our pledges for the last three years." He sealed his happiness with an embrace worthy of a multi-year wait.

A male blackbird flew onto Michael's shoulder and cocked its yellow-ringed eye at his startled blue one before it sounded one "chook" and flew away. He recognized its warning call and flicking wings as a sign foretelling change—trials ahead.

Kiri felt him shiver and sensed his unease. "Afraid of a little bird, my gallant warrior?"

His eyes would not meet hers. "Not this Irishman," he said with less conviction than usual. "I'm waiting for the fairies to gather so we can begin." He took her by the shoulders and stared seriously at her. "Remember our pledges today?"

She nodded. "Of course."

"I promised to raise our children as you would want. I think that oath should go both ways. You must also promise to raise mine as I would."

"That goes without saying."

"But I want to hear it from your lips."

She humored him. "Yes, my wedded husband, I promise to raise our children as both you and I… as *we*… want them raised."

"Good. One more thing." He bent close to her ear. "Don't ever chase the fairies away. Listen for their whispers."

Kiri laughed. "You know I don't believe in fairies."

"When times are harsh and you are sorely tested, you must believe in something. If faith in God fails you, do as the old Irish did and summon the fairies." He kissed her gently. "Now, let's repeat our vows."

They settled themselves on top of their sleeping bag and removed their boots. "I've added something new this year—a candle." He twisted the stubby wax cylinder into the ground to firm it; then, he lit it to spit and dance during their ceremony. He removed the linen and filled the two vessels with their respective waters. They each ran a finger around the rim of the bowl representing a never-ending circle in their lives. They no longer read their Celtic wedding vows; they knew them by heart. They spoke and poured in unison:

I pledge my love to you, and everything that I own.

I promise you the first bite of my meat and the first sip from my cup.

I pledge that your name will always be the name I cry aloud in the dead of night.

I promise to honor you above all others.

Our love is never-ending like a Celtic Circle, and we will remain, forevermore, equals in our marriage.

This is my wedding vow to you.

The couple placed their hands around the bowl, interlocking fingers, to swirl the waters within. "Not only our words, but the elements to realize them are fused forever and cannot now be separated. They become a part of us both with these drinks we take." Michael swallowed the first long one, then Kiri, until they each downed three for their three years of marriage. What still remained, they sprinkled under the tree Aurora, bringing their devotions to an end.

Michael doused the candle, and the young marrieds snuggled down in their bag to end their very long anniversary day. "We can do it, Kiri. We *can* make a difference in our own small way... by being good parents to our own children and to the other children in our family. Maybe I'm not meant to be halfway 'round the world trying to save it bit by bit. Maybe my place is here, with you, guiding this gaggle of beautiful nieces and nephews—along with a few of our own—while their parents are too distracted by the economy to do the job. I'm feeling better and better about the decision I've made... we've made."

"Me too." She felt him relax with her caress. "But I'll hate to give up this special night every year. We're bound to run out of water someday, and we can't leave sleeping babies in the house alone."

"The water is no problem. I had a case of each made up originally because I envisioned more than one use for it. Washing each newborn clean after his first wail—I want to do that one. Slipping a sip down his throat before he takes his first milk—I'll let you handle that end of it. At christenings, confirmations and weddings. And at our grandchildren's births, christenings, and weddings... and their children's... and theirs. Can you imagine passing bits of ourselves and our souls along this way for generations!" He sat up with a start. "I'd better put in an order for our precious 'spirit' waters tomorrow. We're going to need truckloads for the long line of mini-O'Connells we're going to spawn right now!"

Michael clutched Kiri tightly and pulled her deep into their shared bag. He twisted her compass ring around her finger and she, his gold band, as they repeated the inscription inside both. *"Grá anois agus go deo*; love, now and forever, *mo anam ċara."* The two lovers, then, set his plan for that long line of descendants in motion.

In the dead of night, Kiri's voice cried aloud, "Ohhh, Michael!"

Chapter 3

Loud pounding on the front door roused Michael from a deep sleep. Steady ringing of the bell followed. When the two sounded simultaneously, he had the ominous feeling that this was not an overnight delivery from the continent. Barely two weeks after their anniversary, his dreaded summons to depart banged at the door.

"This might be it, Kiri. 'Twasn't my time to leave for a day or two yet, but that persistent knocking sounds like Patrick." He slipped out of bed without turning on the light and crept through the second-story sitting room to a north window. The impatient figure below confirmed his suspicions.

He hurried back to their bedroom, pulled on pants, sweater and boots, and kissed his drowsy wife on the cheek. "I have to go now. Don't worry. See you soon. I love you, Kirin O'Connell." He removed his wedding ring and placed it on her finger. Then, breaking routine, he threw the bedcovers back and buried his face in Kiri's tummy and kissed it. "And goodbye, you!"

"What are you doing? You know I'm not p...."

"Maybe not yesterday, but you might be now. It only takes a moment." With a broad grin, he headed down the stairs to unrelenting knocks.

Kiri never followed Michael to the door when he left on assignment. The couple did not want to give Patrick Murphy, his supervisor, the satisfaction of witnessing their emotional goodbyes. She would listen for the SUV to drive away and then secure the house. Tonight, however, she heard an argument unfolding below, and her name was part of it.

"A little early for a visit, Patrick. Not even 5 a.m. Did you forget your way to the office?"

Patrick attempted to carry his tall, slender frame into the house, but Michael barred his way. "We're headed there together to pick up your papers and get you on a plane within the hour."

"I'm not to leave for another couple of days."

"Wouldn't you know, plans changed. New developments. You're out of here at dawn... and the little wife, too," the agent revealed with no blink in his steely gaze.

"Kiri? She's not part of this assignment. She's upstairs asleep."

"As I said, plans changed. New developments. Call her down, and let's get going."

"I won't! This assignment is much too dangerous. She's not prepared." Michael's bulk did not give an inch.

"You will, or you know what will happen. If she refuses, she'll be cut out of the agency and there goes that cozy deal of hers. She'll have to find a new job in this tough economy—rough for a foreigner—and your 'secret job' will once again be a mystery."

"You're an ass!"

A malicious smirk crossed the man's face. "Call her."

Michael started to close the door and climb the stairs, but Patrick stopped him. "I said, '*call* her.' No offstage devious conniving allowed."

"Kiri," Michael shouted up the stairs. "Come down please. Patrick has something to say."

Immediately suspicious, she donned her robe and walked slowly to the top of the staircase. As Michael's rival and nemesis and her would-be assaulter that New Year's at the castle, Patrick Murphy was not to be trusted despite the title on his office door. "This is an early hour, even for rats. What's up?"

His Arctic ice blue eyes stared hard at her, salivating at what was beneath her robe. "You are. We need you on this mission. Plans changed. New developments. You and Michael must come with me now."

Michael's darting eyes communicated to her: *Don't get close to him, but find out as much as you can.*

She stopped at the foot of the stairs. "I'm afraid I can't oblige without more information. Tell me what's behind this sudden urgency."

"You know I can't do that."

"Then I refuse."

"You know what will happen if you do," he shot back, calling her bluff.

"Exactly nothing." She folded her arms firmly across her chest. "My recently renewed contract stipulates that *you* make no contact with me or demands on me. I answer to Henry Callaghan only, and you know that very well. Unless you have him hidden in your pocket or want me to report you, I'm not moving."

Patrick flushed and fumbled in his pocket. "I'll give him a call."

While waiting a connection, Michael's eyes darted from the molding by the door, to the rings on Kiri's fingers, to the rear of the house and back. When she started to reach for Patrick's mobile phone, Michael shook his head and passed it to her.

"Kiri?"

"Good morning, Henry. Or is it still last night?"

"Sorry about this. I intended to come by for you in an hour, but Patrick apparently jumped the gun."

"Are we surprised?"

"Not really, but his request for your help is legitimate."

"I didn't expect you to need my services until after Michael returned."

"I didn't either, but plans changed. We do need you... now."

"What is the new development?"

"You know I can't tell you over the phone. I can convey only three words: women, children, documents."

"Say no more. I'll come to hear what you have in mind, but no promises."

"If I swing by in half an hour, will that be enough time for you?"

"I'll come with Michael if you convince Patrick to give me five. I refuse to show up in my bathrobe and bare feet."

Henry laughed. "That's the spirit. Pass me back to him. See you soon."

Kiri handed Michael the phone. "Looks like I get to watch Mighty Mike in action. I don't suppose that man will let you come with me to help get ready." Patrick shook his head. "Then I'll be right back," she said, fingering their rings. What clothes she put on was not important; what she did with the time she was supposed to change was. She understood Michael wanted her to leave their rings behind—no personal items allowed—and his glances at the wainscoting near the door warned her to secure the house—a tight lock-up for less than a week out of the city.

Getting to the mudroom to activate their security system was tricky. She climbed the stairs as expected, passed through the sitting room, bedroom and bath to the service stairs, taking her back down to the first floor and the utility area at the rear of the house. There she slid the door's bolt into place and set the others to slide automatically in about ten minutes. She removed the two wedding rings from her finger and placed them in the floor safe on top of her document box. Then she checked for the knife and gun secreted by the service door for emergencies and retraced her steps quietly up to the bedroom. She pawed through their bedside tables for anything important inadvertently left out and was about to head back downstairs when she realized she had not put on clothes yet. She grabbed a sweatshirt, pulled on jeans and slipped into her boots. The agency had their travel clothes and all necessary documents and visas for their destination—wherever that was.

She smiled confidently at Michael as they left their house on Quincy Street. "Let's make this last mission the best! We've got rooms to fill with little feet."

*   *   *

Kiri regularly relinquished her aisle seat to Michael on the first leg of a flight so he could stretch out. He had no problem sleeping in air, and she never could. After his vicious argument with Patrick once they arrived at the network, he needed to decompress. He was adamant that she not go. His supervisor was equally as unyielding; she must. Finally Kiri convinced Michael that with the two of them and Doyle, identity checking would go much faster. Someone must prepare extra documentation for the unexpected addition of women and children in the third group. Twenty minutes for each of the first two lots and an hour for the last. Two days of reporting before, two days after. The whole team would be back in Dublin sharing a celebratory drink at Ryan's Pub in less than a week. Kiri smiled at the thought of one last assignment with the guys she so admired.

The team. The quick and on the sly guys. An elite group of five with Seal Team brawn and University Honors brain whose mission was simple—

to make a difference by guaranteeing truth and safety in reporting. They operated with only two rules in the field: do not use a weapon except in self-defense and do not shoot to kill. They survived by their wits.

Because the guys were not affiliated with any government or military force, no one hindered them. But none helped them either. Once in the field, they were on their own. Their expertise—establishing networks of vetted, reliable and loyal informants and translators, citizens of countries in conflict, to act as eyes and ears on the ground. Their specialty—extraction of associated personnel from a dangerous area on short notice. Their reward—an occasional byline on the evening news.

The team. Secret agents of a secret unit of a secret arm of a secret department of a very public broadcast company that would disavow any knowledge of or connection with its members if a mission went bad. Successes traveled by whisper along news media circuits. The members: Doyle, the congenial one with dark skin, thick black hair and heavy beard, brandished an aggressive nature that carried him to the front of any line. Frank, the active one whose darting eyes kept pace with his words, remained practical in the field—the stick-to-the-plan man. Devin, the nondescript and contemplative one, mastered detail and developed a talent for technological wizardry. Gorilla-man Gus, whose kind heart exceeded the span of his outstretched arms, muscled quick but tender action in complex situations on the ground. Michael, the acknowledged leader of this band of equals, combined all of his mates' strengths and his own to evolve into an imaginative tactical expert who frequently reacted first and let thought catch up with him.

Henry Callaghan, whose slim but solid build and brooding gray eyes masked an inner turmoil that never interfered with the job, demonstrated patience and logical reasoning in his position as liaison between this covert extraction team and the network hierarchy. Patrick Murphy, a man of slick demeanor with a deceptive grin and no particular talents other than being born into a respected network family, claimed the title of department head. At least that is what the plate on his office door trumpeted, but in Kiri's mind he was a pompous bully of little brain—an incompetent supervisor—whose worth counted for less than a ball of lint.

As the plane took off, Michael clasped her hand in both of his, leaned his ginger mane on her shoulder and was out. She smiled at the burly man next to her whose stature belied his gentleness and used her wakefulness to remember their past three years as if they were yesterday.

After their December wedding with Thomas and Paula almost three years earlier, the couple returned to Denver to sort out Kiri's life there. She resumed work in the bank and he, as agreed with his network, reported in and around Colorado. Within a few months it became obvious that he was not happy and that she did not gain enough satisfaction from her job to make up for his lack of the same. They agreed to sell her house. Following their parents' July visit for BBQ and fireworks with both couples barely managing to get along for two weeks in Paula's beautiful home on the hill, Michael and Kiri decided without argument that they really wanted to spend their life in their own cozy home in Dublin. They made the move within days.

They were not home more than two before their elderly neighbor across the road, Paddy, knocked at the back door, cap in hand. This was unusual—not his visiting, but his arriving at the back door and with Maureen, his wife, nowhere in sight. Beads of perspiration broke out above the gray fringe of his balding head. He needed to speak to Michael, he said. After a friendly greeting and setting out tea, Kiri excused herself and listened from the laundry room while the men settled themselves into the nook in the kitchen.

"I hate to bother, you back such a short time and all, but being's we're family now I thought you should know that my Maureen took a turn." Michael seemed confused, so Paddy explained. "At your wedding, Mr. O'Connell said that all who answered 'Amen' to your vows would be family who could call on each other for help."

By the look on his face and the wringing of his cap, Paddy's embarrassment at making such a plea was evident. The two men, young and old and previously neighbors in passing, became partners in Paddy's misfortune—a story repeated by many since the Celtic tiger economy began to gasp. Michael walked the man home and returned to make some calls while Kiri fixed soup from vegetables in the garden Paula still tended.

On her return from delivering the savory mixture across the road, she agreed that Maureen's demented state and the unkempt appearance of the woman and her house needed to be addressed. "But why are we the ones to do it?" she asked Michael.

"He took Father's words as truth, and now he needs help."

"St. Mary's was packed. Surely not everyone there took Thomas' contrived compliance seriously."

"Let's hope not. But our neighbors need help. They have no family of their own, so they've come to us. We can try, at least, to make these last years better for them. I think I've come up with a plan for adjusting my trust funds to work out a deal, but that will require your agreement." At Kiri's surprise, he reminded her that they were partners and he would not take risks—with his life or his money—without her knowledge and consent.

"Maureen never worked, and Paddy's small pension barely covers their living expenses, much less anything for her medical care. They own their home but haven't a prayer of selling it in this market—and they do need a place to live. I've investigated a reverse mortgage kind of deal where we'll hold the papers to the house and pay them monthly toward it. At the end, we'll have a piece of property we can fix up and sell—pick our own neighbors. If we tighten up a bit and pay our house fund a little less, we should be able to make it work," he hastened to add.

When she realized how intent Michael was to aid the older couple, Kiri agreed. She expected elder care to be in their futures—just not so soon.

A couple of days later, with all arrangements in place, Michael summoned the aging man for a "business meeting" in his thrown-together office in the front of the house. "Paddy, I'll be waiting for you at the front door," he said. The man's natural tendency to come to the back with hat in hand for a favor from someone he thought of as superior must be broken. Michael would not offer a handout. Theirs would be a business venture between equals where each gained and gave evenly.

Michael stirred and shifted position in his cramped seat, pulling Kiri's arm with him and cuddling it like a teddy bear. An overgrown child himself who was not afraid to share a few tears, she had no doubt he could handle poopy diapers with dispatch. He was the anomaly in his family, the one who did what had to be done whether or not it was popular or conformed to his gender role. Instinctively intelligent, he handled family issues with sensitivity.

A second call for help came only a few weeks after Paddy's crisis, Kiri remembered. A pub owner phoned Michael at closing hour and asked that he pick up his brother-in-law. "He's in a bad way. We've taken his keys but he refuses a cab." Michael left immediately and returned with Charles in tow. He shoved the unsteady man in the first-floor shower while she made a pot of strong black coffee.

"What's up?"

"His bank took a dive today, and he's worried to death about what that will mean for his family."

"So he came to you?"

His father and brothers are in the same predicament. He's embarrassed to go to my father, so we're the lucky winners."

"But *his* family *owns* the bank."

"That doesn't mean anything. Nepotism. He walked out of school and into a job. My guess is he never learned how to manage money or work for it, only how to spend it to keep my sister Anne happy. You go back to bed. I'll keep watch to make sure he doesn't sneak out once he wakes up and realizes what he's done. We'll all get to work after a hearty breakfast—your job. I only hope he can access his accounts online so we can work from here."

"What about Anne?"

"I'll call her. Convince her we're just a couple of brothers who had too much fun doing the guy thing."

After two long days and nights of Kiri making sense of the numbers and offering numerous constructive suggestions, Michael crunching them and making phone calls, and Charles making excuses for his absence from home and work, a plan for his solvency emerged. "I think we're done,"

Michael finally announced. "Your debt payoffs are on a manageable plan, your mortgage refinance now fits within your reduced salary's budget, and you should be able to handle most of your regular expenses."

"What about Anne's trust fund—down payment on the house?"

"Tell her the truth. When you have the debts paid off, maintain those payments to repay the fund."

"How can I tell her that she'll have to let most of the house help go?"

"Give her a choice: the help or the house. That ought to settle it."

"Thomas?"

"He won't say a word if you demonstrate that you have your finances under control."

Charles and his dignity were saved. Anne complied and never questioned his once-a-month "visits" to Michael's house. She thanked her brother frequently for rescuing them from the brink, but she never acknowledged the part Kiri played in throwing her husband a lifeline.

Michael sat up to flex his shoulders. In an unusually loud and thick Irish brogue, he announced. "Think I'll go for a walk-about in search of the 'little people' while 'tis not raining out. Care to come, love?" Kiri shook her head, hiding her flushed face behind her hands as Michael moved quickly up and down the aisle muttering "tiny tales," bits of Irish lore and limerick, to the passengers. He returned from his stretch and quickly fell asleep again, leaving her to admire his ability to make the best of any situation and put others at ease.

At the sound of his snore, Kiri recalled the spring following Charles' financial catastrophe when she answered a knock on the door to a middle-aged couple she did not recognize. They introduced themselves as the son and daughter of the older folks who lived next door on the west. They asked for Michael. "We heard from Paddy across the road that your husband might be able to help us."

"Don't tell me these people I've never seen before are family," she whispered to him as he came to greet them.

"What can I do to help you folks?"

They looked nervously from Michael to Kiri and back again, several times.

Michael could sense their discomfort and their inevitable appeal. "My wife, Kirin, helps me with all major decisions. What can *we* do to help?"

After taking seats in the living room and accepting tea, the son began. "Our parents finally reached the age when we must move them into a home near my sister in County Cavan. In order to finance that, we are desperate to sell the house here, even at a loss. The banks aren't willing to help, and the realtors say the same. The few buyers there are don't want an older home in an old section of town when they can wait a while longer until prices drop more and pick up a newer home on the outskirts. We're out of ideas, and Paddy told us… said you might have some suggestion to help."

Their intent was obvious, but Michael tried not to make it seem so by conversing casually about family and the neighborhood. Kiri broke in occasionally with more pointed questions which the concerned siblings were now able to answer with ease.

"We'll put on our thinkers and see if an idea or two come to mind. Plan to visit again day after tomorrow, and we'll make some suggestions then. Sorry to hear of your misfortunes. Your parents are good neighbors to us."

Kiri knew what that suggestion would be. After examining where their accounts stood—up, with her working extra hours at the network—and crunching numbers again, Michael announced, "I think we can do it. *We'll* buy the house. But this time we'll put ourselves on a strict payback schedule so we'll be done within five to seven years." When the brother and sister returned, he had contracts ready and a down payment check cut. Elation, appreciation and a few signatures later, the deal was finalized.

"We're now the proud owners of three properties on the same road. Pretty soon we'll have a whole village!" Michael beamed with pride.

"We're still working on our own home. What will we do with a whole village?"

"No worries. I have a plan, but I won't share it until our anniversary."

Michael's kindness extended beyond his family circle, the true embodiment of compassion. She remembered fondly how he revealed through his second anniversary pledge that he intended to convert the property next door into Kiri's business headquarters. "We'll tear out most of the interior walls and create studio space upstairs and down—yoga, *tai chi*, whatever you and Paula want—with a couple of counseling rooms in case you decide to go that direction. In the back, we'll build a huge pool for you to offer therapeutic aquatics. Soon, you'll be busier than I am, and I'll have to be satisfied with listening to you splash around next door. What do you think?"

That pledge became a reality just a few weeks ago when he told her all permits and plans were approved and they could start digging soon after their return from this mission.

During the intervening years, Michael made time to take the nieces and nephews hiking and camping, to America twice to see the buffalo, and into open water for swimming lessons which included throwing the older kids overboard into the Irish Sea to toughen them up. They just learned the rudiments of sailing when autumn set in and he was due to leave again with promises that the fun would resume in the spring. "But you won't get to come," he told Kiri. "You'll be cozy and warm at home incubating."

Kiri chuckled over his now constant references to the future they awaited with excitement. After three years of stalemate on the subject of starting their family, his choice to cut back on overseas work now made that possible. She realized the wisdom of allowing him to come to that decision in his own time, for he was more accepting of it.

Michael took the second shift, staying awake from Geneva to Istanbul on a military transport with webbed sling seats not large enough for his bulk in sleeping position. Kiri tired by this stage and stretched out as if in a hammock. He rubbed her neck and shoulders just so and found the right pressure points to hasten relaxation and sleep. She removed her boots so her feet would not swell and gave in more easily than usual, allowing him to reflect on their last three years together.

Many Irish carry a sense of place and of family wherever they go, but time causes a yearning for their native isle that they cannot ignore. So it was with Michael, he remembered. After a couple of months in Denver following their wedding—the second one—he was anxious to return. Both he and Kiri filled their days with work and the weekends with play, but he continued to nudge her toward his Ireland. When they finally did move back to Dublin, he realized the wisdom of allowing her to come to that decision in her own time, for she was more accepting of it.

Their first few weeks back in Ireland were filled with getting used to each other in their home with the octagonal bedroom he built for her. He returned to regular assignments with the network, first in Dublin and then a little further afield, then the continent and finally back to the Middle East. Kiri returned to part-time work with Charles' bank and, with Henry's urging, spent off-hours working on a procedural manual for addressing women's issues. With Michael gone more frequently and for longer periods of time, Kiri threw herself into classes, both online and at Trinity. With his encouragement, she developed two particular areas of interest: aquatic therapy for geriatric patients and trauma psychotherapy in which she had first-hand experience.

Their first major disagreement turned into more of a discussion. "You're gone so much that when you are home I want us to spend time together," Kiri complained. "By that I mean you and me, not the whole family. I'm tired of the family thing—always doing what everyone else wants and expects of us. We need alone time together." Michael agreed. Being with family was so natural to him, he did not realize it would not be the same for Kiri. They decided to pencil in important events but to beg off casual ones—every Sunday tea, every birthday party and every holiday.

That helped. But when he returned from a six-week stint in the Middle East and found her packed for counseling fieldwork in Glasgow, he was hurt. "When I come home, I expect you to be here so we *can* spend time together."

"I expect the same, and I come home every night to an empty house. Where are you? I'm trying to understand your need for your job, but I have needs too and they aren't being met. I don't like being alone."

"You wouldn't be alone if we started our family. You'd have children to keep you company."

"Well, we don't, and we *won't* until I know you'll be around to help!"

That was their first—and last—grizzly argument. It ended with their agreement to discuss fiery topics during neutral times when they could think critically and not emotionally. Then came the Arab Spring uprisings.

As the network's extraction specialist, Michael was dispatched immediately at the first sign of trouble in Tunisia. Kiri put up no resistance and cancelled their ski trip to Colorado. Within days, Henry contacted her. "We need your help."

"London?"

"Not this time."

"If you think I'll ever put my boots down on Middle Eastern soil again, you're crazy." She rubbed the scar on her arm.

"We're thinking Geneva. If we're to follow *your* recommendations, we need to assess mental trauma as soon after events as possible. We're starting to see more women than we anticipated—and as you predicted— trying to get out of Tunisia, both reporters and informants' family members. We thought we could cut a couple of days off the wait for them to see you in London if we moved you to Geneva for the time being. Now that you're certified, there will be no problem putting you back on the payroll full-time."

"What does Michael say about this?"

"I'm not asking Michael. He's busy. I'm asking you."

"I'll be ready in an hour."

That was when Kiri became a specialist, not in treating, but in assessing mental and emotional trauma and recommending immediate intervention or a regular course of therapy once in London. "Trauma triage," they came to call it. She had a facility for keen and quick analysis, management and referral, and the ability to convey compassion borne of shared experience. She left tissues and warm fuzzies to others.

Michael returned home to find her prepped to pamper him with a sensuous shave and two-fingers-length haircut such as she performed following his full and complete recovery from their ordeal in Yemen and from every major mission thereafter. His transformation from an exhausted, wildly kinky-haired and bearded foreign correspondent into a stylish, handsome manly man became a first step in an affectionate welcome home ritual. When he learned how she helped, he was so proud of her… and showed her in every way he knew once they came together again.

Eighteen days of protest in Egypt re-called the two into service. Kiri went to Geneva for a few days, but when it became evident that a press pass and their gender would not protect female journalists from assault by an angry mob, the team sent her to Egypt—despite the protestations of her boots. She worked near the coast first, then in a small town not far from

Cairo, and finally at the airport where many foreign nationals tried to evacuate.

Patrick objected. "We aren't paying Kiri to help every weeping female get out of the country. She's supposed to take care of *our* people!"

Henry shot back in her defense, "If she treats only those employed by the network, a trail will lead right back here, and we'll be out of business. As Karys Kolton again, she works for a relief agency and fast-tracks our people while processing others. She's a whiz with the documentation needed to get them out, and her improved Arabic gives her a step up when dealing with Egyptian authorities. She earns every euro we pay her."

When Michael returned home to a sensuous shave and haircut and learned how she helped, he was so proud of her... and showed her in every way he knew once they came together again.

The war in Libya called them into action for a third time, this one together. Since Libya was surrounded on three sides by unfriendly countries having internal problems of their own, and on a fourth by the Mediterranean Sea, flights out were an impossibility, so the marine option seemed the best bet. As a British overseas territory with a naval base, Gibraltar provided the most efficient exit for anyone with proper passport and documentation for a direct flight to London. The islands of Sicily and Sardinia were closer but problematic because a stop there involved another country's government. Best to keep their undercover operation in-house. The British Foreign Office was used to unusual requests from its major broadcasting company, so would not object to frequent activity in the harbor. The safety of loyal British citizens was paramount.

For this operation, the whole crew was called in: Devin, to run the networks inside Libya; Frank, to organize a safe house near the western border; and Gus, to run transport from the house to the coast. Michael, the only one with nautical skills and the ability to use them in the dark of night, piloted a 15-foot Zodiac from the coast to international waters to rendezvous with a yacht which cruised to Gibraltar and back every few days for a repeat. Henry, their extra man in the field when needed, met the yacht in Gibraltar to coordinate the last leg to London. Doyle and Kiri were stationed on a relief/medical aid ship anchored just outside Libyan waters to pick up refugees fleeing the war in their country or wounded who were transferred there. Once again, they posed as Welsh medic volunteers... until the dark hours.

Patrick exploded at Michael's initial plan. "You want to buy a yacht!"

"Not exactly. I'm sure we could lease a 65-foot vessel from a tour company. Old yachts are frequently converted to accommodate tourists for short hops along coasts. They should have proper registrations and flags already. We supply the 'tourists.'"

"Ridiculous! Absolutely not!"

"I think that's a clever idea. Might work," Henry nodded. "No one will suspect... except the crew when they embark passengers in the middle of the night in the middle of the sea, but we can probably hire a mute bunch for that as well. How long do you think the operation will take?"

"Figure twelve to fifteen days—four to five trips—to get everyone out who wants to leave. The zodiac can carry eight passengers besides me. You decide who stays and who replaces, and line them up. I'll take whoever's got a ticket, either direction. Devin and Frank should remain for the duration in case we have to slip into action again—the quiet and on the sly guys, remember."

"Excellent. Can't tell how long this one will last. Remember, you'll be reporting as well."

"Absolutely. Can't compromise the cover. I'll swim back to make primetime if I have to," Michael smiled, then his face expressed concern. "'Tis the informants' families I'm worried about—the ones with no travel documents or temporary visas. That's where Doyle and Kiri come in... in the dark hours."

With only Libyan national passports and if caught trying to leave the country, families could be detained in camps, or worse, indefinitely. The trick was to get them into international territory, arrange documentation before they set foot on foreign soil, and then move them along accepted channels—a week of uncertainty at most. Kiri and Doyle spent an inordinate amount of time fishing life-jacketed and –boated refugees out of the water during the dark hours.

Her intensive water training prepared Kiri perfectly for deep-sea rescue. Her facility for battling through bureaucracy was a plus when it came to filing visa applications by fax from the ship's communication center, photos and all. She spent equal time with the families, verifying that they did not suffer mental or physical abuse in the process and assuring them that adjustment to a new life would be difficult, but once they got a taste of freedom, just like strawberry ice cream, they would love it.

She and the others came to realize that their rescue missions were not all water games. One of their camera teams was captured, beaten and subjected to mock executions before they could be extracted, and a Danish evacuation mission ended three lives with the crash of their helicopter, justifying Michael's push for a solution by sea. After a strenuous, but successful, few weeks he remembered coming home to a sensuous shave and a haircut. He was so proud of Kiri... and showed her in every way he knew, once they came together again in Dublin.

Now, here she was, finally sleeping peacefully with her head in his lap, on the way to their next—and last—adventurous assignment together, and she had no understanding of how dangerous it would be. When Patrick first outlined this mission, Michael protested. The team had never done anything like it before—extract two different groups from two different cities at one time. Patrick insisted that the situation grew worse daily and an opportunity presented itself. With proper planning, Michael could make it work. The young agent appealed to Henry who also thought it risky but with budget cuts and limited time, if they could pull off a two-for-one operation, it would be quite a coup and validate their usefulness when all corporations sought to cut expenses and personnel. Reluctantly, Michael agreed if they would give him full control over the operation.

That is why he was so surprised when Patrick showed up at his door saying, "Plans changed. New developments." Michael made the plans, and he did *not* change them. When Henry explained that there was an opportunity for a three-part rescue of non-combatant professional personnel, Michael went ballistic "Why now!"

"A UN envoy will visit Syria and Lebanon this week to discuss peace efforts. We hope for calm while he is there."

"Can't be done! We're the quiet and on the sly guys. We work with our own and take care of our own. We don't trust anyone else! That's what makes us so effective. Two groups make too many variables. Three increase the risk exponentially and spread us too thin. I'm axing the whole deal!"

"It's your job, Michael. If anyone can pull this off, you can. We worked out the logistics for you. Take a look, at least. Your original plan is superlative—no problems there. We just slip the third piece into place following the same pattern, and it's done. Doyle is already in Syria making arrangements. You can do this," Henry assured him.

Patrick hid his devious grin behind his hand.

"Time to wake up, Ms. Karys Kolton, relief worker in disguise. Get your boots on because…"

"…a man is dead in his tracks without them," she smiled.

Chapter 4

Kiri crouched on a hillock and squinted south toward the harsh landscape of the Syrian border not a half-mile away. Michael kneeled, dug into the soft soil beneath a pile of rock and unearthed a case holding a pair of field glasses. "Here. Give these a try," he said, sitting beside her. Wide-eyed, she accepted. "I have a stash," he offered.

"I suppose you have a stash on the other side too," she said, focusing on the border crossing. "These are powerful. I can practically read nametags."

"Not a stash. Over there, I have a 'guy.' Several in fact. Every time I've been here over the past year, I've spent at least a week observing from this very spot all movement in and around the complex in case this extraction ever became a necessity. Use the glasses now to get a feel for the lay of the land. Memorize every detail—guards and their manner, huts and their purpose, roads and their direction, neighborhoods. You may have to use that knowledge when we're separated."

"Separated!" The binocs dropped into her lap.

"Yes. We can't cross together. Too suspicious. I'll go first. If I have any trouble, go immediately to the medical trailer near the refugee camp and wait for word. If all goes well—as I expect, since they don't have fingerprint scanners at this crossing yet—you can follow in five to ten minutes. Once you're in, if you don't see me, go to the second road down, turn left, then right onto the next. See that green storefront? We'll meet there to pick up our vehicle, money, etc. We can't bring anything— weapons, currency, goods, vehicles—into the country, and we can't take them out. Quite a sub-economy has grown up near the border crossings to keep anything of value from leaving the country.

"If you do have trouble at this checkpoint, my guy will try to intercede or, worst case if they won't let you in, go to the med trailer and wait." He hesitated. "The guards will probably search you, you know."

"I'll make sure I have my watch, glasses and phone together in a bag so I won't have to take time to find them."

"No. I mean... really search."

Their eyes met. "Oh." Kiri sighed. "I guess I should expect the same treatment refugee women are subjected to. Do they really search every female?"

"Not every one, but you are ripe for it—a comely, fair-skinned young woman. Try not to show anger, fear or contempt."

"I've heard that advice before."

He gave her time to study the facility and surrounding area. He shook his head at Patrick's hair-brained insistence that Kiri be involved. Michael argued that she could easily do her job on this side of the border. Set up a screening tent near the clinic. No need to take her inside the war-torn country, but rogue Patrick insisted she be on hand for verification of documents.

"Ingrained in that keen mind of yours?" She nodded. He replaced and covered the field glasses. "For next time," he said, patting the soil firmly. "Oh, I forgot. For the *last* time," he corrected with a smile. "Come with me, Ms. Karys Kolton." He grabbed her by the hand. "You get to play my souped-up phonecam person today."

This is BBC reporter Michael O'Connell speaking from southern Turkey near a Syrian refugee camp by the Oncupinar border. What appear as rows of metal freight cars butted end-to-end are trailers—containers—for housing the hundreds of Syrians daily who flee the heightened conflict in their country. Hordes flood in and are funneled from the border crossing nearby to this place. After signing a refugee certificate, they are assigned a temporary home with two windows, a door, perhaps another family, and a central well in a common area at the end of one of the many roads— paradise compared to the squalid, makeshift camps in the south. Behind me, strings of colorful laundry hang across the narrow roads suggesting some semblance of normal daily activity. Even narrower alleyways between the rows serve as playgrounds for the many children who seem happy to escape the sudden thuds of exploding bombs and the sights of their neighborhoods in ruin....

*   *   *

The border crossing did not open until an hour past dawn, despite the throngs gathered to flee the country. Not many waited to get in, so Michael passed through with no problem. His visa was long-standing and in order. Kiri's was recently issued, so they gave her a second look and a search. The guard who did the honors was pudgy-short, had a beaky nose and a bushy mustache long at the sides that jounced when he barked orders. She would not forget him anytime soon.

Michael fell in beside her after she crossed the first road heading east. In short order his guy joined them, led them to a waiting four-wheel drive Land Cruiser, and drove them off the main drag and to Azaz where he disappeared along a back road into the town after exchanging words and supplies with Michael.

"What was..." Kiri began to ask until Michael stopped her with a *shush.* Sometime later he pulled off the road, got out and motioned her to do the same. When they were well away from the vehicle, he explained. "I haven't had a chance to check out this Cruiser. Once I'm sure we're not bugged or tracked, we'll rig ourselves and be on our way."

He examined the vehicle carefully, returned to her and parceled out the supplies: an earwig for each connected to the Dublin office, a GPS disc to feed through a slit into the ribbing at the neck of their T-shirts and a buttoncam to stick into their shirt pockets. "We create our own secure

35

channels of communication." Michael also doled out a knife for each which they slipped into their right boots and a light backpack with food, water, maps, some local currency and a phone.

"I'm #1, then Henry, Doyle, Frank and Gus. Henry and Devin will monitor our movements and communications around the clock. No disappearing from the face of the earth this time," he chuckled. "Remember, we are two strangers sharing a ride. No personal comments. You were directed to report to the Red Cross office in Damascus and were stranded with no bus service, so I was sent to pick you up. I will initiate any conversation between us. Please refrain from showering me with your affections." He gave her a wink. "From this point on, we're all business. Now, I'm going to call Henry to activate our systems and run a test."

During the call, they both responded to commands to speak, answer questions, and focus their buttoncams on one another. "All's coming through loud and clear. Take care, you two. See you in a few," Henry said from Dublin before he cut the feed.

Michael headed for the car, but Kiri stopped him. "If we can't talk freely there, maybe you should let me in on the plan now."

He grew thoughtful and ran his fingers into his hair, scratching above his forehead. "'Twas a good one until Patrick threw the last bit in. We're using a mid-size tour bus originating in Palmyra where it's been under wraps for months. Since that city is a historical tourist hotspot, the folks there are used to seeing tours with foreigners pass through. The bus will collect our charges along the way. Gus is driving and Frank is the director."

"That's ridiculous! The bus will stand out like a giraffe in the desert."

"The best we can do right now. Air and sea options are out, so we have to travel overland. The 'tour' is a special one for researchers following the Euphrates River from Iraq through Syria, and to its source in Turkey. Every time it reaches a checkpoint, 'tis rerouted toward the main motorway in the west—or that's what the paperwork will show, thanks to another one of my guys. The small bus can carry a group of men and women of various nationalities, food, water and petrol without questions, but a convoy of half a dozen jeeps trying to do the same will draw suspicion, strange as that may seem. The added complication of trying to find trustworthy drivers for that many vehicles makes the one-bus option more logical.

"A couple will travel on their own from Homs to our rendezvous in Hama, and now Patrick has thrown in a family from Damascus. I don't like it. I don't know them or their background. Verifying their papers will be your job. That, and warning them of what lies ahead for women at the border. Patrick knows there are only twenty seats on the bus. Now he's added you and Doyle and a family—a really tight fit. If the other guys pick up any extra... well, I don't like it one bit."

"If I'm causing such a problem, why am I here?"

"That's what I keep asking myself. But you are, so we'll make the best of it. Ready, Karys, medic volunteer?"

Midafternoon, as they skirted Aleppo, Michael turned sharply toward the major city and called Henry. "Follow us. Jets headed for Aleppo. Me too." At Henry's protests he laughed, "Can't keep a reporter from a good story," and gunned the motor, keeping his eyes on the sky.

Kiri wrapped her shawl more tightly around her head and neck as she thought, *how can I ask Michael to give up the thrill of the chase? The elation of being first on the scene?*

He pulled up abruptly facing thick plumes of smoke near the ancient city's center and let the motor idle while they witnessed the bombing of a mosque during prayer time, trapping many inside and toppling its walls onto the crowd waiting in the square. He tossed Kiri his specially rigged phonecam and climbed onto the hood.

This is BBC reporter Michael O'Connell on the scene in the city of Aleppo in northwestern Syria. The smoke behind me masks the destruction of a mosque where government forces just bombed their own citizens. The screams are those of women and children, many injured, who gathered in the square while their men were at prayer and then crushed by the rubble— along with their petitions to the Almighty for peace in this war-torn land....

With a dramatic finish, he hopped down from the car and advised Henry, "That's my report for the day. Hold it as long as you can to give us time to get out of the city and past the major checkpoint. But Henry... we'd better be first with this one!"

Speeding south, Kiri noticed many burnt out cars and trucks, others that were abandoned, and stragglers on foot heading north. Some carried weapons and others, bundles of clothing, while holding fast to their children. The couple negotiated the government-held checkpoint with a minimum of difficulty. Michael's documents—at least the ones he used at that moment—confirmed him as a relief agency courier ferrying medical supplies and one female medic bound for the south. The guards searched one of the many cartons Kiri had not noticed in the back of the vehicle and found only water, bandages and antiseptic. After some raised eyebrows and condescending glares, the vehicle was allowed to pass through. Kiri nudged Michael and attempted to mouth questions, but he ignored her for several miles.

Finally, he spoke. "Henry, it's safe to release that broadcast now, but shut the two of us down for a while, please. We'll check in shortly." When he felt certain their mics were cut off so they could talk freely, he answered her. "The government restricted access for foreign journalists some time ago and refuses many of us entry. I can be a correspondent to get in and out of Turkey, but I cannot for Syria without threat of detainment, imprisonment or simple denial to cross the border. The whole team carries dual sets of documents... except you, of course."

"Where do you keep all these papers? Do you have second skins or something?"

"Trade secret. Maybe I'll let you search me when this is all over," he said with a gleam in his eye.

"The medical supplies?"

"We'll set them by a well when we leave our meeting place. Every village is in desperate need. Now, *shush*." He touched his finger to his phone. "Henry, back on duty here."

Michael turned off-road at nightfall just north of Hama and followed a narrow track into a gully. They left the Cruiser, took their gear and climbed up the opposite side to higher ground. "Welcome to your hotel," he said, stretching out a canvas. "Room service brought us some granola bars. Eat up. Then try to get some sleep." He removed a gun from his pack and set it by his side.

"Where did that come from?"

"From my guy."

"Why do you need it?"

"To fend off the snakes and scorpions while you sleep."

Kiri squealed and jumped to her feet. Michael laughed. "I'm only teasing. I've camped here many nights and have always come home to you unscathed." He smoothed the canvas and pulled her back down to it. "I'm glad you're here, Ki... Karys. With you framing the shots, you keep me from cutting myself off at the nose when I get excited and flail my arms. I might have to hire you as my permanent cameraperson. Oh, I can't. Because I won't need one." He smiled and reached for his phone. "Henry? Just making sure you're there, in case we get company in the night."

"Let me take first watch," Kiri offered. "You've done all the work today."

"You? Watch?"

"I've got eyes and ears. Besides, you know I can't sleep when I'm away from home. I'll wake you if I start to get tired... or if a snake slithers in."

"Since you insist." Michael laid his head in her lap, hugged her around the waist and snuggled against her tummy. "Night, night, little pea pod, and *grá anois agus go deo,* to you, little mother. *"*

"And to you," she whispered, bending to kiss the nest of hair sheltering his ear.

"Cut it out you two," Devin scolded into their earwigs. "You're on the clock, remember."

*   *   *

"Patrick! What's the holdup?" Eyes afire, Michael shouted into Kiri's chest so the Dublin contingent could not mistake his anger. "Doyle and his group are twenty minutes late. We're on a tight schedule here!"

"Dunno. Last I heard, they were looking for *you*," Patrick replied from a well-fitted communications center in the deep recesses of the network's Dublin offices.

"They're not supposed to be looking for me. They're supposed to go to the address I gave you, and I will find *them*," Michael shouted in frustration. "I want to speak directly to Doyle. Now!"

"Don't think we can do that." Patrick tried to stall.

"Done!" shouted Devin.

"Doyle, buddy, where the hell are you?"

"Weaving in and out through this neighborhood looking for the bus."

"Well, you won't find it. The bus is waiting for you someplace else. Who said anything about a bus? Did you?"

"No. My driver keeps saying he can't find the bus, so he makes another pass around the area. Why?"

"Stop, get out of the van now and stand by the hood. Only you. Don't say a word to anyone else. Describe your vehicle."

"Tan '97 Toyota van."

While Doyle did as instructed, Michael scanned the area from his perch atop a huge pile of rubble on the edge of the partially bombed out neighborhood just east of Hama, not far from where the highway from Palmyra entered the city. He overturned a couple of scarred stones to reveal a second stash with a second pair of field binoculars among other tools. Kiri shook her head at her squirrel of a husband and peered toward the battered buildings as well.

"That's you? I've watched you weave 'round for quarter of an hour. Thought it was some drunk couldn't find his way. I can guarantee you haven't been followed. Look, I'm uneasy about your driver. He shouldn't know about the bus. Any way you can pay him off and leave him there? You come on alone?"

"No. He claims he was promised a seat, and he has papers."

"OK. I'll give you directions. Don't write them down, don't speak them and don't signal until you are right on a turn. Got it?" At Doyle's thumbs up, Michael continued. "Straight ahead, six roads. Turn right... just a minute... one, two... seven roads... right again... follow around the curve about a quarter of a mile, then right at the well and continue to a burnt out garage on the left. You'll see me. I'll call the bus in now. If you aren't here in ten minutes, you won't find us here either. You can all find your own ride home."

Doyle gave another thumbs up.

"That was rather harsh," Kiri said as they watched the speck of van drive away. Michael put a finger to his lips and shook his head to stop her from saying more. They scrambled down the loose pile of twisted metal and stone while he was connected to, and gave similar directions to, Gus in the bus. When they reached their own vehicle, he covered both buttoncams with one arm, then wrote on a dusty window, *Don't trust driver. Watch him.* Kiri nodded, and he wiped the words away before they proceeded to the abandoned garage.

In Dublin's communication center, Patrick Murphy listened nervously to the conversations, breathed a deep sigh of relief when everyone moved again, and left the room with a smile.

*   *   *

Michael jumped when he heard his phone ring, then felt in his pockets remembering that he carried three at the moment. The shrill sound came from the one he gave his guy in Homs to guide that group to the rendezvous. They arrived first: a translator, his wife and three children. The bus turned up minutes later carrying fifteen plus Gus and Frank: reporters, informants/sources, translators of both genders, spouses, children and somebody's mother added when the father was killed in a bombing a week earlier. They numbered seven men, five women, and three children. Just before the deadline, the van rolled in with Doyle and the driver, an informant, his father and his wife, his two children and... a lanky blond young man? Michael did a double-take. "Where did this clown come from!" he shouted into Kiri's mic with his raging eyeball up against her buttoncam. "Is he on my list? Find Patrick!"

Before the evasive agent materialized, Michael hustled everyone out of the vehicles and discovered yet another passenger—the van driver's son, a frightened little boy of about five clutching a teddy bear. "What the... Patrick! Thanks to the group you added, I have thirty-three people here with their thumbs up their noses wondering how they're going to get out of this godforsaken country and only twenty-two seats on the bus. What do you expect us to do? Draw straws? Pick a number? Women and children first? That golden boy you sent along hardly looks like a Middle Easterner. He'll be the first we toss out."

Michael paced in circles around the nervous group with his hand to his ear listening to his superior try to reason a solution. "I don't care whose cousin Blondie is or how you wrangled him a Swedish passport, he's not getting the first seat. We take care of our own, and the Americans can take care of theirs. Our guys have priority!" he shouted.

Discussion and expletives followed until Kiri burst in. "Shut up and take your team outside."

"How dare you talk to me like that, Ki..."

"It's *Ms. Kolton* to you, sir. And if you don't want *my* agency to come down hard on *yours*, you'll step outside... now!" She gathered the men around her out of the passengers' earshot and ignored Michael's daggered stare. "For a group of professionals, you are behaving as unprofessional as it gets! Twenty-eight people in there are scared to death that this day may be their last, and you are arguing in front of them about who should live and who might die. When they signed on to work with you men, they were assured that when the time came, you would take care of them. Now that time has come! They are giving up their lives here for the unknown. All they have left is faith that you will keep your word."

Doyle, Frank and Gus sobered. Michael tried to hide his embarrassment behind bluster. Kiri continued. "Your responsibility is to come up with a plausible plan, never mind Patrick's ineptitude. Now, what was the purpose of the bus in the first place? To get a group *to* the border or *across* the border?"

"To the border, it looks like now. We didn't see any vehicles moving across yesterday. Any of our people should be okay to walk with proper documentation, but we can't make two trips with the same bus."

"As I recall, you said that a convoy of similar vehicles would be suspect and they would require trustworthy drivers. None of the vehicles here are similar, and if they travel fifteen to twenty minutes apart, they shouldn't be suspect. As for drivers, I see four standing around me right now—four men whose particular talent is extracting their charges from desperate situations. Do your jobs! Put your heads together and come up with a logical cover for getting us all out of here fast. I'm going to do mine and make sure that if *you* can get them to the border, every man, woman and child can legally cross." Kiri turned and reentered the burnt out garage, not waiting for further discussion.

In the network's Dublin communication center, Patrick shuddered every time he heard his name spoken with such disdain. At Kiri's reasoned usurpation of the argument, he clapped his fist into his palm and grinned. "I knew she could do it! That woman has a way of getting right to the heart of a problem."

Henry turned on him immediately. "Are you saying that the only reason you sent Kiri into harm's way was to solve a problem of your making?"

"Not the only reason," he smirked as he left the room.

*   *   *

Kiri just completed the examination of paperwork when the team returned, not elated but resigned. In a form of general announcement, Michael said to the group, "Everyone is going as far as the Syrian border—unless you've changed your minds. The family of five from the car will take the empty seats on the bus, the van will drive out as it came in, and Ki... Ms. Kolton and I will follow in our vehicle. If you have anything you need to do, do it now... over there." He motioned to a small room with only a four-foot wall remaining. A few of the passengers lined up to use it.

"Find any problems?" he asked Kiri.

"Only a couple. All ID's are in order. The van driver and his son have passports but no exit visas. We may have to let everyone else cross first, and then I can help those two try to get one at the border. That shouldn't be too much of a problem if we can come up with… number two… an itinerary document for after they've crossed. You know, like a hotel, train or flight confirmation that states they are headed out of the border area. The folks on tour obviously have them and so does your family from Homs. Good work, guys. But the ones Patrick bunched together don't—not even the American." She spoke louder and with emphasis into Doyle's ear. "I'm sure the documentation could be waiting at the border. That would help the exit visa problem too."

"Good call. Anything else?"

"One of the female reporters has been… compromised. I've asked the older woman who just lost her husband to watch out for her. Sort of a mutual consolation society—shared loss. Seat them together on the bus, please. And…"

"More complaints about the way I handle my job?" Michael asked tersely.

"Just an observation. Ask each group to stand by its vehicle." They did without being asked. "What is your cover for the bus?"

"The same. A research group whose tour was diverted."

"And the van?"

"A Syrian family heading for the border."

"Look at the two groups. What's wrong with that picture."

Michael and his team surveyed the nervous passengers and shook their heads.

Kiri asked, "How many groups of researchers do you imagine have children as members?" Jaws dropped and spirits deflated. "And a family of Syrians is not likely to have an American or Spanish uncle," she said, alluding to Blondie and the Iberian sailor in Doyle's background.

Frank motioned adults to one side, children to the other. The two teens sided with the little ones. The driver stayed with his son and the other children. "The numbers are about right," Michael said, "and that takes care of Doyle and Blondie. But when the government guards stop us at the checkpoint, they are likely to think we're either stealing their kiddies or saving them. If it's stealing, they'll shoot us all. If it's saving… well, we'd better look like we're rushing them to help. Any ideas? How about you back home in Dublin?"

No comments drifted into their ears, so Gus spoke up. "I have eight sisters and tons of nieces and nephews, and they're always getting hurt. You know, scrapes and bumps. Maybe we could say we're taking them to a doctor."

"Without a scrape or a scratch to be seen? That's mad," Frank said.

"It might work if we could make them look sick or injured," Michael said. "We have some medical supplies. What do you think, Henry?"

"Better than the alternative. Go for it," came the word from Dublin.

A frenzy of activity ensued. Frank and Doyle looted the medical supplies and wrapped gauze around heads and arms. Gus examined the van to see if any of the seats could be removed easily for the "wounded" children to lie down and found the stash of tools. Michael siphoned gas from the car to the Cruiser, topped off the bus' tank with petrol from the containers it carried, and emptied the remains into the van.

Kiri asked the women to congregate on the opposite side of the bus, and she gave them a heads up about what to expect at the border. She then gathered the children to explain what was about to happen and how important it was to mind the adults in the van. "If you are touched or poked, it is okay to whimper or cry. That's what children do when they are scared or hurt." With her limited Arabic, she was thankful when one of the mothers came to help.

A couple of the fathers lent Gus a hand with seats, and another swabbed bright orange antiseptic onto bare skin and bandages. A third sorted ID's and placed them in plastic bags around the children's ankles, setting the rest of their papers on the driver's seat. At the end of less than half an hour, Michael scanned his buttoncam around the garage and asked for approval from the Dublin supervisors.

"Looks good. Time to hit the road," Henry replied. "Travel safe, everyone. See you in a couple of days."

Suddenly the plan broke apart like an upended jigsaw puzzle. The van driver refused to get in. He was afraid of the checkpoint; he did not know how to explain to the guards when he did not understand himself. He pulled his son, still clutching the teddy bear, away from the van. The men put their heads together and decided the little boy would look suspect in the bus, so driver and son should travel in Michael's vehicle where he could keep an eye on the untrustworthy passenger. That put Doyle in the driver's seat. Kiri said she would ride shotgun; someone needed to keep the children calm.

"You will not!" Michael objected.

"Oh yes I will. Those kids need a woman nearby."

She started to get in when the Homs translator from the car spoke up. "I will drive the van. I have license and no problem with accent or dialect. Three of those children are mine, so I will stay with them."

Michael nodded, allowing Doyle and the translator to trade places. Then the man's wife volunteered. "I will go with my husband and children. I can speak with all of them more better than Ms. Kolton. Thank you," she said and stood next to the van.

Henry in Dublin objected. "We can't have three of you on the bus and only one behind. We need to maximize our options in case the van runs into trouble. Doyle rides with you."

"Right. Kiri, you are on the bus."

She shook her head. "For the same reason, I should be in the vehicle behind the children. In case of trouble, the more hands the better. The bus, twenty minutes ahead, can't turn around in the middle of the highway without attracting attention and can't get back in time to do much good. That would put the whole operation in jeopardy."

"Kiri's right." To the team's surprise, it was Patrick's voice coming to them from Dublin. "Gus and Frank in the bus up front. Michael, Doyle and Kiri in the rear. That way they can surge ahead to help either vehicle in trouble. Let's get going." He rubbed his hands together in satisfaction at the part he played in the drama.

That left two empty seats on the bus. The two older teens switched places gladly, leaving their bandages behind and reclaiming their papers. Michael started to give the "everyone line up for a pat down" signal, when Devin in Dublin chimed in. "Hold it! We won't have any communication with the van if all of you ride front and rear."

Visibly frustrated, Patrick shouted through cyberspace, "Well, figure it out and move!"

"I'll give up my earwig. That way the van will be in verbal contact at least. If you keep satellite video on them, that should be enough," Kiri said. "I'll be with the other two men, so I won't need it. I still have my GPS tracker, and if I'm in real trouble, I'll send an SOS with my buttoncam," she joked, patting her chest pocket.

"That will have to do," Henry agreed. "We're working on getting a second satellite for the next few hours, so we'll alternate that one between the bus and Michael's rig. Hustle, guys. We need everyone across the border before it closes at dark. Good luck."

Michael strode to the center of the garage. "Folks, this may be the hardest part of your day. Put all your mobile phones, electronic devices, games, cameras, whatever… on the ground. Pen knives, anything metal and/or sharp—just like on a plane—on the ground. We don't want the guards at the government checkpoint to find anything unusual. That goes for you, too, Blondie. No tweets, chirps or letters from home. Nothing to suggest you are American. Keep your hat on, your eyes down and your mouth shut." While Frank bagged the contraband, Gus and Michael started to pat down the passengers from each end of the line. As they boarded, Kiri noticed the violated young woman help the recent widow up the steps and into a seat.

"All of your electronics will be replaced at your final destination. Put on those sunglasses, pull out the maps, and look like tourists. Safe travels." Michael waved as the door closed and the bus pulled away. "Dublin. Vehicle #1 is on the move."

He turned to the remaining passengers. "Same for you lot. Empty your pockets of everything. Toys, games, chewing gum." The translator gave a more detailed explanation about how important it was not to hide anything that might make the guards suspicious. The seven children and three adults complied. The former driver laid his son's teddy bear gingerly on the ground.

Doyle gave the adults a twice-over, while Michael dealt with the children. "Airplane arms." He demonstrated. "I'll try not to tickle you," he winked. Some giggled as he gently felt their trunks, arms and legs. He tousled the hair of the driver's son who still seemed frightened by all the confusion. He examined the sparse collection of toys and a book or two, pushed the teddy bear aside and bagged the rest. "Keep these up front with you," he said to the translator. "Volunteer to give them up at the checkpoint. The guards will probably take a look and let you keep them. Sorry, but I have to take your phone."

"Is OK, Mr. O. I not need it. I can hear you talking in my ear." He smiled broadly. "We gonna be okay. Thank you many times. May your god bless all of you. We gonna be okay." He and his wife helped the children into the van and climbed in themselves. "We go now?"

"Ten minutes. I'll give you a nod."

While they exchanged thanks and shook hands, the former driver took his son by the arm, picked up the teddy bear, lifted both into Michael's vehicle and slid in beside them. The team emptied the bag of contraband and used the building's rubble to smash it into smithereens before dumping it all down the toilet hole. Michael nodded to the van. "Dublin. Vehicle #2 is on the move."

Michael pulled Doyle and Kiri aside. "That driver has me spooked. Where did you find him, Doyle?"

"I didn't. He found me. He said he was sent to drive a van to a rendezvous point, then ride the bus to the border. Since this last group was a hurry-up job, I picked up documentation and procured a van. I assumed..."

"We do *not* assume!" Michael tugged at the errant curl above his right eye. "I want to leave him right here, right now. Henry?"

"Here."

"Shut off the others. We need to talk privately."

"Done."

"What do you know about the van driver. I don't like the looks of him."

"Nothing beyond the fact that he's on Patrick's list and was sent the necessary papers. We weren't aware he would bring his son, but if the boy has papers too, Patrick must have known."

"Can we leave them behind?"

"I want to say yes, but we may not be privy to the man's importance. Maybe he's with the government and a surprise, just like the American. Patrick's not here right now, and I don't think we should hold up your departure any longer. We're behind as it is. I say, go ahead but keep your eye on him. We'll quiz Pat when he comes back and let you know."

"Privately?"

"Privately."

A sudden sharp squeal called attention to the Cruiser. The former driver shrugged and held up a hand apologetically. "No problem. My boy trying to sleep already, and I catch his finger in seatbelt. OK now. We ready to go."

Michael scuffed his boot on the ground. "Henry can't get back to us any too soon. Here's what we're going to do. Doyle, you ride up front with me." At Kiri's surprise, he continued, "We can't have a woman riding in front when there are other men in the vehicle. Get your shawl up around your head and you'll look like a nice little family back there. Keep your hand close to your knife and if there is the slightest hint of anything suspicious, give us a signal. Let's go."

The three comrades climbed into their assigned places, and Michael started the motor. "Dublin. Vehicle #3 is on the move."

Chapter 5

Barely an hour out of Hama, incinerated vehicles and bullet-riddled pickups with gun mounts in back bounded the pocked roadway, bearing evidence of recent battle and bombing. Patrick's driver leaned forward and found himself nose-to-nose with Doyle. "May we stop one minute?" the nervous man asked. "I need..." He glanced away with embarrassment.

"Make it quick. We're way behind schedule," Michael replied. His vehicle's occupants did not speak until that moment.

Kiri stared out the back window. "Something's wrong. This little boy hasn't moved a muscle since we left, and I've never known a guy to walk a quarter-mile to relieve himself. It looks like he's taking out a pho...."

Michael darted out of the vehicle, gun in hand, before she finished and Doyle jerked off the shirt covering the boy to expose his limp body with the teddy bear tightly seat-belted to him. "Bomb! Get out now!" he shouted. The sounds of explosion muffled his warning.

Patrick's phone rang the instant Doyle shouted. "Yes?" He nodded his head at the sound of a loud burst. "Thank you." He put his mobile away in an inside pocket and waited a few seconds until he heard confusion break out in the communication center down the hallway. Then he wiped a self-satisfied smile from his face and entered. "Trouble?"

"We heard a blast and then lost all contact with Michael's vehicle. We're trying to raise him now," Devin replied, sweat already beading on his forehead.

"I'd better let them know upstairs. Let's hope we aren't dealing with another kidnap for ransom situation." He left abruptly and closed the door firmly behind him, allowing that smile to return.

Kiri did not wait for Doyle's warning. The instant she spotted a wire sprouting from the bear's stomach, she bolted from the vehicle and toward the cover of battle wreckage. A millisecond later a heavy weight hit from behind and toppled her to the ground, forcing her face deep into grit. The earth lurched at the first, and then a second explosion shooting thick black smoke into the air. When the rain of road scrabble and flying metal subsided, she tried to raise her head to shout for Michael, but a firm hand held her down and a voice barely whispered, "No talk!" A head pressed close to hers and allowed the harried conversation in Dublin to come through loud and clear.

Doyle rolled the two of them slightly to the side, pointed to his ear, put a finger to his lips and shook his head. With panic in her eyes, Kiri nodded and then mouthed, "Michael." The agent on top of her pointed south where a lone figure sneaked swiftly from cover to cover away from them, parallel to the road. Doyle grinned and mouthed back, "OK."

Kiri calmed and pressed her ear closer to Doyle's to listen as Henry and Devin tried to make sense of the jumble of signals in front of them. At a lull, the agent flipped her quickly to point her chest to the sun. "Oh! What was that flash?" she heard via Doyle's ear. Then she felt tapping on her front pocket.

"Buttoncam malfunction. Can't tell whose," Devin replied from Dublin.

"There it is again. Regular pattern. A signal?" Henry asked.

"I can make out the distress sign, but that might be wishful thinking. Hand me pencil and paper in case."

"If it is intended, it's not making any sense. Just a scramble of letters."

Devin chuckled. "Gotta be Doyle. Only he would mutilate Gaelic like this. Hey, buddy. That you?" He watched the screen carefully and read to Henry as the flashes came through: "*Y.* That's yes. *Bomb. 3 alive.* If that's correct, give me two." Two bright glints, then darkness confirmed the time-tested transmission.

"Go ahead. *Pat.* He's not here. *Cutwigcs.* Done. *Cut GPS.* We don't like it, but we'll do it unless we lose contact again. *Cut recording.* You know we can't do that. Evidence. *Later. Later. Later.*" At Henry's nod, Devin shut down everything except the office's audio to the three stranded in Syria and their buttoncams to use as virtually indecipherable communication.

Michael's camera came to life in a flurry of less garbled signals: "*No IED. Bomb on boy. Suspect P.* Impossible! You are crazy! *P P P P P* OK! but I don't think he'd sabotage this mission. Too important. *Not mission. Me. Check in 2.*"

"What does 'check in 2' mean?" Henry asked.

"You spend too much time behind a desk and not conniving with the rest of us. It means, every quarter of an hour plus two minutes, like 3:02, 3:17 and so on." He checked the time signature in the lower right of his screen. "We'll get a flash in about twelve minutes. In the meantime, we should decide what to do about Patrick. He could walk in any time," Devin said.

The two men huddled to discuss plausible reasons for Patrick's involvement and how to convince him that none of their communications or the satellite could find the lost agents. Twelve minutes dragged by, then a flash from Michael. "All's clear here. Go ahead. *Where are we?* Don't tell me all your phones are out too. *All OK. Danger to use. Location.* You're about ten kilometers south of Maarat al-Numan. *Check in 2.* 'Til then."

Kiri lost track of Michael but tried not to worry as long as she could hear Devin's voice repeating his communiqués. His shadow, approaching from the opposite direction and behind, startled her. He sat on the ground beside her. "A sight for sore eyes, but I'm happy for it. Any injuries?"

She shook her head. "Doyle fell on top of me, and... oh my gosh, I didn't even ask if he got hit. I'm so sorry."

The big man laughed. "I'm fine, but I'm anxious to hear how this guy of yours plans to get us out of here."

"You joke. But I do have a plan... and a surprise for Patrick!"

Kiri clasped her knees and listened to the two men at her sides deep in analysis of the events of the last few days, searching for hints of guilt. Silent, she longed for a cuddle or even a pat on the back, but they remained unaware of her until her head fell forward in sobs. "How could he do it?" she cried. "How could a father blow his own son to bits like that? It doesn't make sense."

"None of this made sense, but it is beginning to." Michael held her now. "The boy was probably orphaned in the fighting, and the driver lured him away from his village with promise of more than a teddy bear."

"That doesn't make the memory less horrible. I can't forget..."

"I'm not suggesting you forget. I won't. But you need to counsel yourself right now so we can get through the next couple of days. Compartmentalize like I do. Find a space to fold tragic events away until you can deal with them from a different perspective. Tuck what happened today way back here." His fingers tiptoed a path through her snarled curls to find that sensitive place at the base of her skull. "Thanks to Patrick's talent for hiring incompetents to do his dirty work, we may have enough proof to link him to this fiasco once the vehicle cools and we can take a good look." He gave her a big hug, assuring that he had not forgotten her. "For now, we all have a job to do, so let's get on with it."

She smeared her tears across her sooty cheeks and fell in behind the two as they crept toward the smoldering remains of the vehicle, careful not to attract attention from passing traffic. At a scheduled signal to Dublin and after determining that Patrick was long gone, Michael requested that all audio, video and recording be resumed until he told them to cut it again. The three gave running commentary while they filmed the site. Michael exclaimed at the foolishness of their would-be assassin to leave incriminating evidence inside the vehicle. Doyle focused on the exterior, and Kiri recorded the environs, including the two agents scouring the area for clues.

"Enough explosive to kill the three of us, but not to destroy everything—as a smart man should have." Michael finished and called his two sidekicks in. "We'll bring the bits and pieces we can. This recording goes in the vault until we're back. We'll start for Maarat soon. Cut all communication as before, and need I say, not a word to Patrick. Check in eight." Before they left, he buried the bits of boy he could identify.

The small band of survivors trekked north through calf-high scrub along elevated ground with only a half bottle of water from Doyle's pocket and two granola bars from Kiri's to share. They were not the only souls seeking refuge at the border, as the few cars they spotted were loaded with families and other refugees traveled by foot. Michael threw an arm around Kiri's shoulder and nuzzled her grit-filled ear. "Good job today, love. Good job."

On the third check-in, they learned that the bus cleared the government checkpoint. "That deserves a celebration!" Michael allowed them a swallow of water each. A half-hour later, they were told the van also made it through without incident. *Great. In eight.*

"I'll call my guy in Azaz to meet them at the border. He'll need to commandeer the van to pick us up tomorrow," Michael told the other two after they celebrated with a bite of granola bar and another sip of water.

"I thought it was too dangerous for you to use your phone," Kiri said.

"Not this one. 'Tis only for me and my guys. We may have a success after all!"

Their elation was short-lived. On the outskirts of Maarat al-Numan where they learned that all charges arrived safely at the border, they heard the scream of fighter jets overhead. Warplanes dove to hit an area of housing complexes, dust and rubble fountaining skyward in their wake. Michael took off at a run—toward the havoc—with Doyle close behind. Kiri tried to keep up. "Stop! It's too dangerous!" The whir of low-flying helicopters dropping internationally banned cluster bombs drowned out her shouts as she watched the armaments split in half to release a rainfall of bomblets. Mini-explosions guided the three to a devastated residential area where men raced to tear away rubble trapping women and children who took refuge in their mosque.

Arms, legs and bones sheared of flesh emerged from the debris. Men worked feverishly to uncover bodies, hoping to find life. They carried the dead a respectful distance away before returning to the mound, Michael and Doyle among them. Kiri, conspicuous as the only woman combing the debris for survivors, hefted rubble as well as she could until she overturned a large stone. Her hysterical screams brought Michael in a flash. The severed head of a boy lay at her knees.

Michael cradled the curly-haired sphere in his cupped hands, and with dignity overshadowing his anger, climbed past the little one's feet twisted into the spokes of his bicycle. He handed the piece of boy off to a cortege of men, equally aghast at the horror. He scrambled back to find Kiri retching into the hollow that once held innocence. Pulling her up and to him, Michael gripped her so tightly that barely a grain of sand could pass between them. He screamed toward the sky, calm and blue now as if tragedy were nowhere near. "Stop! No more children! No more dead children!"

* * *

A later check with the team revealed that all in their care gathered at the border. Occupants of the bus waited for the van so families with children could cross into Turkey together. Michael passed his consent to cross the border on to Frank and Gus. When they learned of the failed car bombing, Volcano Gus erupted and jerked Michael's guy from the van, primed for a second rescue mission. Frank barely stopped him. "Our job is to get these folks across the border before you go ripping down the road after Michael. Besides, it's too late to make it that far and here again before dark and too dangerous to travel at night." Gus backed down, kicking at the tires and nearly puncturing the hood with his fist.

His stranded friend did not share the afternoon's horrific rescue experience—not yet. He did reveal his surprise. *At check 2. Live broadcast. Set it up. Secret from Pat. Resume all communs then. My guys too. P must must must be present.*

"Are you crazy?" Devin asked from Dublin. "He thinks you're captive again. He'll explode!"

Right. Watch face. Eyes.

"Good luck with this. I hope your scheme won't backfire before you've had a chance to make a firm case," Henry added.

Record P reaction. Evidence. At check 2 in six.

At the appointed time, with all systems up and running, Patrick hurried into the network's Dublin communication complex. Lights on throughout the building indicated that no one had left for the evening. The executives feared that the rumored live feed might be a ransom request. "Do we know yet who is broadcasting or from where? Can we track this in case it concerns Michael?" he asked, feigning worry over a man who was supposedly eliminated earlier that day.

Henry and Devin shrugged and watched Patrick's face turn from shock to horror as a disheveled Michael incarnate crackled into view.

This is BBC reporter Michael O'Connell speaking to you live from Maarat al-Numan in northwestern Syria where just hours ago government air strikes turned a quiet neighborhood into rubble. I sit atop one such pile now and see nothing but devastation in all directions, a tragic sign that the visit of the UN's peace envoy these last two days brought no ceasefire to the brutal fighting throughout this area.

'Tis never wise for a journalist to become a part of his story, but in this case we had no choice. We witnessed nosediving jets shower bombs on this housing complex and were shocked to discover they were Russian-made. Structures collapsed like sandcastles under a giant's foot, trapping those seeking shelter inside. This reporter and his crew lent their hands to those of townsmen searching frantically for wives and children. In the end, only a few survived. Near fifty lay lined up in the dust at the foot of this heap

awaiting identification, made difficult because so many bodies were torn into pieces. Mourning will follow, but recovery will remain elusive.

In the dark of night, scavengers will descend to scrape through the rubble once again searching for anything of use—shoes, strips of cloth, pieces of metal. But unknown dangers lurk. Many of the dropped bomblets failed to explode and could burst at the slightest motion, causing more injury and death of innocents. Tomorrow some will rope off the unsafe areas and puzzle over how to clear them. Others will bury their dead, and still others will pack up to start the long trek north to the border, leaving their demolished homes and lives behind for lack of flour, fuel or family like tens of thousands before them.

I've stared into your warm, safe homes many nights over the last several years offering a stagnant refrain. Dates, times and places may change, but even without me to report it, the story remains the same: destruction, displacement and death. Any small child could predict its ending. As the sun sets on this horrific scene, one wonders what it will take to cause societies who call themselves humane to rise up against such inhumanity. What do we want our children to learn from us? This is Michael O'Connell wishing you good night... and good conscience... from war-torn Syria.

Kiri pulled the shot of Michael back until he was but a dark silhouette against the golden sky. When the screen went black, Henry let out a deep sigh. "That report was a prizewinner. The execs will be happy. There's our job security." Devin nodded and turned to gauge Patrick's reaction, but he was long gone.

*   *   *

.

In a demolished mud brick hovel on the edge of the bombing site, Michael stared at the black sky, impatient for morning and the promise of rescue. He scraped the ground with his boots to clear a smooth space. The couple removed their jackets and spread them out on the ground as a buffer against the grit. They pulled off their boots and set them beside their makeshift bed to grab at a moment's notice. Michael lay down first and drew Kiri alongside with her head in the crook of his shoulder.

"Too cold?" He ran his hand up and down her scarred arm.

She shook her head. "Not now."

"Tired?"

"Exhausted. I'll sleep all they way home—even on the plane."

Michael chuckled and pulled her closer. "I won't. I'm too excited. Just think, tomorrow brings a new dawn... a new day... a new chapter in our lives. I can't wait! Happy?"

She barely nodded. "A little sad still."

"Me too. A little. But we need to make peace with what happened today and move on. Celebrate the lives saved. We can't let this one day cloud our dreams." He placed his hand over her heart to feel its beat. "Let's look at those beautiful stars springing out and count a blessing for every one… and when we reach an end, we'll create a little blessing of our own right here on earth."

"But we're in the middle of nowhere… dirty… exhausted… exposed."

"What's wrong with that? What better time and place? With cruelty and chaos all around us, why not make a statement for what is right in the world. Wouldn't it be fantastic to leave death behind and create new life in this wretched place?"

Kiri squirmed. "I don't know if I can…"

Michael gazed tenderly at her. "Lots of children are conceived on the ground and in places foreign to them. Close your eyes and pretend we lie on a luxurious buffalo robe. Open your eyes and soak up the exquisite skies above. Imagine you are in your Colorado mountains, inhaling the piney scent of home. Relish in the touch of the man who loves you more than anything in the world." He turned her to face him and caressed her neck and chest. "Savor the sweetness of my kiss…" He leaned in slowly, inviting her lips to reach out for his. "…and if you listen hard enough, you'll hear the whisper of a fairy in your ear…" He blew gently through her hair. "…telling you that in this moment, all's good in this world… and with us."

They ignored their discomfort to twist around one another in passionate embrace until Michael jumped to his feet.

"Where are you going?"

"Outside to check with Doyle about our ride home tomorrow." He smiled lovingly at his wife, beautiful even amidst the rubble. "Give you and that fairy voice time for a little chat."

Kiri watched him walk away, then noticed and shouted after him. "You forgot your boots!" He was too far away to hear her call, so she lay back down, gazed up at those stars and waited for a tiny whisper. This morning, she remembered, they were two professionals doing a job. Tonight they were husband and wife. Tonight she was dirty, tired, smelled of sweat and vomit, her hair tangled from wind, smoke and dust, and she just wanted the night to be over. Her husband survived a worse day than she. He fulfilled his responsibilities with precision and honor and was then betrayed by his boss. He witnessed the deaths of children and his own wife in mortal danger and was powerless to change either outcome.

They trudged miles and were hungry and dispirited. All he asked of her now was a little tenderness—the awareness of what he felt and the willingness to convey that understanding. He needed to feel like a man, to regain some control over the life that nearly slipped away from them. The man she loved—that strong, courageous romantic—needed to feel her care and respect and love. He needed his wife—the one who shared his dream. That was her job tonight. No, that was her *privilege*.

She breathed deeply to relax, loosened her clothing and listened for a fairy's whisper. An ear-splitting burst accompanied a violent jolt beneath her. A lone voice cried out in the dead of night, "Kii...rii!"

*   *   *

The thunderclap brought Kiri to her feet and into her boots immediately. She stumbled through the darkness, guided by Michael's voice, and nearly tripped over his inert body. Doyle, only steps behind, shouted "Oh, God! Michael! No!" He pushed Kiri aside. "Don't touch him 'til I've had a look."

She could not if she wanted to. She froze. Her heart glaciated, a chunk of ice broke off and crashed into the pit of her stomach, and her throat choked with frosted slurry.

Doyle turned Michael over gently and winced at the sight of the cavity where his lower extremities used to be. Kiri dove to his side and cradled her husband's head in her hands.

He focused on her panic-stricken eyes. "I'm sorry, love. Forgive me. When I saw him pick up the bomb, I prayed. 'Not that boy. Not one more child.' ...and He listened."

She shook her head, unwilling to accept the inevitable. "I should have held onto you longer... kept you next to me."

"No difference. 'Twas my destiny... sooner than expected."

She zeroed in on his wounds and worked frantically to stop the bleeding by tugging at his belt, at hers and motioning for Doyle's to reverse Michael's fate.

"Stop! No tourniquets. No golden hour for me. Only minutes... Stay with me to the end... Hold me. No one else but you. Your touch only... My hand on your heart and yours on mine. Pass life between us with each beat."

Kiri appealed to Doyle, but the helpless cohort watched blood spurt from his friend's femoral arteries with no ambulance or helicopter for miles and shook his sorrowful head. She turned back to Michael and nodded her resignation, holding his weak hand to her heart and placing her hand on his, sobbing.

"No tears. My last earthly sight your sparkling blue eyes... dancing hazel flecks... smile as broad as my hand."

His faint smile coaxed one from her. She pressed her body against his chest to hold their hands firmly in place and rubbed her face against his shoulder to wipe away her tears.

"That's better. Can you find the strength to hang on 'til the end... until I'm gone?"

"I'm right here," she nodded. "I won't leave you."

"No. I mean, 'til I'm *really* gone... cold in the ground. Allow time for our souls to twine together. Do you have that courage?"

Michael was in shock, she realized, and did not know what he asked. "I'll hold on to you every step of the way. I promise. How can I ease your pain?"

"No pain. No feeling. Adrenaline." He struggled to inhale deeply. "Our last minutes. Fill with promise... your promise... to make our dreams reality. Your pledge. You are bound... your rules."

"Save your breath, Michael," she pleaded.

He tried to shake his head. "Too many words unsaid." He swallowed hard. "Live your name. Kirin Aurora. Unicorn. Chaste and faithful sentinel. Welcome each new dawn."

Blood slugged through Kiri's veins to carry life to both of them, giving him strength for more words. "Tend our village and watch it grow. Circle your arms around our family... Nurture the little ones... Provide a safe place... a joyous and loving one... Reconcile."

She shook her head again. "I can't. Not without you."

"Yes! Be strong. Fold friends into family." He rested for a few seconds, then licked his lips. "Greatest challenge. When you come to a good place... live by your pledge... Nourish my seeds... and bear my children... Raise them... as we envisioned." Michael labored to lift his head and shouted with an intensity beyond his strength. "Promise me now... in front of God... that you will live by your pledge!"

"I promise I will live by my pledge!" she cried out in answer.

Michael heaved a relieved sigh. "All you need in our safe place... St. Kevin. More than you can bear..."

"I know. Call for help," she finished, to spare him the effort.

He drew in shallow breaths. "Remember my name. Michael... Protector at hour of death... You will not serve alone. I'll join you... on our unfinished mission... from the other side... of the thin space between us."

His mind played tricks on both of them in his last moments, and his delirium spoke through a feeble voice. "Don't fight fairies... Listen for whispers... Connect circles..."

In a final burst of renewed energy and consciousness and with a clear voice and focused mind, he made a final request. "Help me die the way I prayed I would... just not so soon... in your loving arms... passing my last breath to you. Take it in deeply... Hold it until it infuses you... becomes part of you. Just like our souls mingle... let my last breath... remain a part of you... to pass to our children. Let my last breath of life... become their first."

He begged a last concession from his devoted wife. "I love you, Kirin Aurora... Please give me permission... to go now."

She inhaled deeply and nodded. "Thank you, Michael Killian, for every blessed moment we've spent together."

"*Grá anois agus go deo... mo anam čara.*"

"My precious Michael. My first, last and only. Love, now and forever, my dear mate... in body and soul."

His eyes fought to hold Kiri in view as he whispered, "Take my last breath… and live for us both."

She felt his lips quiver as he struggled to inhale deeply. As she pressed her mouth hard against his, she felt the force of his breath fill her lungs, rise to the upper regions and circle her heart, then sink into the depths to massage her womb. She held it there until she could no longer and fought against releasing it, letting only the slightest wisp of air escape before she sucked in again and again while their two limp bodies lay together.

Kiri was completely oblivious of Doyle's filming their last and most intimate moments as the crew in Dublin looked on in disbelief. Grown men wept openly. Michael. Gone. Impossible. A primal cry chased Gus to the van, brought to life despite Frank's warning. A father clutched the son who tossed the bomblet at Michael and bowed his head in thanks to the stranger who saved one more child that day. Women in purple headscarves printed with white flowers emerged from makeshift shelters, surrounded Kiri and pulled the resistant young woman from her dead husband while their own men sprinkled his mangled remains with a violet powder and wrapped him in white cloth. They bound around his neck and hips, then carried the shrouded body respectfully to a place in line with the others who died that day. The women sat on their heels with their arms around the young widow, rocking and wailing with her and with each other.

"This is the closest to keening I've seen," Doyle said through his own tears. "I don't know what to do."

"You keep that little lady safe! I'm on my way!" Gus shouted into his ear.

Frank channeled his nervous energy into a plan to carry a body across the border.

Patrick, roused from sleep by a frantic call from the office, breathed an unexpected sigh of relief.

Chapter 6

Kirin Aurora watched dawn creep across the dirt road like a cat, slither over a wall leveled to its foundation, and paw-to-paw bat light from stones to leaves on the uneven floor until it settled at her feet in the roofless hut she called home for the night. A new dawn. A new day. A new life. One for which she was completely unprepared.

Ringing in her ears became the all-too-familiar scream of jets back for another round of pulverizing defenseless neighborhoods. Ground trembled, pitching stones around her. Dust danced in the sunlight. Frantic cries drowned out birdsong. The sound of a vehicle approaching at high speed turned into a screeched stop in front of the ruined shelter. A gorilla of a man jumped out, clasped his friend in an embrace of shared sorrow, and burst across the threshold of what once was a doorway. "Oh, Kiri. What a sad, sad day this is." Gus choked back tears.

"Stop right there!" a voice demanded from across the vacant space.

Gus found himself staring down the barrel of a madwoman's gun. Her back against a crumbled stone wall and her boots outstretched toward the sun, the determination in her animal eyes signaled a definite red light. Clothes, face, hands and her long brown curls were crusted with dirt and dried blood. Michael's shrouded head lay in her lap, and her left hand rested on the cloth covering his chest, massaging it as if she could force his heart to beat again. Her right hand held the weapon, and a knife lay at her side. "I'm a crack shot. You taught me."

"Oh dear girl. I've come to bundle you in my arms and take you away from this horrible place." He started toward her again.

"Not another step! I'm not giving him up. I won't let go. Michael told me not to let them take him... not to let anyone touch him. I know you're really here to take him away from me... to separate us... like all the others."

He turned to Doyle who shrugged. "I don't know what she's talking about."

"What others?" Gus asked a resolute Kiri.

"Doyle, for one. He keeps asking me to go outside. The men out there. Guards at the checkpoints and border. Your precious network. Family... Thomas. You'll all try to take Michael away from me... and I promised not to let go of him until he's ready to leave."

The two men exchanged quizzical glances. Gus tried again. "What do you mean?"

"Michael is not at rest yet. I can feel... sense the tension in his body. His soul is frenzied... lingers...."

Doyle whispered, "I tried to warn you. We've got a problem. This won't end without someone else getting hurt."

"How long has she been like this?"

"All night. She hasn't moved all night. Her hand hasn't strayed one inch from Michael's chest. She snarls at me when I take more than two steps inside. She's kept a constant monologue going… and she hums a lot."

"Has she cried?"

"Not once the village folk left and we dragged Michael in here."

Gus squinched his eyes and scratched through his bushy black beard. "She's not going to give in to us easily, you know."

"What makes you the expert?" Doyle smoothed his.

"I have eight sisters, so I know a woman won't change her mind just because you tell her she's gone a bit looney. You need to gentle-talk her into believing you've come 'round to her way of thinking." He held his hand up toward her. "I'd like to pay my respects to my mate… my brother. Would you let me give him a hug?"

Her back stiffened and her eyes narrowed.

"You're not going to use that gun on me, now, are you?"

"Will you try to take it away from me?"

Gus shook his head. "Not on your life. You win this one. But I would like to come sit next to you, then… share a few thoughts about my friend."

She hesitated, then nodded and lowered the gun.

Gus lumbered over and sat by her right side. "We loved him, you know. He was a good friend and a great leader. We all thought he was crazy to lease that yacht for the Libyan scheme, and the tour bus for this one. But both plans worked. Twenty-eight happy people are on their way to London today, thanks to Michael. And to the rest of the team too, of course—you included. We do good work when we do it together. God, I'm going to miss your man." He rubbed his eyes. When he put a hand on her arm, she gripped the gun tighter. "Why do you keep your other hand on his chest?"

"So he can sense my presence. That's how we connect. I don't want Michael to feel abandoned… alone in the dark… like he did in Yemen. He needs to know I'm here… and will be… until he's ready to go. I told him I would hang on 'til the end."

Gus raised his thick, black eyebrows and put a muscled arm around her shoulder. "I hear that you talk to him. And hum."

The faintest smile played around Kiri's lips. "The sound of my voice relaxes him. He teased me once about using too many words. But when he feels tense, he asks me to talk… talk about anything. At night in bed, we listen to Celtic music. He likes the Irish harp best. Says he can feel the vibrations inside his body. They soothe him. That's what I'm trying to do. Soothe him. Soothe his lingering soul."

Gus pulled her closer. "Would you have a good cry with me?"

"I can't. I can't show weakness. I'll be eaten alive back in Dublin, if I do. I'll cry after Michael's gone. I'll have a lifetime alone… and plenty of tears to fill it."

Gus' free hand pulled her head to his chest. "Let me hug you tight, then, and shed a few for both of us. You're stronger than I am, for sure." He remained silent as dampness spread across his cheeks. "I understand why Michael loved you so much, and I know you mean to be loyal to his wishes, but no matter how long you sit here and wait, he won't find peace. Not here—ever. And I know why."

Kiri looked up at the massive man with the tender heart.

"It's an old Celtic notion, I know, but the way and time a soul leaves a body is different for each person. The body must be in a familiar place for that to happen. Michael needs you to take him home... home to Ireland... before his lingering soul will feel free to go."

He patted her hand, then held it. "Doyle and I will plan a way to get all four of us to the border... together... but we have to hurry. Those jets may decide to flatten this place even more than they already have. Take a few last minutes alone here with Michael to let him know we're leaving. Then, we've got work to do." He gave her another hug, got up and walked to Doyle, guiding him out of hearing range.

"Do you believe that stuff about lingering souls?" Doyle asked.

"I don't know what the Church says, but Kiri believes it, and that's what we must work with. She's like a lioness guarding her cubs, staying calm but watchful, ready to spring at the slightest threat. Right now, we're that threat. So yes, for the next few days, I do believe in lingering souls." He gave his friend a slap on the back. "And so do you. Now, let's figure out how we're going to get Michael out of here without touching him."

"Strange how there's no stench of decay from the body yet."

"Some never do. They give off a sweetness instead. Michael's would be one to do that." Both men nodded in accord.

Gus opened the stripped-out van to expose the supplies he and the Azaz contact hurriedly assembled near the border before dark: buckets, rags, bread, water and scraps of medical supplies. "We sucked the bus dry of petrol. Should have enough to get us back—barely—if we aren't rerouted due to a cratered road." The men briefly discussed how to handle a distraught Kiri, then put their hands to their ears as a second wave of bombings began, toppling loose stones from the remnants of walls. "Time to get out of here before we're a permanent part of this miserable place. We'll work on a story to get us through the checkpoints as we drive. Ready?"

Doyle nodded and picked up the buckets, water, and wads of gauze. Then he looked toward Gus for encouragement. The burly man heaved a sigh. "Tough love will only work if you back me up. Let's go."

The two men reentered the demolished home to find Kiri exactly as they left her. Ignoring the gun, Gus strode confidently up to her, stood with his feet shoulder-width apart and his hands on his hips. "Getting us all home is a job... an assignment. I'm in charge. You will take direction from me. Is that understood?" She nodded.

"It takes a team to save a team. You know that better than most. It also takes sacrifice on everyone's part. I will not compromise the safety of three live bodies for one dead one, but I will respect your wishes for Michael's treatment so long as it does not jeopardize this mission. Do you understand that?" She nodded.

"Now, put down the knife and gun." Her eyes grew defiant, so he explained. "A woman with weapons in this country is a dead giveaway that we're involved in something we shouldn't be. Put them down." She complied.

"Next, clean yourself up." She shook her head, so he continued. "A bloodied madwoman as messed up as you won't get us through one checkpoint, let alone all of them. The guards will think you're our victim, or we're your prisoners. Either way, they'll throw us in a dungeon and Michael in a ditch with the rest of the men they've massacred. You're a medic. Bloody clothes are expected, but the rest of you better be squeaky clean."

Her gaze focused on Michael's chest as she hesitated. Gus started in on her again. "You have ten minutes. Get over in that corner and start scrubbing. If your touch is so powerful, Michael will sense it ankle-to-foot while you're doing all the things a women needs to do after being on the run for the last day."

Doyle unloaded the supplies into the corner and left. Gus marched right up to her and took the weapons. "We need these to stand proper guard. No one's going to be staring at your naked body. Now move!" he barked as he walked out.

Nine minutes later, Kiri called from inside. "Ready."

The two men brightened at her transformation. Her hair, still dripping from a good soak, was tied up in a ponytail with a strip of gauze. She turned her T-shirt around to expose the cleaner backside and scraped most of the mud and vomit from her shirt, jacket and pants. Hands, even fingernails, were scrubbed clean; likewise her neck and ears. Her face was as beautiful as always, the only evidence of trauma being a firmly set jaw and dark circles surrounding her tormented eyes. She knelt beside Michael, her hand again on his chest.

"Perfect," Gus smiled. He explained how they would move the body to the van. "We'll try to respect Michael's wish not to be touched, but if we have to, we will. Your man is a husky one, so he'll be heavy. Doyle will carry the hip bindings. You'll hold his head. I'll take his trunk."

Doyle wrapped several layers of gauze around the chest still shrouded in blood-brown and purple. Then he tied a handhold and Gus grabbed it to test its strength. They heaved on "three" and, with labored steps, Michael's bearers transferred him from stone floor to van.

"That was the easy part, Kiri," Gus said. "We have checkpoints to get through. We don't know who will be in control of which ones today— rebels or the government—so, be ready for anything. The guards are likely to poke or jab Michael to confirm he is dead. They may ask you to unwrap his head to expose it. If you flinch, cry out, shed a tear or try to stop them, they will arrest us all and throw your man aside where you'll never be touching him again."

Gus gave his warning time to sink in. "You must be strong for a few more hours. As you said, you have a whole lifetime to mourn." He was about to climb in and close the door behind him when Doyle started back to the hut. "Just leave it all," Gus said. "No one will know who left that mess." Doyle shrugged and took a step toward the vehicle.

"Wait!" Kiri cried. "His jacket. Phones and cameras. Papers. I need his boots!"

Gus looked at the body of his friend and shook his head. The items that held information made sense, but what would a woman do with boots and no feet to put them on? "Bring it all," he ordered.

With arms loaded, Doyle returned to the van to witness a shouting match.

"What is your name?"

"Kirin O'Connell."

"What is your *name*?"

She looked at him, confused, and shouted back, "Kirin Koyle O'Connell."

"Damn it, girl! *What is your name*?" Gus screamed at her.

Kiri looked for an answer in all four corners of the van. Then she calmed and looked him straight in the eyes. "Karys Kolton, sir."

"Why are you in my country?"

"I'm a relief agency medic."

"What are you doing with this van?"

"Returning the body of a fellow aid worker to his country. He was killed accidentally when he picked up an unexploded bomb."

"Do you have papers that allow this?"

"We have identification, but we did not wait for papers. We thought it wise to remove his body from your country before his death provoked an international investigation. A UN peace envoy is visiting now."

"Where do you work?"

"Near Damascus where many humanitarian agencies are headquartered, but..."

"Then why are you on the road heading north?" Gus challenged her. "Jordan is closer to Damascus."

"...but we were in Maarat. We entered from the north. Fewer questions if we use the same border station. An embassy rep from Ankara will meet us there with papers. Jordan is more strict than Turkey, and we want to avoid trouble, as I said."

Doyle leaned into the van, facing the verbal combatants. "Where did all that come from?"

Kiri was as surprised as they. "I don't know. It just popped into my head like a fair…"

"Well, there's our story… and a plan. Frank! Where are you? Get to work! Can you repeat that?" Gus asked her. She did. "How about in Arabic?" She stumbled through a rough translation. "That's way better than yours, Doyle, and mine too. Can you keep yourself together enough to do the checkpoints for us?" At her nod, Gus climbed behind the wheel and passed back her shawl, water and bread. "Wrap up and eat up. I don't want two bodies on my hands. Hey, Dublin!" he shouted. "Anybody there? Vehicle is on the move!"

Chapter 7

Son Tommy was the first to learn of the tragedy. From his executive office in the Raidió Teilifís Éireann building, he glanced at the news services' streamers crossing his big screen. *Oct 19, 2012: Reporter killed in Middle East.* He did not think too much of it. Several met a similar fate as Arab uprisings spread. Moments later he read, *BBC reporter killed in explosion in Syria.* He picked up the phone to call his father but was routed to voice mail.

*   *   *

"Thomas? Henry here."

"Henry, good to hear from you. It has been a long time."

"Gather your family, Thomas. All the adults. One hour. Your house."

"What hap…"

"One hour." The call cut off.

Thomas turned to Paula. "Something's wrong. Something happened to Michael. This time I'm sure of it."

"You can't know…"

He flung his arms around her and nearly choked her with his embrace. "I *do* know. For this Irishman, the ominous words 'Gather your family' can mean only one thing. I'm not prepared for this, Paula. I thought Yemen was the worst of it. I must call the children immediately. Henry wants all of us here in an hour."

"I'll help."

"No. If you call, they'll think I've breathed my last. I'll do it. God, give me strength in this moment."

"I'll call Kiri and Kurt, then."

"Kurt?"

"He's part of this family too. If it's tragedy we're facing, he needs to be here."

"How?"

"Skype?"

The two agreed to describe the unusual request for their children's presence as a conference to discuss "family matters" and regrouped after short conversations with too many unanswered questions. Paula was more distraught than when they started. "I can't reach Kiri. Her phone is off. Even the agency won't say whether she's in their office or not. Oh, Thomas, you don't suppose… There's been no hint that she goes beyond London for them."

He grabbed her hand and collapsed on the sofa. "Let's not assume the worst. Let's pray that both children come home to us."

63

Son Tommy arrived first, obviously anxious. Thomas met him at the door. "You haven't told anyone? Margaret?"

The eldest son shook his head. "She's coming with Meghan. Do you know any more than the streamer I saw?" Thomas embraced his son and did not let go. "Then hold on, Father, until we know more. Could be anything. Since reports slipped out, the network might be running damage control to keep others involved from harm. Hope for the best. Charles and Anne are here."

Thomas freed himself and left to wipe his eyes and dab cold water on his face. Meghan and Margaret were not far behind, and finally Stephen and Emily joined the others in the living room where Paula fiddled nervously with a laptop.

"Are we all here?"

"Michael's not. I saw him on the news a couple of nights ago, so he is probably still out of town. Kiri?" Emily asked.

"In London again, no doubt. She spends more time there than at home these days. Not very good for a marriage, if you ask me."

"We're not asking you, Anne." Thomas uncharacteristically barked at his eldest daughter. "Our guest will be here in a moment."

"Hi, Mom," Kurt greeted from the laptop. "What's up?"

At that familiar voice, Meghan whipped around in her chair to see Kurt with his wife Tanya next to him in what looked like a classroom. She turned back around with her eyes downcast.

"What are *they* doing here?" Anne asked Meghan. "I thought this was a family conference."

"Kurt and Tanya *are* family, just as much as your spouses are, and right now we need every member we can summon." Thomas' second sharp outburst in as many minutes unsettled his children. He removed his handkerchief from his cardigan pocket, blew his nose and left the room.

Paula quickly interceded. "Let's all calm down. Our guest will be here shortly."

Thomas escorted that guest, Henry Callaghan, into the room. In his black suit, white shirt, grey-striped tie and highly polished shoes, he also wore the most somber countenance the group had ever seen on a man noted for his unflappable demeanor. He remained standing, facing them all, while Thomas took a seat beside Paula and gripped both of her hands.

Henry cleared his throat—twice. "BBC reporter Michael O'Connell died last night while on assignment in Syria," he announced as if he were reading a bulletin and not delivering the most dreaded news a family could receive. "He was in the city of Maarat al-Numan working on a story when a bomb exploded."

Tommy's face turned ashen. His wife grabbed for his hand. Anne cried out, and Charles put his arm around her shoulder. Meghan clutched the seat of her chair and started to shake; she had no partner to help her through this crisis. A slow trickle of tears flowed from Emily's eyes toward the lower lip she bit to try to stem them. Her husband Stephen, unsure how he was expected to respond, stuffed his hands in his pockets and studied the floor. In Colorado, Tanya clapped her hand over her mouth, and Kurt dropped his head into his hands and shook it.

Thomas emitted a low moan... and then another... and crumpled into Paula's arms. He sobbed openly without embarrassment, continuing to moan, "My son. Not my baby boy. Not another son." There was not enough of her to surround his entire body and shield him from the tragedy of losing a child. His remaining children witnessed their father lose complete control only once in their lives, and that was when their mother died.

Paula did not try to stop him. She continued to console and comfort him, weaving her fingers into his thinning hair to hold his face close to her chest. "I'll call Bishop Byrne, Tom. He can help you." She fumbled for the phone, and after a short exchange she whispered, "He's on his way." As she glanced over her grieving husband's shoulder, her gaze met Henry's. "Kiri?"

He coughed into his hand. "She's bringing him home."

"Was she...

"All I can tell you is that Kiri will escort Michael's body home. It may take a couple of days. I'll call the minute I hear." Henry scanned the tattered remains of a family and excused himself, the business of secrets and lies weighing heavily on him.

*   *   *

Two evenings later, Henry stood in light drizzle at the airfield, awaiting the arrival of a C130 transport aircraft with no climate control. Frank made the request, "to keep Michael as cool as possible. We have him on ice, but Kiri refuses to leave his side." Within minutes, a hearse pulled in bearing the name, *Groton & Sons*. Henry approached and tried to explain to the confused driver that there was no need for a hearse; there was no coffin to transport. They should return to the city.

Their dismissal was the result of a heated exchange with Kiri during a layover in Geneva. "I don't want to see one ambulance, one hearse, one box, or any men in black suits at the airport. Michael comes *home* with *me*. If you won't drive us, I'll strap him to my back and carry him there myself. You know I will!" Henry was certain she would. Dressed in navy blue jacket and slacks, he returned to his vehicle and leaned against its side.

While awaiting the solemn arrival, visions of Kiri flashed through his mind. The first time he spotted her entering Copley Castle four years previous, he was struck by her appearance, not her looks—although they were striking—but her demeanor. She was different from the other women who frequented their social circle—wholesome, genuine, spirited and without an ounce of pretension. She was the first woman he sought to know, and he tried several times that weekend.

His attempt to introduce himself at the social was foiled when Kiri came in on the arm of Patrick. Henry assumed she was a tag-along relative of Michael's and, when he tired of dragging her around, he would ask someone to take her off his hands—keep her out of trouble and having fun. Henry positioned himself to oblige, but Michael kept her close. Henry approached his friend to offer to take care of Kiri while he disappeared with Alice Richardson, his on-again off-again flame of many years, but Michael did not take Alice's bait. At the Ball, Michael did ask his friend to dance with Kiri. Their bodies moved completely in synch. He knew in that moment he could give up his confirmed bachelorhood for a future with her, but Patrick's uncle in the red sash interrupted them. Henry never got a second chance.

When Michael disappeared in the Middle East, Henry coaxed Kiri back to Ireland—twice—to help find and rescue the missing reporter. He could have kept her safely in Dublin, dependent on him, but she was so eager to go… to be a part of the action… that he let her. When the couple returned, he expected their relationship to fall apart since Michael refused to acknowledge her. Henry primed himself to step in and take the tormented man's place, but next thing he knew they were married.

Henry imagined all the times he could have played it differently with Kiri. How he might have taken her arm to escort her to her car, called to check up on her when her husband was overseas, held her hand when she was upset about Michael's frequent absences, hugged her now and then—in a friendly way, of course. He imagined all the chances he missed, and now with the tragedy of losing Michael, all the chances that would never come his way again. In a fair fight, given Michael's neglect or wandering eye, he could take a chance on winning Kiri, but he could never win a contest against the memory of a dead man.

The drone of an incoming aircraft caused Henry to steel himself for the ensuing battle between Kiri and the O'Connell's. He could not imagine remaining neutral. He wanted to favor Kiri, but knew that would be suspect. He decided to take Michael's side in the conflict as one did for a best friend. No one could fault him for that.

When the cargo hold opened, Frank was the first man off the plane. He called to his superior, "Are you sure we want to do this?"

Henry nodded. "Our friend, the doctor, said he could buy us three more days with a new death certificate to replace the one that was… inadvertently misplaced between Ankara and here. He's waiting for us at Quincy Street. Says he brought everything we need to clean Michael up."

"Kiri won't let you touch him, you know. We've had a heck of a time at the airports. That's why we requested the transport—so she could stay with him in the hold. Gus finally rolled her up in a blanket so she wouldn't freeze and made her rest while she lay beside him."

"Has she slept?"

Frank shook his head. "Nor eaten. She takes water when it's forced on her, but she refuses everything else. At least we have Michael on a stretcher now so he can be moved easily. I'm supposed to be checking for unauthorized persons before she'll allow him to be carried from the plane."

"I'm the only one here. Thomas has no idea I sent the mortician home. Signal the all clear."

Frank waved his arms, and the three bearers emerged from the hold: Doyle at the foot, Gus at the head, and Kiri side-stepping in the middle with both of her hands on Michael's chest, her lips moving rhythmically and her soiled clothes hanging from her diminished frame. "She's probably explaining to him what's happening. She tries to keep up a constant chatter... and humming. I don't understand the point."

"If it helps her feel better, the point doesn't matter."

The two men slid the stretcher into the back of Henry's SUV. Kiri climbed in beside it, and they closed the door. "Rough few days for you two, but a stellar job. Cudos arrive from all corners," Henry told them. "Go home and try to shake it off. We won't debrief until after the funeral."

Gus swung the door back open and clambered in. He grabbed Kiri and hugged her hard and close. "I don't care what you say. I'm giving you a hug goodbye. You stay strong now, and if anyone tries to give you guff, you give a whistle. Gus'll set them right." He backed out again, and wiped his cheeks. "She hasn't cried a'tall, not since the first night. Says she won't until after the funeral. You keep good watch over that little lady, Henry. You keep good watch."

I will, he thought to himself. *I'll keep very close watch.*

Henry pulled onto the motorway toward Dublin. "Kiri, I don't know what to say. I can't tell you how sorry I am."

She answered from the back. "I understand. Words aren't adequate. Please, just keep to business for the time being. I don't want to be distracted. I won't be able to hold myself together if my mind starts to wander. I must remain strong for a few more days."

"Agreed."

"Is everything ready?"

"The doctor is waiting at your house." Silence. "You do remember that you were not in Syria with Michael."

"Oh really, Henry. Then where was I? Tell me. Tell me I didn't see him blown to bits in front of my eyes. Tell me I don't have my hands on his lifeless body right now!"

Anger. Good, Henry thought. "You were here in Dublin. Took two friends to lunch. Then you went shopping and bought a dress. It's in a bag here on the seat, along with all credit card receipts appropriately dated on Friday morning. I sent you to Geneva to identify Michael's body and bring him home before I informed the family. Your boarding pass is in the bag too."

"I'll swear, you don't miss a thing, do you Henry?"

"I miss Michael. I can't tell you how much."

"Me too," Kiri said and was silent for the rest of the trip.

*   *   *

Thomas paced from living room to den and back. He drew the curtains aside and peered into the drizzly evening, watching rivulets of water pool on the windowsill and spill over. Grief for his son was the same—spilling over, too much to hold inside. He was drowning in it. Paula reminded him to be patient. Word would come from Henry that Michael was home. They would see him soon.

She was anxious too, anxious to hear her daughter's voice, to take her in her arms and comfort her. Watching Thomas dissolve before her eyes, she could imagine what her daughter must feel. Paula wanted to fly to her, help her bring Michael home, cuddle her, but Henry insisted that was not possible. Too much international red tape. If only Thomas would stop pacing. His constant shuffling drove her mad. She turned on the fire.

At the first ring of his phone, Thomas pressed it against his ear. "Henry, are they home?"

"It's Alec Groton, Mr. O'Connell. I don't know if the plane has arrived yet. A tall man sent us away. I thought I should call and let you know."

"Henry what! He sent you away? By what authority?"

"His, I guess. He said there would be no body to transport, so we might as well leave. Something about an investigation and needing a death certificate. We can't transport a body without a death certificate, sir. I'm sorry."

"When and where *will* you pick Michael up? Did he say?"

"We won't be doing that, sir. The man said Mrs. O'Connell would take care of any arrangements."

Furious, Thomas shouted at Paula. "Since when do *you* make arrangements for the disposition of *my* son's body? That is *not* your responsibility!"

She was as surprised as he. "I have no idea what you're talking about. I haven't asked anyone to do anything."

A voice interrupted from the phone, "No, no, sir. Not *your* wife. Mrs. O'Connell. Your *son's* wife. She's taking charge of arrangements. We've been released. I just wanted you to know."

Plum-faced, Thomas turned on his wife. "How could your daughter do such a thing? Deny me my son's body? What a hard-hearted child you raised!"

Paula tried to calm him, but getting near enough was a challenge since he backed away from her and pointed a trembling finger. "Kiri is as much your daughter as mine," she reminded him. "She has a kind heart and a reason for what she does. I know this is a sorrowful time for you. It is for me too... for Kiri... and for the entire family. We need to remember that now. We need to hold together as we did three years ago. Henry will call us soon with an explanation. I'm sure of it."

Thomas collapsed onto an ottoman, his head in his hands and tears streaming down his arms to his elbows. "You have no idea what it is for a father to lose a son."

Yes, I do, she thought. *I know how painful it was for this mother to lose our son over forty years ago.*

* * *

Centuries of women the world over prepared bodies for burial. Kiri's intention to do the same was only unusual for the time and place. She gazed down at Michael's shrouded body on the floor of their bathroom. She knew what to do; the doctor prepared her for what she would see. He came with potent salts from the chemist to clean and disinfect decay. The gentian violet powder sprinkled on Michael in the village, an ancient ethnic remedy, retarded decomposition and sterilized the egregious wounds, he told her.

"Take your time. Celtic custom allowed seven days for a body to be laid out to give far-flung relatives travel time. With history on your side and this new certificate to buy you three more days, no one can question your actions." He and Henry waited in the upstairs sitting room to help move Michael from floor to tub to bed, as she wanted.

Kiri was exhausted, frightened and her hands began to tingle like her feet did when she curled them beneath her while reading. She rubbed her palms and warmed them under her arms, but the feeling did not dissipate. For a moment, she imagined that their two souls mingled as Michael once described, causing the frenzied sensation in her fingers. The closer to his body she moved her hands, the greater the tingling—all those speckles of soul dancing together. "Help me, Michael. I want to do this for you, but I don't know if I have the courage." The prickling guided her hands to his shroud, and she began to remove it.

Once in the tub laced with scented oils, she gave him the shave and two-fingers-length haircut he so coveted on his return from every mission. She wound her favorite curl—the one that danced above his right eye when he became excited—around her finger for the last time. She soaped, washed and massaged his body, running her fingers over all the familiar places that remained to commit that touch to memory. She dressed him not in white linen or his proper Sunday best, but in tone and texture that suited him, that would bring out the color in his eyes if ever they could open again. She bedded him beneath their quilt of wildflowers pulled up to mid-chest and bunched below, giving the impression he was whole. She played his favorite harp music, willing the vibrations to soothe him. When she placed her hands over his heart, she was certain she felt him sigh and relax. *Grá anois agus go deo, mo anam čara*, she whispered in his ear and fell asleep on top of the quilt next to him for the last time.

* * *

After the bishop calmed Thomas and left, Paula led her grieving husband by hand to their aromatic, frothy tub. "Slide in, Tom. A hot soak will help you relax."

"You're not coming too?"

"Not tonight. Tonight is about you. Lean back." She pulled him gently to the end of the tub to soap and massage his chest. "Your body is turning on you. Your grief is consuming all your energy, so you body won't function as normal. You must take care of it." She laced her fingers into his hair and massaged his temples, front to back, gently, her thumbs making their way to his neck. "Give yourself permission to sleep, to eat. Sacrificing your health will not bring Michael back." Her hands reached his shoulders. She worked them rhythmically. "Cry, Tom. Weep. Overflow the tub if you must. Mourn your boy, but let the anger go. You are trying to find guilt, place blame. As far as we know, there is none. Channel your hurt, your frustration into constructive action. Let's make this farewell to Michael a dignified, crowning moment."

"I'm sorry, Paula. I have been angry and blameful. I shout at you. Snap at my children. Accuse you and Kirin of conspiring. What am I thinking?"

"You're not. That's the point. Feel the hurt in your heart, but give your head a chance to find reason for what you say and do."

"Right as always, my love. I could not survive this tragedy without you by my side, *mo anam čara.*

*   *   *

Kiri's world trembled violently. She threw herself on top of Michael to protect him from dust and falling debris. The shaking came again. "Kiri, wake up. You're dreaming. Wake up and have some tea and toast."

"Henry? Have you been here all night?" She cocked one eye toward the figure at the side of her bed.

Embarrassed, he nodded. "The doc stayed until you fell asleep. I covered you up, then dozed in the recliner. I didn't want you to wake up cold and alone in an empty house."

"Very thoughtful. Thank you." She rolled to sit on the edge of the bed, straightening the quilt across Michael's chest.

"You did a masterful job with him. How did you achieve his fearless look?"

"He was courageous, wasn't he? But I did nothing to create that impression. When a person is at peace, his true countenance shows through." She smiled, then turned toward Henry. "I appreciate your approval, however, and I suppose I owe you for this tray, too, but I really can't eat a thing."

"You must. Thomas and Paula are due in an hour and a half, and you need your strength. He is angry as a fighting cock, and if he sees you looking like a madwoman, he won't wait for a starting bell to attack."

Kiri glanced down at the bloodstained clothes she had not changed in a week—a dead giveaway that she was not lunching with friends. "I'll have to clean the bathroom too, I suppose," she thought aloud.

"Done. Bagged up and ready to stow with your rubbish."

"Very kind. Thank you again. But please don't. Don't leave the bags outside to remind me. Take them with you. Take my clothes too. I could never wear them again." She stepped unsteadily to the dressing room and returned wrapped in a robe, with her clothing neatly folded.

Henry worked his fingers through the shirt's buttonholes and around the ribbing of her T-shirt. "We can't let your electronics get away. High-end British forces stuff."

"You'll want Michael's too. We'll have to go through…"

"Done. All electronics retrieved and accounted for."

"Not his earwig, surely. I threw it hard across the room."

Henry nodded. "All retrieved. The guys brought Michael's jacket, papers and the 'evidence' he gathered when they stopped by at dawn this morning to check on you."

"You told them to go home for a couple of days."

"They can't stay away. You are as much a part of their team as Michael. They're worried about you and want to help you through this terrible time in any way they can… with any task, no matter how small. They want to share your sorrow."

"How kind. I've been pretty hard to handle, I know."

"Gus wanted me to pass on this advice: 'Keep the frenzied, lingering soul bit to yourself for the time being. It won't sit well with old O'Connell or the cleric.' I haven't a clue what he meant."

Kiri smiled. "I do. Tell him I'll save my fancies for *our* next conversation. Excuse me. I'd better see what I can do to disguise this madwoman."

"Right. I'll dispose of… take a few things with me. I'll pop home to change and return before Thomas arrives."

"You're coming back?"

"Absolutely. You need someone to stand with you before the Inquisitor, to fill in if your mind goes blank when Thomas presses you for details."

"That's right. I was lunching with friends. I know nothing."

"Good girl. Oh, the guys said you wanted these."

"Michael's boots! They didn't throw them out." Kiri grabbed and clutched them tightly to her chest, forbidding even one tear to slip away. She leaned her forehead against Henry's shoulder. "Thank you, Henry. I'll never be able to show you how much your friendship means."

For now, he thought, *this will do.*

71

Auxiliary Bishop Gregory Byrne, a life-embracing sort of a man, gazed out the car's window, his slight frame nearly disappearing into the back seat. His pointed chin angled downward toward his long, thin fingers nervously pulling on one another, the twinkle in his eyes at rest today.

Paula drove the familiar route to the house on Quincy Street. Thomas had neither the energy nor the reason to steer himself, let alone passengers, anywhere but off a cliff. Poor man. Bishop Byrne ministered to the O'Connell family for more than four decades and pulled them through many trials, but this day would test everyone's strength and faith beyond any other challenge they faced. Today he must minister to a family in deepest mourning... and at odds with one another. Seems the daughter/daughter-in-law refused to release the son's body to the father. Both Paula and Kirin were unconventional in their interpretation of God's place in their personal lives and His workings in the world, but they usually devised a way to fall in behind the patriarch when family loyalty and decorum demanded it. The cleric doubted that would be the case this day.

Embracing life commanded every ounce of the bishop's strength when Michael's death glared down at the sorrowful trio from everywhere. Newspapers, information boards, and storefront televisions constantly reran his international broadcasts as a tribute.

Auxiliary Bishop Byrne was the first out of the car, even before it stopped. His crisp gait carried him to the door ahead of the bereaved couple. He wanted to gauge the widow's temperament before the altercation began—to judge the strength of her conviction. An official-looking man dressed appropriately in grey trousers, knit vest and sport coat opened the door to him and stepped aside. Shocked, the cleric outstretched his hand and searched for words to describe the young woman standing before him. Strength was not applicable.

Dressed in the expected black, Kiri's skirt and sweater hung from what was once a comely frame. Her lusterless hair, pulled severely back into a sock bun at the base of her skull, provided no framing for her face. Sunken cheeks exaggerated her prominent cheekbones. Dark circles surrounded her eyes devoid of expression, their vibrant blue faded to a steel gray like an ailing *American Gothic* come to life. Her pallid complexion bespoke the depth of her sorrow. Even a whisper, the bishop thought, would blow her to the ground.

The cleric's caution to Thomas to greet his son's wife with an embrace of shared sorrow and to allow mother and daughter a moment of comfort was ignored as the man strode into the living room, eyes afire and fingers shaking toward the willow of a young woman. "What have you done with him! Where is my son? What right have you to take him from me?" he shouted as he came close enough for the bishop to feel the heat of his breath.

Unbent, Kiri summoned a firm and steady voice. "*I* haven't taken Michael from you. Your Almighty managed that on His own. Please lower your voice. This is a house in mourning, and you will respect that or leave." She challenged Thomas to lose his bluster and back down. "A black wreath may hang on the door, but that is no excuse for poor manners. I will greet our guest properly, then I will address your concerns."

She gestured for the bishop to have a chair near the fire. "Welcome to our home, Bishop Byrne. I'd like you to meet Henry Callaghan who agreed to act as liaison between the network and the family." Henry nodded but did not outstretch his hand.

"Mother...

Paula wanted to rush to her daughter, but Thomas grabbed her arm and set her soundly on the sofa. She gazed at her child longingly and realized that her joyous, spirited little girl disappeared from their lives as swiftly as Michael.

"...Please calm your husband. This conversation will be much easier for all of us if he remains quiet for a few minutes while I clarify the Church's standing on a point or two." She seated herself opposite. Henry stood behind her with his hands on the chair's back. "If I remember from the lessons you've given both my mother and me over the past three years, at the time of death, certain responsibilities fall to the Church and others to the family. Is that correct?"

The bishop nodded, recalling a similar squall over Michael's baptism—his rebirth. Now he headed into another over the young man's untimely death. He nodded. "That is correct."

"Laying the body to rest—prayers at the Vigil, the Funeral Mass and the Rite of Committal—is entrusted to the Church, and preparation for the rituals falls to the family. Is that correct?"

"Yes, but as a Catholic now yourself, you have no choice in the proceedings."

Kiri brushed his reminder aside. "As Michael's lawfully wedded spouse—remember, you married us twice—and therefore his nearest living relative, at his death I became head of *his* family and bound to assume the family's responsibilities. Would you agree?"

The cleric gave a reluctant nod, but the memory of a similar conversation with Kiri sparked Thomas' agitation.

"As spouse and head of his family, I may also ask for advice and assistance in any of the areas for which I feel unprepared. I could ask his father, for instance, to collaborate with you in planning the familiar rituals. Is that true?"

Very clever, the bishop thought. Assume the upper hand, then ask the adversary for help. He nodded again, his fingertips nervously dancing on one another.

"As his family's head, I have the legal and moral obligation... no, privilege... to carry out Michael's wishes insofar as possible, even though I may not personally agree with them, so long as his remains are handled and disposed of in a reverential manner."

Thomas tilted on the edge of his seat. "What wishes? How do you know what my son wanted when he stared death in the face!"

Kiri felt Henry's hand on her shoulder and his thumb dig into her muscle. She took a deep breath. "After Yemen, we both realized that death might come without warning. The 'what if' conversation became the inevitable 'when.' Michael's requests of me were very specific, and I will try my best to honor them. I expect nothing less from his father." Henry's hold on her relaxed.

"You've incinerated my son! You've turned him into a handful of ashes!"

"No, Thomas. The bomb nearly accomplished that. I tried to put him back together so you would not think him corrupted."

"Where is he? Where is my son!"

"Upstairs, resting... "

"Don't be glib with me, young lady. Michael is *dead*!"

"Have you never wished the departed to rest in peace? Your son is peacefully resting... in the place he loved best, surrounded by light and music, and soon by the people he loved most." Kiri stood and extended the tortured father her hand.

Henry spoke softly into her ear. "Good job! Where did that oratory come from?"

"I have no idea. It popped into my head like a fair...." She stopped herself. No one present would believe those were not her words. She turned toward the astonished priest. "You are welcome to perform a Gathering in the Presence of the Body, if you feel it appropriate." She ushered Bishop Byrne, followed by Thomas and Paula, up the stairs and into the octagon Michael built—the mystical shaft of space bridging the terrestrial and celestial, as he once described it to her.

The priest drew in an exclamatory breath, startled by the scene. He attended many a deathbed—in homes, hospitals, and long-term care facilities—but none outside a church so hallowed as this. A collage of mountain peaks covered the three interior walls surrounding the head of the bed where Michael lay as if snoozing in a sunny field of wildflowers. The three walls opposite were glass, save for a narrow chimney leading from a small fireplace nestled between deeply cushioned window seats. An octagonal skylight joined with the lofty windows to invite light into every corner of the room despite grayness outside.

Sill-wide molding above the window seats and through the mountains along the walled sides of the bed held softly-burning, pine- and cedar-scented candles in glass holders interspersed with mementos—a pressed flower ornament, a small Celtic cross, and a set of five miniature harps diminishing in size, carved from green Connemara marble and unearthed from Thomas' attic. The mournful wail of Irish pipe and soulful strains of harp played somberly in the background. The room was an interweaving of vibrance and solemnity in a never-ending circle of life and death.

"You captured a spiritual quality in this space, my dear," the bishop said squeezing Kiri's hand. "The octagon is a medieval symbol of rebirth and renewal, you know, the squaring of a circle to join the physical to the spiritual. Most appropriate. Michael could rest in no finer place for now."

"He designed and built it himself—a fusion of O'Connell Celtic spirit and Koyle sentiment, he joked. Michael will not be moved from here until the funeral."

Thomas entered next, prepared to be aghast but overcome by the ambience. He dropped to his knees by the bed and wept, one handkerchief not near enough to absorb his emotion.

Paula, last to enter, finally embraced her daughter. "Oh, my baby. Is there anything I can say or do to help ease your pain?" Looking deeply into her child's tormented eyes, she understood there was not. "I'll hold you tight for a long, long time to let some of your sorrow spill onto me."

"You can't possibly carry both Thomas' and mine. He is too fragile and has given in to his sadness. I haven't even started."

Paula rubbed her daughter's steel-rod-stiffened back. "This is your severest test, Kiri. You have to let go. I want to help you."

"I don't dare lose control for even one second... until Michael is in the ground. I have a lifetime left for sadness and I need to concentrate now on making his journey easy. Thomas needs you desperately. You tend to your husband, and I'll tend to mine... with every minute we have left together."

Bishop Byrne bent to help the grieving father back onto his feet. "Shall we begin? When we're finished, I'm certain Kirin will allow you private time with your son for as long as you wish."

Thomas nodded, and the mournful family gathered.

Paula fixed tea and sandwiches that went untouched by all except the bishop. Henry accepted a cup but sat aside, well out of the conversation with the cleric. Thomas descended from his lone visit with his son by noon. Resignation signaled that he was ready to face the woeful tasks ahead. "Thank you, Kirin. I'll call Groton to come for Michael," he said on his way to the door.

"Don't bother. Michael will stay here until the service. The dead cannot be left alone during their transition to eternal space, as the Celts said, and I will not be separated from him."

"You can't be serious!"

"Very! How would you like to be handled by strangers, pushed around on a banquet cart and stuffed in a box or a meat locker to lie cold and alone in the dark? Michael deserves better. Bishop Byrne, is there any doctrine to prevent my tending Michael as pre-modern Irish women did their deceased?"

The cleric shook his head, certain that Kiri knew the answer before asking.

The fight faded from the aging father. "I... You are right. But we do need to gather as a family... to plan for his... Will you come to the funeral home with us?"

"No. I will not leave Michael, and he will not leave *his* home until the last minute. You are welcome to have the family here to make your arrangements. You may stay as long as you wish."

"No children!" Thomas exclaimed, then shook his lowered head. "My son is not... No children... until the funeral."

The bishop laid a comforting hand on the grieving man's shoulder. "I suggest we meet here this afternoon, Thomas. We will discuss particulars in the car. I'll follow you in a moment."

When the older couple left, Bishop Byrne took Kiri's hand in both of his. "Thank you, my child, for making my sorrowful task less painful today. Facing Thomas as you did cannot have been easy. I never quite agree with your conclusions, but I cannot find fault in your logic nor in what you have done for Michael. I don't know how you pulled this off."

"*You* taught me well."

Chapter 8

Henry assumed the role of doorman as one sibling couple after another arrived: temperate Tommy and Margaret, arrogant Anne and Charles, emotional Emily and Stephen, and mellow Meghan alone. During the interim between Thomas' departure and return, the news exec convinced Kiri to rest, so she would be at her sharpest, he said. He manned the phone to record messages and condolences, and he made arrangements for Kurt to be picked up at the airport. With all assembled, Bishop Byrne took charge of the uneasy discussion. Anne held pad and pen to record decisions. Kiri sat to the side, stony, and nodded when asked for her approval.

Anne dominated the proceeding, suggesting music, greeters, ushers, readers, ministers of the Eucharist, persons to place the pall (sisters, of course), and pallbearers...

Kiri, subdued until then, shouted "NO! Absolutely not! Patrick Murphy will take no part in this funeral!" Henry gave her a sharp look. "Tommy, Charles, Stephen and your Killian cousin are fine. My brother Kurt will represent the Koyle side of the family. The last place..."

"But Patrick is the obvious choice. The network should be represented."

"It will not be represented by Patrick!"

"Really, Kiri. Do you still hold a grudge over his slight indiscretion at the castle nearly four years ago?" Anne smiled smugly.

Kiri caught a second warning look from Henry when she opened her mouth to speak again. "What I feel personally about Patrick is unimportant. I represent Michael's interests, and they will not be served by Patrick's participation in any form. No reading, speaking, ushering, bearing, nothing. In fact, he should not even come!"

"But what will I tell his family? I promised Alice..." Anne simpered.

"You should never promise what you cannot deliver! He can develop bronchitis, a sprained wrist, a sudden call out of town. Patrick is very good at making up stories."

"Then who will represent the network?"

Kiri turned to the man standing beside her. "Henry, will you act as pallbearer to Michael?"

Caught off-guard, Henry's hands began to shake. How could he refuse? How could he say no to Kiri? He found his voice and answered. "I would be honored."

"Thank you. Settled. Now, let's move on. What's next? Time and place for the vigil? Here tonight?"

The family gasped in unison. Bishop Byrne leveled a stern look at everyone. Tommy suggested. Anne objected. Meghan proposed. Anne shook her head. Emily wanted. Anne laughed. Thomas wrung his hands. Paula tried to hold them.

Kiri suddenly rose from her chair and shouted, "Stop! Everyone! You do not honor your brother with your bickering. I'll listen to one sentence from each of you. Choose carefully. Say what is most important to you. Then *I* will make the decisions."

Anne rolled her eyes and protested. "You obviously know nothing about an Irish vigil—or a Catholic funeral, for that matter."

"Is that your one sentence, Anne?" Kiri asked sharply.

The chastened stepsister clapped her mouth shut and waited for her name on the roll call.

After eliciting one suggestion from each including Henry, Kiri left the gathering swiftly saying only, "Don't anyone move. I need Michael's input too."

With Kiri out of earshot upstairs, Anne complained. "Michael's input? She's clearly delusional and incapable of making one cogent decision, let alone several!"

Safe in her bedroom, Kiri placed her hand on Michael's chest and felt his agitation. "You're upset. We all love you, but we aren't working together to show you how much. Guide me. Give me a sign." She rubbed her hand across his chest again and examined the elements in the room: candles, flowers, cross, harps, compass necklace, sunlight and her hairbrush on the dressing table. A plan started to form. She pattered to her desk and back with index cards and a pen. She sat cross-legged on the bed next to the body and began to write. When finished, she held them up to Michael's face. "What do you think?"

Before an answer came, Kurt tiptoed in. "You all right, Sis? Lots of frustrated people downstairs. Whoa! You have Michael *here*?" She nodded. "So that's what you mean when you say you're staying with him. You really are. No wonder everyone is so on edge. Is this legal?"

She nodded. "For two more days."

Kurt studied the pewter-sheened visage closely. "So this is what death looks like."

"Yes."

"Pretty harsh."

"Michael wouldn't want to be plumped up or prettied just to satisfy someone else's idea of what he should be. He met life head on, held dead children in his hands, and knew that reality is sometimes really brutal. Yes, this is what death looks like, and it's time we all recognize that fact. Let's go."

"I apologize for the delay," she announced to the gathered relatives. "As much as I want Michael's death and burial to be a private affair, I realize that his family has different expectations. Thomas said it the night before his wedding. We don't have to love, or even like, one another, but when we took a vow to be family, we agreed to respect our differences and to show up in times of crisis. We all know where we are at odds... and so does my neighborhood now. This funeral is a test for us. Can we live up to our vow?"

The stepsibs shifted uneasily in their seats, but Kiri plunged ahead. "We're all running on nervous energy. We say we're grief-stricken, but we won't really experience our loss until we expect Michael to take his usual place at a family gathering and he doesn't show up. I suggest we channel that nervous energy into action. Give our minds something constructive to work on while our emotions are tumbling about."

She shuffled the index cards in her hands. "We need a plan. I divided up responsibilities and hope you will agree to take them on. If you do, I trust you to keep Michael's best interests at heart and to follow through." She turned to the mortician seated quietly to the side of the group near Bishop Byrne. "Mr. Groton, you've been so patient to wait through our arguing, wondering what your role will be in this saga. You have the most urgent and important job. You must find the perfect casket. With every corner of Ireland only hours away, I'm sure you can discover it somewhere."

The nervous man glanced over the specifications on the card she handed him, raised his eyebrows and hurried out.

"For the rest of you, most will work with a partner." Kiri passed similar cards to each person present including the bishop, Thomas, her mother, Kurt and Henry. After allowing a few seconds for them to note their duties, she continued. "The ground rules are these. Do not involve Patrick Murphy in any way. No filming, broadcasting or electronic devices are allowed. Music must include a harp—an old Irish Celtic one, if possible. Thomas decreed, no children here tonight or at the Vigil. Their attendance at the funeral is your choice as a parent. Do not put your personal interests before Michael's. Consider what you want your *children* to remember about this wretched experience."

Like ready-set-go in a game, excited exchanges and pairings replaced disgruntlement until Thomas summoned his children to the bedroom for a private service. They reappeared much later, visibly shaken but regrouping to begin their tasks. Tommy lagged behind for a word with Henry. "Dueling networks; same purpose. I'm grateful for your offer to stage a public vigil at your network's reception hall considering the crowd we expect. Most fitting," the brother said as he left.

Kiri's brows rose up. "Really? Instead of the church?"

Henry nodded. "We received many inquiries from... we'll call them associates... in other parts of the world who would not be comfortable in a Christian church. This compromise seemed a perfect way for the network to show appreciation to the family for sharing Michael with us for the last several years. He loved his work and we loved him."

"I'm impressed. How did you come up with that idea?"

"I don't know. It just flashed through my mind. Will you be all right if I take off?"

She nodded. "Kurt will stay with me tonight. Thanks."

After everyone departed, Kiri returned upstairs to survey the bedroom. Cushions piled for kneeling were scattered on the floor, some near the bed and others by the window seats. She straightened the wildflower quilt and rubbed across Michael's chest. Not as agitated. Music was fine. No candles needed replacing. Then something caught her eye—or didn't. Something was missing. A marble harp. Second largest. Second in line. Second child. Anne. Kiri felt her blood pressure surge. How dare Anne take something from her home! She inhaled deeply. Don't upset Michael. Anne must need it more than she, but her stepsister should have asked. Just one more strike against their ever becoming friends.

*　　*　　*

Alone. Family gone. Henry gone. Kurt gone. For the first time in a week—and now for the last—Kiri and Michael were alone in their home. She did not know whether to be frightened or relieved. She knew she should try to sleep. Her body cried for relief. But she also knew that every minute of sleep was one less she could spend with him. In barely twenty hours he would be carried away from their home, and he would not walk through the door again. How should she spend these last hours?

With each family visit—Thomas in the morning and the rest of the O'Connells in the afternoon—Kiri sensed more of Michael drift away. His presence was still active in the room but it lessened with each intrusion into their private sanctuary. He was almost ready to leave. How should she spend these last hours—make every second count? Thanking him for giving fullness and meaning to her life? Expressing her anger at being abandoned? Repeating promises? Recounting favorite times? Recalling his stories? She finally decided to read to him—one of his favorites, John O'Donough's *Anam Čara*—about souls existing outside the body where they touch, interact and become a part of one another.

That is what kept her going now, why she did not fall completely apart yet—the belief that Michael's soul still tried to mingle with hers to leave a part of himself with her to communicate to and through her until they were together again. That's what she would do—reaffirm that his death was not really the end for them, that somehow they would remain a part of one another.

She planned for the coming day. She must dress Michael to suit Thomas. A Celtic warrior was often buried with his sword or shield, but Michael did not use tools of war. He used his wit, words and wisdom… and his boots. He always felt prepared for a journey if he wore his boots and joked that he would be dead in his tracks without them—a prophecy fulfilled.

His ring? Some men were buried that way. He always left his ring home, on her finger, when he went on assignment—his promise that they would be together again—their souls reunited—their pledges kept. She decided to keep his ring and wear it. Where was it? She felt her hand. Where was hers? She hurriedly put them in the safe the morning they left and had not missed hers yet. She rushed to the mudroom, opened the safe and found them where she left them—on top of her box. How could she forget? Maybe that is why Michael was still agitated. She slipped them onto her finger, his ring closest to her heart and hers snug enough to secure them in place.

The doorbell sounded just as Kiri started up the stairs. She tried to pretend she did not hear it, but the noise persisted. Numb but resigned to what was expected of her, she gave in and answered it to find Paddy from across the road. The poor man stood slumped, head down, with his cap in his hands. "Come in, Paddy. What can I do for you?"

"I came to pay my respects. Michael is all over the news, you know. And there's been folks in and out of your house all day long. But I suppose you know that too. A sad, sad thing it is that your man should be taken from us. I don't know how you can bear it. When my Maureen...." He stopped to wipe a tear with the back of his hand.

"How is your dear wife doing?"

"Not so well. I'd bring some fresh bread over, but she hasn't baked in many weeks now. Just sits in front of the window in her rocker and stares out at passersby."

"You have the social services you need to keep up with the laundry and cleaning? Meals?"

"Yes, Ma'am. But..." He wrung his cap nervously. "But I don't know how long we can afford to keep that up, now that Michael is gone."

Kiri suddenly realized that she was not the only one worried about what would come next—how her husband's death would change lives. Others depended on him too. She put her arm around her neighbor's shoulder. "Don't worry one minute. Michael set up your account for the bank to continue payments, no matter what. You let me know if there's a problem... but there won't be."

Relief immediately washed over the man's face but not enough to remove the grief. "I don't know how to thank you. If only I could do something for you, mourning deeper than m'self right now. My garden is done until spring, or I'd bring over some fine squash."

"Having you come to pay your respects is enough. Would you like to say goodbye to Michael now?"

"He's here?" He softened at her nod. "Then I'd like that very much. I'd be honored."

Kiri led the old man upstairs, stayed with him for a few minutes, and then left him alone for a final goodbye while she disappeared into Michael's office.

Paddy came down the stairs, using a handkerchief to wipe his face. "Thank you so much. You have no idea what that meant to have a few last words with your husband... to thank him for all he's done... and you too... for me and my Maureen. He's a good man, gone too soon. I only wish I could do..."

"Paddy..." She looked into his sad, gray eyes. "I wonder if you could do something for me?" His eyes brightened. "I wonder... You know our house will be empty for long periods of time over the next few days, and you know how worried Michael was about snoopers. I wonder if you could watch over the house like you do when we're out of town?" The man nodded gratefully. "I have a card here with a couple of contact numbers in case you can't reach me, and the information I'd like you to write down."

"Oh, I know that as well as I know my name: vehicle license and description, date and time, and the culprit. Would we be lookin' for the same young man with the light hair and the sly eyes?"

Kiri chuckled. "The same... and he may send others, so you'll need to be on your toes."

"Oh, I will. And my Maureen can help." He smiled at the thought. "We can sit by the window together and watch. We'll be honored to help out."

"I'd like you to take Michael's binoculars to..."

"Oh, I couldn't do that..." The man shied away.

"Take these. He'd want you to have them. He felt a man should be well prepared for an important job. These glasses will help you describe more completely. If you see anything suspicious, write it down and slip the note through our mail slot... in case we don't see each other for a few days."

"I will, then. I'm happy to lend a hand in your time of need. And a shoulder to cry on, should you need one after... should you need it. Just give ol' Paddy a wave."

"Thank you. I know I can count on you." Kiri hugged the old man goodbye and watched him walk back across the road standing a little straighter, with his cap back on his head.

Kiri climbed the stairs to the bedroom wondering where the idea came from to give Paddy a job and a token remembrance. She was not capable of a single original thought at the moment. She sat beside Michael and twisted their rings around her finger. The doorbell sounded again. She wished not to be home alone after all. Having Kurt or Henry in the house would save her from dealing with people before she was ready—if ever. The bell sounded again. She returned to the door and opened it to find four solemn men standing with their hands folded.

"I've been wanting to come since we arrived home, but Henry said to wait 'til the whole team could visit together. You didn't want to be disturbed. But we couldn't wait any longer. Oh, Kiri girl. Come to Gus." He scooped her up in his massive arms before she could refuse, and he sobbed the sorrows he could not verbalize.

The men expressed their condolences and their guilts. One after another, each confirmed he would have traded places with Michael in a minute. "If only Gus and I had given our seats on the bus to you and Michael," came from Frank. Gus said he should have driven the van back the instant he learned of the car bomb. Doyle said he should have dismissed the van driver when Michael expressed suspicion or he should have lunged for the bomblet himself when he saw, slow motion, what would occur. "If only I kept my eyes on Patrick, not let him out of my sight until the operation was complete," Devin lamented. "If only there were something we could do to share your burden."

"If-only's won't change the facts. But I appreciate your sentiments. You've been good and faithful friends to both of us. You may visit with Michael, if you'd like."

"He's still here?" the surprised men chorused.

"He's upstairs waiting for you to say goodbye. Follow me."

The loyal comrades trailed after her, handkerchiefs in hand, unprepared for the tranquil setting. She turned up the music to mask their speech and offered them places on the window seats or pillows. "I'll leave you alone. Stay as long as you need," she said and retraced her steps downstairs.

She went to Michael's office and found another card, wrote on it and carried it with her up to the library. She searched the shelves for *Anam Cara* and flipped through its pages without focusing on the words. The guys found her there rocking gently with a serene smile on her lips and fingering an index card.

"Kiri," Frank said. "You've been more than kind to have us here. If there is anything... *anything* we can do for you, please just say the word." The other men nodded in agreement, unable to express how useless they felt.

"As a matter of fact, there is one task I haven't assigned yet. How are you with a shovel and spade?" The men traded confused glances. "I'm trying to keep Michael's burial as simple and true to the old ways as possible, so I've forbidden the use of a backhoe or any other mechanical device. I have a card here with the dimensions and a contact number for the groundskeeper who can direct you to the site. Or I could find some others... if you'd rather not."

When they finally grasped her meaning, Doyle plucked the card from her fingers while Gus blubbered, "We'll be honored to dig his grave! Sides squared. Corners sharp. Not one finer since the old days." He squished her into another tearful embrace.

Devin confirmed that the team was at her service. "You have no idea what helping in this way means. You are very generous to include us when you have so much on your mind right now."

"Michael and I are both grateful for your support. Yes, there is much to do before Groton's arrives at noon tomorrow, so why don't you go raise a glass in his honor and plan how four grown men will work together in one modest hole in the ground."

Their laughter followed them as they waved their goodbyes and let themselves out.

Relieved to be alone at last, Kiri carried the book into the bedroom, set it near Michael's head, and rubbed his chest noting how his agitation diminished with each visit. She straightened the pillows and checked the candles for any that needed replacing. She moved the rocker from the sitting room to rest beside their bed and pulled an ottoman nearby for her feet. She lowered the music and heard the doorbell sound for a third time. She dealt with the neighbors and the team. She wondered, who else was left?

Persistent knocking drew her downstairs once again. She opened the door to find Meghan's oldest son standing alone. "Brendan! I'm surprised to see you. Is your mother with you?"

"No. She's at Aunt Anne's getting an okay on the prayer cards. I took a taxi."

Her eyebrows arched. "I see. Why are you here?"

"I came to visit Uncle Michael. Mother said the whole family prayed over him this afternoon, but that is not true. My cousins and I weren't here. Why?"

"Your grandfather decided that viewing your uncle was not appropriate for children, and I agree. Your mother will determine whether or not you come to the funeral."

"I'm not a child. I'm twelve, and I've been confirmed."

"Yes, but in our opinion you are not old enough."

"I'm the oldest grandson, so I represent all of my cousins. Only a couple of us were alive when Grandmother O'Connell died, and we don't remember much except all the grownups cried a lot and didn't let us say goodbye to her. The littlest ones don't understand what is happening, and the middle ones are curious but no one will talk to them. As the oldest, I think I should be allowed. Someone needs to explain to my cousins."

"Your grandfather would scold you for coming and tell you to ask your priest about what happens when a person dies."

"We've heard all that stuff before. If death is *not to be feared*," he emphasized by spreading his fingers wide beside his saucer eyes, "then why can't I see what it looks like? The truth, Aunt Kiri. You always tell us the truth."

"When a person dies, his body doesn't always look the same as you might remember. Even some adults find that change disturbing. Your uncle would want you to remember him as he was."

"Everybody changes, even when they're alive. Think of Grandfather, for instance. He is much older now and has more wrinkles and brown spots and less hair than when I was a kid, and that doesn't bother me. Please. Uncle Michael let me touch his scars once... when he came back from his dangerous job helping other people."

"What did you learn from that experience?"

"That even if you try to do a good thing, sometimes a bad thing happens instead, but not to let that discourage you from trying. I think he'd be fine if I saw him now, too."

"I'm afraid you'll have nightmares, and I cannot allow you to see your uncle without your mother's permission."

"I won't have bad dreams, I promise. And I'll call and get permission right now." He dug in his pocket for his cell phone and soon had his mother on the line. Excited, he stated his case again and finally convinced Meghan that if she agreed, Kiri would too. "Do you need to talk to her?" he asked.

Kiri shook her head. "Tell her I expect a prayer card with her permission and signature on it."

Brendan made the arrangements, put his phone on the console table by the stairs, and straightened his sweater. "I'm ready to see my uncle now."

"Are you too grown up to take my hand?"

The adolescent, trying so hard to be a man, looked his aunt squarely in the eyes. "If that will help *you* feel better, I am happy to escort you upstairs."

Kiri almost smiled. She stopped Brendan at the door of the bedroom to allow his nose to adjust to the strong pine, cedar and sickly sweet scents, and his eyes, to the dim candlelight and to the sight of his uncle's form so still on the bed. Uncle Michael was never still. She felt the youngster's hand tremble in hers. "Do you want to leave?"

He shook his head. "I'd like to move closer, if that's okay."

"You're sure?"

When he nodded, she let go of his hand and watched him step slowly toward the head of the bed to face the stark reality of a dead body. He studied his uncle for a long time. "How did he die? I tried to find out on Google, but no site had details."

"He was doing his dangerous job helping people find a safe place."

Brendan looked her squarely in the eye. "You can do better than that, Aunt Kiri. I'm twelve now."

She took a deep breath. "He saw some boys... a little younger than you... playing with an unexploded bomb... and he tried to stop them."

"Did they die too?"

"No. They were not hurt."

Brendan gazed on his uncle again and thought for a long time. "He was very courageous, wasn't he, to do what he knew was right even though he might get hurt?"

"Yes, he was," Kiri nodded. "Is that how you'll remember him?"

"That, and how he used stories, games and adventures to teach me and my cousins to be good and to take care of each other." He paused pensively again. "You must be our guide now."

When Kiri registered shock, Brendan gave her an "it's so obvious" look. "Barely three weeks ago we played St. Kevin and the Blackbird. Remember? But my uncle switched it up. He said when we have a burden more than we can bear, we need to holler for help. You were the first one in the game to help, so that means if we run into trouble, you are the first one we should call and you will help us. Paula is second."

Kiri swallowed long and hard and asked herself, *Who do I call for help, now that Michael is gone?* "I'm not sure that's what he meant..."

"I am." He was very matter-of-fact. "Uncle Michael would never leave without someone special to watch over us." He pulled a rosary from his pocket. "I think I'm supposed to say a prayer for him."

Kiri listened to his earnest entreaties and expressions of thanks, particularly to his uncle for all his kind deeds and guidance. One tear dropped, then another. He wiped them away with a fist and kept going—praying, wiping, praying. "I'm sorry. I can't help it."

"It's okay to cry... even for a young man of twelve. Cry as much as you want." She moved a box of tissues closer to him.

"But you aren't crying."

"I can't. I know that when I start, I won't be able to stop. I think your uncle wants me to be brave until after the funeral. I'll have a good cry then."

Brendan blew his nose and sniffed. "Can I touch him?"

"Only from the shoulders up."

He put his hand on Michael's shoulder and then stroked his uncle's cheek with his fingers. Tears fell again as he continued stroking. "I'm afraid I'll forget what he's like. I'll never forget what he's done for me, but I'm afraid I'll forget what he's like. I hardly remember my grandmother. I don't want to forget my uncle too."

"I know you don't believe me right now, but you never will forget. He was too big a player in your life." She moved to the other side of the bed and picked up Michael's boots. Brendan's eyes grew wide. "I can't give you these. They are going with Michael. But I can give you..." She removed one kinked and worn leather lace. "...this to help you remember."

Brendan wiped his face again and looked at her quizzically.

"Your uncle always wore these boots to help him feel strong. Wrap this lace around my finger and tie the knot your uncle taught you to moor a boat firmly to shore."

Brendan did as instructed—twice. His nervous first try was not up to his uncle's standards, he decided. Kiri pulled it off her finger and handed it to him. "Keep this close. Reach for it whenever you feel like you might forget or when you need guidance or encouragement. I'll bet just touching the knot will help you feel better. You can imagine what your uncle would tell you to do."

The young man pressed the lace between his palms. "Can he hear us talking?"

"I believe he can sense what we say."

"Then I'd like to talk to him for a few minutes, if that's okay with you."

"Your uncle would like that. I'll leave you two alone for a chat, and I'll wait downstairs."

He surveyed the setting again, the body reposed beside him and the knot in his hand. "Aunt Kiri?"

"Yes."

"Uncle Michael would approve of how you are handling his death."

Kurt returned from running errands for his mother as Kiri reached the bottom step. "Hug time, Sis. Feeling any better?"

"Not much. How's the rest of the family?"

"The same, but busy. Mom had me driving all over for chairs and cups. Thomas assigned my reading for the funeral. Meghan gave me a short course in Catholic funeral etiquette. I'm whacked!"

"Don't collapse yet. I have another errand for you. Brendan needs a ride home. He showed up to see his uncle."

"I thought Thomas said 'no children.'"

"He did... but Brendan made a good case. I sensed I should make an exception for him. He'll be down in a minute."

Just then, the boy finished blowing his nose and started down the stairs.

"Hey, buddy. I sure could use a hug. How about it?"

Brendan flew into his arms and held on tight. "I'm glad you came to help Aunt Kiri. I think she could use the company. It's kind of lonely here now."

"I know. We're all going to miss Michael very much. It was thoughtful of you to come pay your respects."

"I wish I could do more... help, like the rest of the adults. Everyone got a job but me."

Kiri had a thought and sent Brendan to the kitchen for a leftover sandwich before she headed to Michael's office. She returned with a card at the same time he returned with crumbs on his chin. "Brendan, I wonder if you would be willing to help Uncle Kurt. He's never done a reading during a Catholic service before, so he needs someone to show him what to do. Maybe you would even agree to alternate lines with him."

Kurt latched onto the hint. "Yeah. Your mom tried to set me straight about the kneeling stuff, but I'd feel so much better with you right by my side to keep me from embarrassing myself. Because I'm a teacher, I got the longest reading, so I'd like to split that up if you are willing."

The excitement in the boy's eyes nearly spilled over like his tears as his head bobbed up and down. "I'm very good at the church stuff, so I will be glad to help you."

"Your cousins won't be too jealous?"

"Not when I explain to them that since I am the oldest, I was asked to represent them. I'll show them this card with my assignment on it. Then they'll believe me."

"You'll have to get written permission from your mother, since your grandfather forbade children."

Brendan nodded. "Thank you, Aunt Kiri. I won't let Uncle Kurt down. He'll do a fine job. I'm ready to go home now." He headed out the door.

Kurt spoke softly to his sister. "Where did such a harebrained scheme come from?"

"I don't know. It just popped into my head, like a fair...."

He laughed. "I don't know how you can hold yourself together. Lock up after us. That scoundrel Patrick is parked down the road. Wait for me, Buddy. Let's go face your mom." He started for the door, but Brendan darted back in to grab his phone.

"I always forget this thing when I'm on an adventure with Uncle Michael." He stopped suddenly and his eyes saddened. He gave his aunt another hug. "I have an idea. I'll call you if I have a nightmare, and you can call me if you need someone to cry with." He held up his phone and smiled. "Call for help!"

"Sounds like a grrrand idea."

"That's exactly what Uncle Michael would say."

Kiri turned the lock, took a deep breath, then clenched her fists, opened them to shake her fingers, clenched and opened again to calm herself for the night ahead. The doorbell sounded again. Kurt had a key so would not ring, and she could not imagine anyone else who might visit at the late hour. She did not want to speak to one other person but aware of her responsibility, she peered through the security peephole to see who wanted her this time. Patrick Murphy peered back at her! She jumped, flattened against the door and slid to the floor with her hands over her ears to block out his frantic pounding.

"Kiri! Please! I know you're there. I must talk to you. Now. Before... I want to express my... my sympathy, to explain about the American. Kiri, please!" He pounded and pleaded, pounded and pleaded.

She crawled away from the deafening racket and up the stairs to the sanctuary of her bedroom. Her body shook violently. She collapsed on the bed near Michael, willing herself not to lose control. When the thumping stopped, she raised her head and noticed the book *Anam Čara* open to a passage she never studied before... about the soul at death... with Michael's notes in the margin. As she read them, she could almost hear his voice speaking to her.

As I see it, Anam Ċara expresses the Celtic spiritual belief that souls connect and bond in an ancient and eternal way. They form an infinity chain along which they ebb and flow into one another. Time, distance and separation cannot alter their joining.

One's body is merely a covering—a clay shape—with his soul radiating around it, animating it, until death when his soul is freed for its eternal journey through a thin space to its new world. But the dead's invisible form remains attached to a place—the place where it was happiest and felt the love and connection with his anam ċara. 'Tis the presence of the departed we sense in that place if we are open to it, for we live in a circle of eternity where 'tis the dead who guard and take care of us.

* * *

Paula opened the cedar chest to remove two bolsters and other yoga props and to release a soothing scent into the bedroom. She buried her nose in the soft blankets and inhaled deeply to fill her lungs with the relaxing aroma now infused in her equipment as well. She spread two blankets on the floor, then raised the bolsters to a gentle tilt with blocks. She finished strapping herself into *supta baddha konasana* when Thomas entered from the bath and lowered himself carefully into his place beside her. She gave his arm a tender pat. "How are you tonight?"

"The epitome of fatigue. But I do feel some better... after seeing Michael and praying with the family." He tossed his strap aside and rolled a throw under his knees, rested his ankles on a small pillow, and pulled a blanket to his shoulders. Paula tucked it tightly around him. "Kirin helped by putting us all to work—an inspired idea. I was comforted to ponder not only the readings the Church recommends, but to consider what Michael might select for one of us or for the grandchildren, to console them."

"The music. What set you off when Kiri mentioned music—the Irish harp? Is that inappropriate?"

Thomas sighed deeply. "Not at all. If I were told so, it would not make a difference. The harp we shall have. I was moved because Kirin thought of it, that she understood how meaningful that instrument was to Michael."

"Is there a family secret lurking?"

"The truth?" He studied candle flickers on the ceiling. "The Irish harp was Kathryn's favorite. She couldn't play, but she so loved the sound. She said it filled her with 'vibrational energies' that invigorated her soul. Michael must have remembered how dear the harp was to his mother and incorporated it into his own life with Kirin."

He wiped away a tear. "There was a time when Celtic harps were banned, harpists killed and their instruments destroyed, you know."

"Really!"

"Those few who survived wrote down their music for future generations, so some strains still exist—weeping, merriment and sleep. I've chosen one piece for sorrow and one for rest to be played at the funeral. Today, many fine musicians play harp, but few use long fingernails to pluck metal strings, and fewer claim to be born with the soul of the music in them. Kathryn always felt some connection but never could play herself. She was disappointed to miss out on that gene. After each of our children was born, she had a miniature harp carved from Connemara marble in the image of the Brian Boru."

"The one on the Guinness label and the Irish euro?"

"The same. We saw them in the bedroom today among the candles. Michael must have found them forgotten in the attic. I'm comforted to know that he carried pieces of his mother with him."

Thomas allowed one tear to escape from the far side of his right eye. "If there is one positive in Kathryn's early death, it is that she was spared the grief of losing a child. Losing a spouse is devastating, even when expected... but a child? That made me think of Kirin, and how much she must need you right now and how selfish I've been to keep you to myself. I couldn't bear this without you, Paula. I couldn't." He reached for her hand.

"What must Kirin feel without her mother to comfort her? Who is taking care of her? I don't think I've even held her and told her how sorry I am that Michael has left her life too... that I understand her despair. When this is over, you and she must spend more time together, and I will help her too. I'm afraid she'll find herself at such loose ends without Michael... that she'll drift away from us. I need to show her how vital she is to our lives—to both our lives—so she'll find comfort in our company. Once we make it through the vigil and the funeral...."

Paula listened as his breathing grew deep and steady and his hand fell lax in hers. Let him sleep here on the floor for a while, she decided. Thomas had not slept soundly for several nights—and would not for several more.

Chapter 9

Kiri awoke with a start. The bedroom was cold and dark, all the candles burned to their wicks' stubs. A sudden chill scurried up her spine. She reached for Michael but could not find him—only a form, stone cold and still. She brushed her hand across what used to be a chest and felt nothing. No tingle, no flutter, no sense of essence. Michael was gone... and his soul with him. She kept her left hand in contact, just in case, and waited expectantly through the rest of the night.

At the first peek of dawn, Kiri felt a quiver in the palm of her right hand. She looked down to find a small feather, velvety, from the belly of a bird, black as night but iridescent when held in the sunlight where it changed to a striking midnight blue, an even darker hue than her ball gown. The fluff of the feather waved with her breath as she brought it near her cheek to feel its softness. She twirled it between her thumb and forefinger to watch the down dance in a circle as she remembered Michael's lesson from St. Kevin... *more than you can bear... ask for help.*

"I'm betting you can hear me, Michael." She addressed the feather. "I'm betting you know what I'm going to say because you put words into my mouth and the mouths of Henry and Kurt as well these last few days. I don't know which thoughts are my own anymore, but the puzzle pieces are falling into place now. You knew this was coming. Why didn't you warn me too?"

She tickled his nose with the feather, but he did not sneeze. "Your forcing a promise from me to bring you here and keep you close was no accident. The intrusions into our sanctuary of our neighbor, your team of friends, your family, and a child were not coincidences. They were reminders of the pledges we made to foster a village and guide its inhabitants. Only problem is, you won't be here to help, and I'm not much good on my own. Leave the others to the songs of angels; let me believe in the magic of a fairy's whisper. Is that what this feather represents?" She waited for a sound that did not come.

"*What do we want our children to learn from us?* When you asked that in your last broadcast, could you sense what was in store? Don't answer. I couldn't accept that this end was part of your grand plan. For the present, I'll do my best. I'll devote the next twenty-four hours to the formalities, but beyond that... no more promises."

Kiri set the blackbird's feather on Michael's pillow and went to work preparing him, and then herself, for the interminable hours ahead. Careful not to awaken Kurt, she tiptoed downstairs to the pantry for a bottle of each of their anniversary waters. She mixed a little of each in the glass bowl, cut a piece of linen cloth and carried them to their personal sanctuary. She gently sponged Michael's face one last time with the spirit water he created to hallow all significant transitions in their lives, then sprinkled the rest in a circle around his body—another Celtic tradition. Touching the last to his lips with her fingers, she whispered, "You never imagined that our spirit water ceremonies would begin and end with you."

Her mission thus accomplished, the unicorn stepped slowly from the spring and eased the gallant warrior from her back to lie beside the still waters and await the restoration of his soul…

Words and efforts became mechanical now. Dress Michael in a suit and tie and, of course, his boots. Set those near the foot of the stretcher supporting his body. Shower. Do her hair. Take a deep breath. She sat at her dressing table using the hazel wood wedding gift from her new husband to brush her long curls. She remembered telling Michael that every time she did, she would think of his fingers running through her hair. She closed her eyes and imagined him grooming her while the minutes flew by.

Kurt called from the landing. "You up, Sis? I brought some peanut butter toast and OJ. I'll leave it in the sitting room. Try to eat something. I'll wait downstairs for Groton's."

"Thanks" was all she could muster. Another sock bun. A bite of toast. Pack a few necessities into a small zipper baggie. Find an appropriate outfit for vigil and funeral. She had never attended a vigil before, so how would she know. Kiri perused the contents of her closet. Professional, yes, but refined, no. She spied the sack of dress Henry gave her the night she returned with the body. Hmm. Michael had become "the body." She emptied the bag and shook out the garment. Perfect! No doubt Michael had a hand in its selection. At least she felt better to assume that he did. Fit exactly, even allowing for the weight she lost over the last week. Henry did not know, so Michael must have guided him. Shoes. Rings. She heard noises downstairs. Grab the baggie. The feather? Grab the feather, give Michael a final pat, and go!

Astounded by Kiri's transformation, the group below stood agape at the apparition on the landing. Dignified and serene came to mind. Her flight down the stairs created buoyancy causing the two tiers of long ruffles at her hem, elbows and neck to flutter like a bird on the wing. The sheer crinkled fabric moved freely over a slightly fitted lining, allowing ease of movement. The mid-calf-length dress appeared to be the expected black, but when she stepped into the sunlight, a mottled pattern emerged showing splashes of midnight blue that brought color to her eyes. She tucked the small feather into her bun as her only accessory.

"Wow, Sis. You look terrific! Where did you find that gorgeous dress?"

Doyle, Frank, Devin, Gus and Henry exchanged cautious looks.

"Hen… At a little shop around the corner from my lunch with friends… the day Michael was killed."

"Well, he would be proud that you pulled yourself together for the rites ahead."

Devin stepped forward. "Speaking of ... We would like your permission to say goodbye to him here, in our own way. We placed the casket on your dining table in front of the fireplace, if you'll allow us a few minutes with him."

"It's beautiful, Kiri. So fine, just like the man," Gus broke in.

She ran her hands over the beautifully grained and polished hazel wood, symbolic to the Celts. She inspected the work carefully to assure that all seams in the octagonal box—three short sides at the head and foot and two long ones joining them—were fitted with wooden pegs, no metal. She felt the white linen lining the interior. Simple, dignified and all Irish. "I'm sure this is exactly what Michael wants." She tried to smile, but one would not come. She met each man's eyes with her own. "Michael is gone, you know. He left in the night. I would appreciate your help bringing his body down. You may touch it now."

Frank nudged Doyle. "What's that about?"

"Don't ask. Just go with it," Doyle replied as he fell in line with the others climbing the stairs.

"He does look ready to go, in his suit and all," Gus said as he moved around the bed to take up a handle of the stretcher. "But I wonder about the boots. Won't Mr. O'Connell object?"

"Michael never left on an important mission without his boots, and Thomas won't know if we close the lower lid before he arrives." She tried another smile.

"I take your meaning. He's missing a lace there. Should I...?"

"No. It's in good hands."

Gus nodded, then gave a signal to heft the litter and bear the body of their comrade to his coffin.

With Michael situated therein and the upper lid left open, the sober group took their places around him with Kurt and Henry at the foot. Devin began. "We're gathered to say farewell to our Celtic brother in spirit, Michael O'Connell. A true Irish hero of old preferred an early, glorious death to a long, unexceptional life and claimed sacrifice as his duty...."

*   *   *

Thomas walked into the bedroom to find Paula already reclined in *supta baddha konasana,* her eyes closed and the cedar chest open again. A similar set-up for him was right beside. He wrapped his robe tighter around his middle and lowered his stiff body into the contrivance. "You're going to have to help me with this, my love. I can't pretzel myself like you can." She barely stirred. He tugged at the strap in frustration. "Help!"

Paula opened her eyes and tried not to smile. At times like this when he was more dependent on her for support, he also was more likely to comply with her demands without argument, accepting that there were times when she knew best where mental and physical health were concerned. She patiently untangled his strap and adjusted it to his body, supporting his thighs and forearms with rolled blankets and his head with a small pillow. She pulled a coverlet up to his chin and resettled herself. "Relax like this for at least five minutes. Today was a long, difficult one, but you held up well. You need rest so you'll be strong enough to face tomorrow."

"I dread tomorrow… you have no idea how much. The finality of it. But for a bad day, today was a good one. To witness the private ceremony Michael's friends conducted around his open casket was a treasure. So typical of the old style. Kirin even allowed me a last kiss to his forehead before she closed it, and the men invited me to help carry my son to the hearse, passing three times sunwise around the evergreen tree in the back on the way—another ancient custom. How kind of the neighbor Paddy to come out and stand respectfully with his cap over his heart. His wife dressed strangely though, in bathrobe and slippers with a hat plopped awkwardly on her head."

Thomas adjusted his coverlet. "Kirin was right, of course. Being an active participant is so much more meaningful than merely observing passively. Those few emotional moments set a tone that carried me through the day."

"The casket was beautiful—simple but elegant. Where do you suppose Groton's found it on such short notice?"

"Handmade in the West, I reckon, where many of the old crafts are still practiced. Some father and son likely have several starters on hand to finish with ornamentation as ordered, so it wouldn't take them too long to add the sparse Celtic interlacing along the seams to represent the never-ending thread of life and then polish it up."

"Hazel wood has such a glorious grain. The simple intertwining decoration made the coffin look stitched together by a skillful and loving hand—the perfect surrounding for a long, peaceful rest. Now, *shush*. Clear your mind. Let your body relax." Paula took in a deep breath and slowly released it.

"This evening's vigil gave me great comfort. So many friends came to console us. Tommy's remarks touched a chord, and the grandchildren did a wonderful job displaying their tributes to Michael. All those thank you cards for their favorite times with their favorite uncle gave many a mourner a chuckle in the reception room."

"That was Emily's idea."

Thomas was astounded. "My Emily?"

"Of course your Emily. Who else's? She came out of her sister's shadow and found her own mind last evening after trying to explain to Meggie about death and funerals. Most of the grandchildren are too young to understand the solemnity combined with a flurry of nervous activity. Meggie apparently surmised that if Uncle Michael were going away for a long time—maybe forever—she should make him a going away card to celebrate. Sensitive to the little ones' needs to express their confused emotions, Emily decided that creating something positive in their uncle's memory was a constructive way to do so. Shortly after dinner, she arrived with a carload of kids and headed for our well-stocked playroom upstairs."

"Really! Where was I?"

"Lost in your own thoughts. That's where you'll be tomorrow during the service if you don't get some rest. Now, *shush.*"

"Standing or sitting, Kirin was a statue from three this afternoon until we left, with no signs of breaking for a rest or something to eat. I don't know how she maintained her strength. She said she was determined to attend Michael until the last. Such devotion. I worry about her trying to stay through the night. Reporters wander in and out of the building twenty-four hours so there is no danger, but the brothers will take shifts—and Michael's friends, too, I understand—so she won't be alone. The line was endless when we left an hour ago. Hasn't been a good old Irish funeral in this city for many years."

"*Shush.* Five minutes. Clear your mind. Let your body relax." She took in a deep breath and slowly released it.

Thomas squirmed in his bindings and emitted a harrumph. "Michael's four friends showed up late afternoon looking like farmers with mud on their boots. They cut in line to talk with Kirin—the first time I've seen her smile since... since she came home. Can't imagine what they were up to."

Paula rolled her eyes beneath closed eyelids.

"Patrick Murphy came through with his arm in a sling. The story is he dislocated his shoulder. Didn't stay long. His wife, Alice Richardson, wept the whole time as if she were the grieving widow. There was a time we thought she and Michael... that she might become part of our family, but.... A young man was with her, a blond I haven't seen before. He seemed rather disturbed by the whole affair."

"*Shush.* Five minutes. Relax."

Thomas chuckled for the first time in a week. "Those boys—Tommy and Henry—know very well that alcohol is not allowed at a public vigil, but they also know that Michael would find a way around that if his friends were gathering. My first sip of cider set me spinning, and I started to call Tommy out for it. He said they had the keg tested. The beverage was still legal... barely. Hadn't quite turned. Henry knew a guy with an orchard." He chuckled again. "Michael would love it."

"*Shush.* Five minutes. Clear your mind. Let your body relax." She took in a deep breath and slowly released it.

"Did you notice Brendan come in after the short prayer service? He looked very smart in his new suit—quite the young man. When Kirin shot him one of your stern grandmother looks, he promptly presented her with a prayer card—his permission slip, I learned later."

"I thought you said 'no children.'"

"I did, but apparently he showed up at Quincy Street last night and pressed his case as the oldest grandson. To give Kirin some relief, I took Brendan into the reception room to introduce him to some of the mourners.

I thought he would keep silent, but he was very sociable, even telling tales on his uncle. After a time, he politely excused himself to 'keep watch' with his aunt. He'll grow to be a fine man, just like Michael. Only one thing will be missing—the name O'Connell. I cannot accept that when we bury my son tomorrow, we bury his line—and possibly my own as well."

"Thomas! Be quiet!"

Startled by the sudden command, he rolled off his bolster and flailed about on the floor. "I feel like a bloody frog tangled in fishing line. Get me out of this contraption before I strangle myself!"

Paula reached to help him and found herself in the same predicament. Soon they were twined just like a Celtic knot and collapsed in snorts and giggles. "Oh, Paula, is it okay to laugh again?"

"Of course it is. Can you imagine Michael, of all people, putting a ban on laughter? Stop wiggling so I can release your strap. Then we are going to bed!"

The couple continued to scuffle and trade a jab or two until their laughter turned to tears. After several minutes consoling one another and feeling exhaustion from the emotive workout, they made their way across the room, shutting off lights and blowing out candles along the way. As Paula turned on soft music, Thomas climbed into bed and opened the covers for her.

"Your music reminds me. I caused quite a stir at the choir's rehearsal this morning when I changed musical selections. Kirin and I often sing 'Panis Angelicus' for a friend's funeral, as you know—and I so wanted to do it for Michael's—but I knew when I opened my mouth for that first beautiful phrase, nothing would come out. If I were too emotional to sing, I couldn't expect Kirin to either, so I made a different choice. Then, after our talk last night, I realized the 'Panis' by harp would be perfect for Michael—no voice needed. The choir didn't object to the change, but the harpist was all in a fluster until I assured her she could play like an angel. I cannot wait to feel my soul elevated by that beautiful piece of music."

"What a lovely thought to take to sleep with you."

"I can't sleep—not when I'm saying goodbye to my son for the last time tomorrow. I've left so much unsaid… undone… I don't…."

Paula turned to him and pulled him close. "Thomas, listen to me. You cannot dwell on all the things unsaid and undone. Think about what you *did* do with Michael… the opportunities seized, not the ones missed. Listen to the music. Take a deep breath and stretch out completely. Sink into the bed. Imagine the last time you and Michael sailed together on a blue-sky day with a warm sun overhead and a hint of salt in the air. Picture him climb onto the boat in his bare feet. Curl your toes and tense your calves like he would… *Relax*…When he shoves away from the dock, tense your thighs as he would… *Release*… Watch him pull off his shirt and flex the muscles of his abdomen and broad chest in readiness for the task ahead. Do the same… *Relax*… See him hoist the mainsail with his muscular arms and shoulders. Help him by tensing yours... *Release*... Return his excited smile and wide-eyed sparkle by tensing every muscle in your face... Enjoy the feeling of relaxation as you head for open sea... together."

Assured by his deep, steady breathing that Thomas and Michael skimmed across the water, sea spray pelting their happy faces, Paula turned her head into her pillow and wept. *I want to drift in our canoe... on a crystal-clear lake high in the Colorado mountains... and hold my baby girl.*

Chapter 10

Henry Callaghan stood outside the cathedral on a gray autumn morning awaiting the arrival of the coffin bearing his friend Michael O'Connell. The BBC exec and undercover operative known for impeccable dress and manner with every action timed and deliberate, every detail exact, every emotion in check—a control freak of sorts—gazed up at the imposing portal to St. Mary's... completely out of control. His hands shook. Perspiration beaded on his forehead. His eyes blurred. His knees weakened, and his stomach rose in his gullet as he imagined the marble exterior topple onto him, crushing him with its weight and assaulting all of his senses.

The same visceral reaction overwhelmed his body more than thirty years previous when, as an innocent boy of eight, he suffered abuse in a chapel by the priest who had been like God to him. Still, any house of worship and the music within recalled the setting. His throat choked from memory of dry wafers, and the smell of incense permeating the man's stiff clothing nauseated him. Worst of all was the touch. Those that were meant to be comforting—beads, kneeling, the hand—induced disgust. The same fingers that abused him, offered the Host. His place of sanctuary became just the opposite for the young victim when his confessor mutated into his assaulter.

Once he and his mother left that village for Dublin, Henry vowed never to cross the threshold of a Catholic church again and to keep his views about God to himself. He was faithful to those promises until the day Kiri asked him to act as pallbearer for Michael. He could not refuse. As the hearse rounded the corner and he awaited the call to take up the coffin, for the first time in thirty years he prayed... that he would not dishonor himself in service to his friend... and especially to Kiri.

*   *   *

Kiri's memories of the funeral were scant—her mother's hand that never left Thomas' shoulder or the back of his head, the crowds that oppressed her and the lone harp playing "Panis Angelicus" that uplifted her. She felt Michael beside her at that moment... and only that moment. For the last twenty-three hours, fifty-nine minutes and fifty-nine seconds she felt nothing, as cold and dead as Michael's body in the box, as she went through the motions of grieving wife throughout the night at the vigil and that morning at the funeral—no eating or sleeping in between. Finally nearing the end of the formalities, she stood at the head of his empty grave, awaiting the casket.

Her finger-tip length black cape billowed in the cool autumn breeze, another of Henry's acquisitions on her behalf. Before they left the house on Quincy Street, he placed it around her shoulders and handed her a black half-circle mantilla of Cluny lace edged with embroidered Celtic designs.

He had a sense for the appropriate when it was warranted, she thought. He even remembered a handful of hairpins in case of gusty weather. She pulled the cape tightly around her as he and the family's chosen bore Michael's coffin on their shoulders to his final resting place.

At the end of a brief committal service and lowering of the casket into its grave, mourners queued around it to cast handfuls of soil onto the coffin. A sudden shriek halted the procession. "No! Stop it!" Little Meggie's astonished eyes filled with agony. "You can't do that. Uncle Michael can't get out if you cover him with dirt. Stop it!"

Emily tried to shush her disturbed daughter, to no avail. "He promised. Uncle Michael promised to take me to see the buffalo. He can't breathe if you cover him up. Stop it! He pro... missed!"

Her father, Stephen, stepped in and shouted to the frightened little girl, "*You* stop it, right now! You're embarrassing the family." He grabbed her by the arm, jerked her away from the site, and dragged her swiftly away, her tiny feet barely able to touch the ground. Ignoring her protests, he shoved her into a waiting vehicle and returned. Her muted cries continued as the mourners finished paying their respects.

Kiri, the last left beside the grave, barely noticed the figure sidling up next to her. "Aunt Kiri, are you okay?"

"Brendan, you and Kurt did a very nice job today. He appreciated your help."

"I was honored to take part. I'll never forget the opportunity you gave me. You're here all alone except for Mr. Callaghan and those guys over there with the shovels. Do you need help? Should I stay with you?"

"Thanks for the offer, but I want to be alone for a few minutes to say goodbye." He stood stiffly with eyes downcast. "But if you want to be of help, you have a little cousin over there who could use a loving word and a hug."

"Meggie?" He turned to see her weeping face pressed against a tear-smeared car window. "I can take care of her. Thanks, Aunt Kiri. I know you feel bad too, but she's more confused than you are today." He ran to the vehicle, opened its door and picked her up. The family standing nearby paid little attention as he wiped her nose with his sleeve and spoke soft, reassuring words to her. The young man let her down, then the two ambled off, hand-in-hand, to investigate the graveyard's beautiful plantings.

Confident that she was truly alone, Kiri kneeled near the edge of Michael's grave. She scanned the surroundings and wondered if a blackbird were hiding in a bush nearby. From her cape's inside pocket, she removed a small pouch made of Irish linen and emptied its contents—soil containing the remnants of three years' pledges from beneath their tribal tree, Aurora—onto her husband's coffin, releasing the bag to flutter down into the hole. *Grá anois agus go deo, mo anam čara,* she whispered. As she struggled to her feet and limped away, the breeze played with her cape, giving her the look of a delicate little bird with a broken wing.

The reception gathering at Thomas' was well underway by the time Kiri arrived with Henry. A few guests mingled in the dining room by the refreshments. Most of the crowd congregated in the living room/den area for more animated conversation. While parents were occupied with friends and relatives, their children wandered at will. A baby cried, reaffirming that life goes on.

Kiri barely reacted to the activity around her. Exhaustion descended, causing her limbs to grow heavier with each moment and the roller coaster inside her to lurch with every movement. She was counselor enough to know that her delayed reaction to the pain of Michael's death would strike without warning, like a bolt of lightning. The last of her mandatory social obligations could not end soon enough. As she gave them, she ticked off in her mind the thanks expected by each member of the family: to Meghan for the prayer cards with a rendering of St. Michael on the front and an appropriate prayer on the back, and additional "in memoriam" cards personalized with her husband's picture and brief biography meant to be keepsakes; to Anne and Emily for the lovely vigil setting; to Tommy and the husbands for arrangements and set-up; to Margaret for staging this gathering.

She purposely avoided Bishop Byrne and Thomas and was about to search out her mother, when a small hand took hers. "Meggie! I love the card you made for your uncle's vigil."

"Thank you. Did you see the flowers I chose for him?" she asked, pulling her aunt back to the dining room.

Kiri regarded the pot of tiny white flowers snuggled in bright green. "These are very lovely."

"I told Mother we needed shamrocks with white flowers on them because when Uncle Michael took us to the park he'd always say…" She imitated with gruff face and pointing finger. "'Watch where you put your feet. Don't be steppin' on any bloomin' shamrocks!' Even when they didn't have their white flowers yet."

Kiri could not stop a chuckle. "Well, thank you for that nice memory."

"You're welcome, very much," she smiled and ran off toward a cousin.

Kurt came up behind her and they walked back to the living room together. "Hi, Sis. I'm surprised you're still on your feet."

"Barely. Thanks for helping today. Your friendly face was a comfort in that sea of strangers."

"My pleasure. At one point I thought I would have to do double duty. Henry turned all pasty as we entered the church. I was afraid I might have to hold him up along with Michael. He was fine by the time we reached the gravesite, thankfully. I should probably say goodbye. I'm booked on the late flight, so I've got my backpack with me. Who is staying with you tonight?"

"No one, thank goodness. Not that I don't enjoy your company, but I need time to myself now. Thanks for coming. Tell Tanya I appreciate her giving you up for these few days. Our long talks really helped ground me."

"I still think you should have someone around for a few days. Here are your keys and... oh... these are from Brendan."

Kiri took the three prayer cards with permissions written on them: one for his secret visit to the house, one for the vigil he was not supposed to attend either, and one for participating at the funeral. "Thanks for taking Brendan on today. He was thrilled, if you can call such a somber duty thrilling. I hardly remember a thing."

"The service was great, if anyone asks. I can't believe you still require permission slips from the kids. Isn't that getting a little old?"

"The kids don't worry me; their parents do. I'm never going to make assumptions or give the stepsibs a chance to get the better of me like I did that first Christmas." She started to put the keys and cards in her cape pocket when she realized that she still wore it. She looked down at her clothing—the same as when she left her house before the vigil—and shook her head. "I've got to go home. I am a mess inside and out."

"Not as much of a mess as we are, little lady," Gus smiled as he walked in. "You're lookin' at four men who are dirty and ache to the bone, but, oh... it hurts so good!"

"Who are these barbarians?" Anne asked her weepy friend Alice standing nearby. "Every time I see them, they're covered in mud."

Henry joined the little group as Doyle shared details. "We laid our spades and shovels on top of the mound in the form of a cross, just like you said. Don't share this with any of his family, but besides our tears, we left a pint down there for Michael."

Kiri blurted out a single laugh. So fitting. No sword or shield needed, but after a job well done Michael could always find time for a drink with friends.

Anne rolled her eyes at the inappropriate response and followed Patrick as he led his wife toward the widow and the team. He extended the hand not in a sling. "Kiri, I can't tell you how sorry I am."

She refused to take it. "That's because you aren't. You're relieved that Michael *didn't* return. You planned perfectly."

Patrick took the bait. *"You are* wrong for once in your life. If my plan were so perfect, *none* of you would have come back!"

Henry clapped his hand over Kiri's mouth to prevent a reply, but the others whipped around to face Patrick. Eyes afire, Doyle leaned in to challenge their nemesis. "Did I hear you say you wanted to take my life and Kiri's too?"

Patrick stepped back and stammered. "I said... nothing... that can be proven." Then he straightened smartly and with a devious grin added, "Simply put, you wouldn't want Michael's team dismantled over the hysterics of a grieving widow... would you?"

Kiri, now free of Henry's grasp, faced the scoundrel's wife. "How does it feel, Alice, to learn that the man you married ordered the murder of the man you still love?"

Alice burst into loud sobs, causing Anne to come to her defense. "How dare you speak to my friend that way. Your disrespect is disgraceful! You Americans have no manner. You ruin everything. Why don't you all go back where you came from!"

Her shouts brought the rest of the immediate family on the run—all except Thomas who was too far away to notice. Paula dove in first. "Kirin Aurora Koyle! Show a little respect. Thomas just buried his son."

"And I buried my husband today. How quickly you and the rest forget that Michael and I were married."

Paula clutched at her heart. "Nothing can fill the space of a lost child."

"Or the hope of ever having one!" Kiri cried through tears.

Thomas finally entered the fray. "What's going on here?"

"Kiri started it. She insulted Alice," Anne said.

In a spasmodic rage, Thomas looked squarely at Kiri. "This is no time for a childish spat! You dishonor my son with such behavior!"

"Mother…"

"Enough! Paula, grab your coat. We're going home!"

"We can't leave…"

"Don't contradict me!"

"Thomas! This *is* your home!"

The sorrowful man slumped into a chair, his head in his hands, weeping.

Kurt scrutinized his sister's tortured face and nodded to Henry. "Kiri is about to erupt. Get her out of here… *now*!"

The newsman and his team formed a Spartan wedge to protect her from the minefield of family in the heat of choosing sides, and they swiftly escorted the wailing widow out the door.

*   *   *

Frank pulled up in front of the Quincy Street house to find Henry standing outside. "Where's Kiri?"

"Inside already. She jumped from the car as it stopped and was through the door before I could grab her. She threw the bolts and ran upstairs. We've got to get in there and figure out how to dismantle Michael's crazy security system. Any ideas?"

"We'll work on it, chief." He nodded toward Doyle, Gus and Devin as they arrived.

"Kiri is alone, and she shouldn't be. Not now," Henry said to the team. "We need to keep watch for a few days at least. We need to keep an eye out for Patrick too."

Doyle heaved a deep sigh. "Good thing none of us mentioned Blondie's relationship to Patrick—that he's Alice's American cousin. She'd have made a meal of him right there in Thomas' house and exposed us all."

"Good thing none of you told me! I'd have ripped him apart myself and smeared the old man's carpet with his blood!" Gus shouted. "How do you figure?"

"As soon as Michael expressed reservations about the kid, we checked into his true identity," Devin said. "Seems he's the son of an American diplomat on holiday after college graduation and looking for some action. He found it all right and ended up where he shouldn't have with no way to get out of Syria."

"No question the US government didn't want to get involved, so Blondie's father contacted his sister here in Dublin who passed the problem to Patrick, her son-in-law. They both assumed that through his connections in the news business he should know someone who could pull strings to get the boy out," Frank added.

"Bloody family connections!" Gus pounded his fist against the car door.

Devin continued. "As soon as Michael suspected Patrick behind the car bomb, we checked his phone calls. He tried to play the hero and arranged the van group precisely to get Alice's cousin out. When he realized what trouble he was in and that Michael was sure to make the connection, he went overboard to cover his tracks."

Frank drew his lips tight and shook his head. "His actions were against policy on two counts: using our team for private ends and involving another government without sanction."

"Michael would have severed Pat's head for that, no matter the fallout." Gus spit on the ground. "Our mate saved two boys that day and paid Pat's debt to family with his life!"

Devin revealed new information. "We intercepted a letter from the US State Department thanking Patrick and our division for intervening. Better not pass it on."

"Right," Henry said. "Keep it in our private file until we can make a stronger case for his complicity in the bombing. And not a word to Kiri."

"Patrick will try to get to her to prevent her from exposing him. How can we keep our little lady safe?" Gus clenched his teeth.

"You'll take six-hour shifts," Henry replied. "Listen for signs of trouble inside and keep Patrick from the door on the outside. I'll stop by when I can to give you a break, but I want to get right on finding the van driver. After today's blowup, Patrick will be one nervous fellow and bound to try something. Who'll take first shift?"

"I'm the man for that!" Gus answered.

Henry nodded. "Right. Let's run an audio check before we leave. Channel 6.5 should pick up Michael's earwig. I hid it in the upstairs sitting room. I don't know what range we'll get here in the city without satellite access, so sounds may be faint but enough to get the drift of what she's going through. That'll have to do for now. Everyone in his car, and let's see what we've got." Henry climbed into his vehicle and activated the system. The others did likewise. They all gave a thumbs-up, then to a man, froze.

Blood-curdling screams crackled through the airwaves. "No... o... o! He's not dead! Michael can't be dead! Don't leave me alone. I need you. Ohhh... Mi... chael!

Chapter 11

Desperate to reach the sanctuary of their bedroom before she lost all control and in a sudden burst of energy, Kiri threw the safety bolts with a bang and raced up the stairs. She dove for their bed and molded her body to the impression left on the mattress by Michael's. Her hands grabbed for something, any small thing left behind that retained his scent. They found his hoodie tucked near the wall. She stuffed it beneath her face and chest, clutching it so tightly she almost cut off her breath. Then it began. Convulsions wracked her body so fiercely she nearly lost hold of the hoodie. They rose from her gut to her chest and finally escaped her throat in tortured wails, piteous cries she did not recognize as her own. Violent physical and emotional wave followed on wave as she fought against the inescapable truth: Michael was dead!

Daylight turned to dark, and her turbaned Yemeni assaulter reappeared brandishing his *jambiya*—at Michael—and every time, its curved blade found its mark until her partner was cut down to nothing but a pair of boots lying in red soil. Her cries did not diminish; they shifted from woeful to frightened. She clutched his hoodie tighter, wringing her tears from it until she was soaked in them.

Dark turned to daylight, and her howls did not cease, echoing off the walls as if she were surrounded by a pack of wolves waiting to attack. She wanted to twist off her head and throw it at them to stop the violent thrumming between her ears, but she did not dare let go of the hoodie. It was all she had left of Michael.

Daylight turned dark again and her limbs, so heavy until now, melted away, leaving her unable to clutch, hold, touch or even feel his garment against her face. Her eyes sank into her brain and rolled around in her unconscious mind.

Darkness still engulfed the room when her first conscious thought broke through. *Water. Go to water. Go to water in stress.* She rolled from the bed, leaving the cape and hoodie behind, and crawled into the bathroom. She turned on the faucet and lifted her face to it, lapping at the cool liquid like a dog at a water hose on a summer day. Then she switched the temperature to hot, closed the drain, activated gentle waves and pulled herself in to lie face down on the bottom of her oversized tub.

As gentle undulations rocked and warmed her, she recalled evenings that she and Michael spent in this same soothing water washing their frustrations away with some Celtic storytelling. A true hero, he said, welcomed death and the hope of immortality in an afterworld, a joyous region of vibrant color where a man retained his form and ate, drank and loved until his return at the time of his loved one's need. *I need you now, Michael. Come. Take me with you to this land of joy.*

Water continued to run and circulate, becoming hotter and deeper. Good, she thought. Hot water makes the blood run faster, using up oxygen. I'll help. She willed herself not to lift her head.

Frank arrived for his second 3 a.m. to 9 a.m. shift. He brought a cup of coffee for Devin and sipped his own. "Any change?"

"The crying stopped a couple of hours ago, and I heard water running. Probably the bath, but I didn't see any lights go on. Not a sound since."

"She must be exhausted. Probably sleeping it off, and will do for a long time yet. You take your own sleep, now. I'll see you back at the office at 10."

Devin drove off, and Frank settled in for what he hoped would be a peaceful shift.

Kiri shivered. Then shivered again. Despite the sun streaming in the open window, she was cold—hardly what she expected of a colorful, joyous afterworld. She felt her environs. Smooth, curved and wingspan-wide like her tub... but dry. Her hand found the faucet—turned off, and the drain still closed. Where did all the water go? Didn't matter. She was alone. Michael didn't come for her... his afterworld, a fantasy. She felt the welling up in her chest that comes before tears, but they stayed lodged hard against her heart. She fell asleep, still shivering.

The sun was at noon when Kiri opened her eyes. She pulled herself to sitting, then to the edge of the tub and swung her legs over. She stepped onto the mat and felt a sharp prick beneath her heel. She brushed the bottom of her foot and found the annoyance, a small black feather. Must have fallen from her hair, she thought. She raked her fingers through her brown snarls. The tubed sock fell out, and along with it, a black feather. No mistake. Two soft black feathers lay side-by-side on the mat.

Kiri slapped her cheeks. There must be a logical explanation—the open windows, maybe. Or was Michael playing some game? "You are not funny, Michael. Why waste time with games? Why not take me with you?" She blinked and set her jaw. "If you won't take me, I'll come by myself. You know I will."

Her threat spurred action. She ran through the bedroom, down the stairs and out the kitchen door. Halfway to the garage, she turned and ran back. Keys. She needed keys to the car. Locked in the safe before they left. The spares. Where did they keep the spares? In the mudroom. She ran to the mudroom, rifled through drawers, and with keys in hand headed for the garage again. "You can't outsmart me. If you won't help me, I'll do it myself. 'Sonnet 116,' Michael. ...*even to the edge of doom!"* she shouted as she ran out the door.

Doyle phoned the office where Henry and the other three team members worked on their reports of the fatal mission. "We've got movement. Kiri's in the garage ready to head out. No place fancy, I hope. She's in the same dress, no shoes and hair a mess. Should I follow?"

"Any clues as to where?" Henry asked.

"Not really. The only words I could make out were 'Sonnet 116, Michael' and 'doom.' I looked that up on my smartphone, and all I got was Shakespeare and 'Let me not to the marriage...' Any ideas?"

Devin chimed in. "That's how the sonnet begins, and line twelve ends with 'even to the edge of doom,' referring to love, I think."

"Doesn't sound good to me," Frank added. "Any way to get a tracker on the car?"

"Already there," Henry said. "I put Michael's on the Lotus and Kiri's on hers. We won't be expected to account for that equipment. Lost in Syria, if anyone asks."

"Wup, there she goes in the Lotus. I'll follow, but someone else may have to intercept if I lose her in traffic."

"We'll go," Frank nodded to Gus. "Devin has more experience with tracking."

"Doyle, stay on the phone with me."

"Right, chief. She's headed for the M3. Jeez, she takes corners fast!"

Kiri was completely unaware of being followed until she turned away from Tara onto a lonely road that appeared to lead nowhere. Two vehicles made the same turn. She and Michael never encountered any traffic when they drove this way. She slowed down to let them pass, but they did not. "They may be able to go slower than I, but they can't possibly go faster," she muttered as she unhooked her safety belt and gunned the motor.

The sprawling oak tree—their 'live or die' oak tree—was barely two miles ahead. Frequently she and Michael drove out here when they had problems. They named the old oak "doom" and laughed as they passed it by, reminding themselves that they both chose "life..." with each other. For better, for worse. *...even to the edge of doom.* Live or die... together. Now, the decision was hers alone.

"Jeez, she's heading for that tree!" Doyle shouted. "Spread and wedge. I'll take the left."

"Michael will kill us if we put a scratch on his racer," Frank said as he veered to the right.

"He'll kill us if we don't!" Gus replied.

Kiri thought she saw double when her rear-view revealed two cars on her tail—one on each side—slowly gaining on her. The one on the left pulled so close, she was forced to take the center of the road. The one on the right kept her there. Then they pulled even, and she caught familiar faces out of the sides of both eyes. "Don't even try to stop me," she mouthed.

The two pulled a couple of feet ahead. "Now!" Doyle shouted, and they inched inward until they made contact, all three adjoined. "Wedge!" The two tails moved out while the front fenders pressed in on a slant, trapping the Lotus and crushing its front end. "Brake and hold!" The three vehicles skidded, tearing up the gravel roadway, until they came to a stop.

Gus, the only one not behind a wheel and situated closest to Kiri, jumped out of his door and tore hers open. He grabbed her from her seat and threw one powerful arm behind her neck and the other around her waist, pressing her into his chest. "Not today, little lady. Your number's not up today."

Kiri survived without a scratch, her only injury—a broken heart. She burst into sobs.

"Doyle! What happened? The Lotus stopped." Henry could be heard shouting from the phone.

"Good thing, chief. She headed for a tree. Gus has her now." He joined the others near the Lotus. "No injuries. All three cars are pretty banged up."

"Bring them into the shop after you take Kiri home. The least we can do for Michael is fix up his baby. We'll put one of you 24/7 on Kiri inside."

"Gus here, Henry. Beg to differ. We should all meet at Ryan's Pub first. Bring the doc."

Silence on the line. "OK. Call when you're ten minutes out."

The two outside vehicles jockeyed free and headed back to the city. Gus seated Kiri on the passenger side of the Lotus. "You handle this racer mighty well, but I'll be takin' the wheel on the way back." She leaned her head against the window and cried softly.

Gus lagged behind the others to give them time to set up at Ryan's. When he and Kiri arrived, Henry and the doc, and Doyle, Frank and Devin were already seated with pints in front of them. Three empty chairs, two full pints and an empty glass were waiting. Kiri lived this scene occasionally over the last four years—every time Michael and the team, then she, Michael and the team returned from a big assignment abroad—as a celebration of sorts.

Kiri sat in the chair with the empty glass, as was her habit, in between Gus and the empty one. Her half-pint was passed around the table, and each man dribbled a bit of his Guinness into it, including a few drops from the one by the empty chair—Michael's. This respected her desire to limit her intake to "two fingers," but share in the celebration. Departing from the usual hearty cheers for a job well done, each man in turn offered a toast to his absent comrade, extolling his virtues and bravery and raising a final glass to their departed friend. Kiri tried to curb her tears, but that made no difference to the men who openly wept themselves.

Fond memories and storytelling followed with each man adding a tale or two and other pub regulars joining in. Tears flowed as freely as Guinness; laughter puddled them around rosy cheeks and noses, a mix of merriment and sorrow. Music played; voices joined in song. Kiri relaxed, and a smile crept onto her face.

"Now, that's a true 'gathering,' little lady, an honorable celebration for a fallen friend," Gus said when the room finally quieted. He scooted their two chairs to face one another and pulled her onto his lap. He guided her head gently to his shoulder and tried to smooth back her tangled hair. Noticing her gestures of embarrassment at her disheveled appearance, he said, "You're as beautiful as the first day you walked into our lives to help us. We're your family now. Even that rag-tag bunch." He nodded toward Ryan and a few others at the bar. "There's not a man among us who wouldn't come to your aid or fight to protect you, if it came to that. But you have to let us in."

He juggled her weight and pulled her closer, resting his bearded chin on top of her head. "I have eight sisters, you know." The five others rolled their eyes, but Gus ignored them and pressed on. "And oftentimes one would come running through the door all red-faced and weepy. Ask 'em what was the matter, and they'd shout back, 'Nothing! Go away and don't bother me! I want to be alone!' Then she'd run up the stairs and slam her bedroom door."

The big man squeezed her tighter. "What she said was only a half-truth. She didn't want to be bothered, for sure. But she also didn't want to be alone. She really wanted a silent presence to share her unhappiness... maybe with a pat on the shoulder or by holding her hand or just sitting still nearby and breathing in and out without questioning her. I'm blessed to claim you as my ninth sister. We're family." He turned her face and forced her eyes to meet his. "You saved my life once. Now, I'm here to help you save your own. We all want to help you. We won't judge."

The doc moved around the table to sit in Kiri's chair facing her, their knees touching. He held both her hands. "You will experience a range of emotions as well as physical and mental symptoms of your grief. Don't ignore them and don't feel guilty when you give in to them. Most are typical of the grieving process so don't feel like you are crazy. You're not. Be aware that depression is likely, joy absent from your life for a while. You may become anxious and irritable, feel helpless, experience pain or headaches for no reason, even get very sick when you usually do not. Your eating and sleeping patterns may change. Dehydration is a danger. You may not be able to focus or concentrate or make decisions... and you shouldn't for a long, long time.

"You may try to isolate yourself from those who care about you most. You'll ask a million 'why' questions and find no logical answers. Finally, you're likely to experience short-term memory loss and not remember a thing I've said, but try to hold onto this. If you feel you're losing control or experience any discomfort you cannot explain…call me. I'll come immediately to listen and try to diagnose where you are in the healing process. You've witnessed atrocities no one should and performed impossible tasks for Michael that cannot be expected of any loved one. They *will* take their toll. I would offer you medication to help but I know you won't take it, so make friends with your phone."

He gave up his place to Doyle. "You and I have been through a lot together, Kiri. We both nearly bought it in Yemen, but you found the strength to pull us through, and Michael too, from the depths of his despair. Life is terribly unfair. You never imagined you would be here with us tonight to mourn his passing, just as you can't picture a life different from the one you've known. That will take time. We can't wipe away the pain of his loss, but we can be patient and listen while you work your own way through it. Patience is a byword for guys in our business… for everyone but Frank, that is." The whole group laughed at that truth.

Frank took his turn. "I may be the anxious one, but I get a lot done with that nervous energy. If it's clutter, dust or mud you've got, I'll take care of it in no time. Tell me the day the collectors come and I'll have your rubbish gathered and out on the road for them. I even do laundry and windows. And if you have a craving, I'll find the best there is. Just tape a note to your window… lettuce, for instance… and you'll find a bowl on your doorstep the next morning filled with leafy organic reds and greens… or apples, and there will be near twenty local varieties waiting for you with the sun still on them."

Devin elbowed in for his turn in the chair. "Companionable solitude is my specialty. I can play an entire game of *fidchell* without moving a piece or saying a word, simply by staring into a fire. I find as much delight in watching a flower grow as I do in marching in a parade. I can be alongside or follow behind for a walk down the road or through the park and never make a sound."

Henry coveted the ease with which Gus bundled Kiri onto his lap and the others took her hands to comfort her. He was the steady, serious one, afraid to allow too much emotion to break through his steely demeanor. "The doc warned you not to make decisions for a long time… until you feel up to it. You won't have to. The nightmare of paperwork surrounding Michael's death, insurance and compensation is handled. Nothing is so urgent as to require your signature within days, weeks or even months. We're looking out for your best interests. Your job now is to try to eat, sleep and find some measure of comfort in knowing we are available to help you in any way you need." He nodded to the doc who went to settle up the tab and place an order.

Gus squeezed her tightly again. "If it's a plumber or electrician you need, I'm your man. Or when you feel some better and have one of those happy/sad moments you want to share, I'll join in. From time to time you'll have a little griefburst. You'll hear, see, smell or even touch something that triggers a memory—an emotional reaction that'll have you laughin' and cryin' at the same time. That's a healthy response, and I'm very good at it. Sappy is my specialty."

"Hear! Hear!" the others cried and summoned another round. Gus set Kiri back in her chair. A dish the size for kitten's milk appeared before her with a few spoonfuls of beef and Guinness stew. She shook her head. "Oh, yes, you will," ordered the doc. "And this full glass of water too. You need to keep up your strength for some more healthy crying." She picked up the spoon and when she finally set it down with her empty glass, another hearty cheer saluted her as the men thrust their glasses down on the table with a bang, signaling the end of their "gathering."

They led Kiri from Ryan's Pub, barefooted and bone-weary. She looked back and noticed, with a sudden pang, Michael's glass—empty and turned upside down in front of his chair. For a passing instant, she smiled at her good fortune.

Chapter 12

Day One: Actually Kiri was not sure which day it was, but *Day One* would do.
One sun salutation; one downward dog
One wholesome meal—Henry said he left a carton of Guinness stew in the frig
One constructive chore—sort through the mail. Paddy left lots of notes

Day Two:
Two sun salutations; two downward dogs
Two meals, minimum
Two constructive chores—make a grocery list and tape to window; find thank you notes

Day Three...
Kiri awoke to the painful realization that she would never bear Michael's child. She reached in her drawer for her calendar and confirmed she was right on time. They did not conceive a child before Michael died. Now *all* of her dreams were dead!

She ran from the bathroom to the stable—their pet name for the nursery—and grabbed the rocking horse Dreamer. She lifted the antique wooden toy and heaved it out the window. Shattered glass punctured her skin causing little trickles of blood on her arms and legs. She ran down the stairs, out to the garage with keys in hand and came to a dead stop. The guys put a boot on her wheel.

Desperate for an outlet for the hopelessness that engulfed her, she cast about for an alternative. Her eyes spotted the chainsaw and an axe. She grabbed for the saw, ran into the yard and summoned enough strength to yank the starter. Neither the sudden roar of the motor nor the vibration deterred her from hacking away at Aurora, their beloved tribal tree.

Two limbs crashed to the ground by the time Gus reached her. He jerked the chainsaw from her hands and shouted, "What the hell do you think you're doing?"

"Michael and I... all of our dreams are gone. I can't fulfill my promise. I have no reason to live!"

"In that case, let me help," he said, reaching for another branch. "How about this one? Or this one?" He continued to cut small gashes in several limbs around the tree. "Why bother with this little stuff. I'll just chop the whole bloody tree down!" He started in on the trunk.

Kiri pulled on his shirt, then his arm, crying. "No! Stop it! Not our tree!" She sank to her knees beneath it, her fingers scratching through the soil. "Our promises! Our dreams! Michael, I'm sorry. Forgive me." She sobbed uncontrollably.

Gus cut the motor and dropped the saw to the ground. He picked Kiri up and carried her to the kitchen where he washed the blood and dirt from her arms and legs. Then he swaddled her with a throw and lifted her next to him in the recliner. He pulled her tight against him and rocked her gently like his sisters did their babies. "You go ahead and cry, little lady. Cry an ocean if you want to. Gus is here, and he's not going to make you stop." He let his head fall against the back of the recliner and bit his lip while he wept with her.

Henry watched Patrick's vehicle round the corner just as he drove up to Kiri's house. He noticed Gus' car sitting empty across the road and the gate to the back garden open. Frantic that trouble preceded him, he rushed through the open kitchen door and stumbled on a pile of blood-spotted and muddied towels. He walked cautiously toward the living room and found Kiri and Gus... asleep in the recliner.

He shook his friend's shoulder and Gus jerked to "on guard." "What happened here? The floor is a mess."

"You should see the back garden. Kiri took to trimming the tree this morning." Gus proceeded to relate the events of the early hours.

"Patrick drove away as I pulled up. Do you think he came in?"

"Doubt it. The old fellow across the way keeps pretty good watch."

"Where did you say the crash came from?"

"The other side of the house. Had to be a window, the way she's all cut up."

Henry investigated the main floor first. Nothing seemed amiss in Michael's office or the guestroom. Upstairs, the first room he entered was tidy, but the second was empty except for a party hat on the floor and shards of glass beneath the broken window. He peered out to see the splintered remains of an old rocking horse. That triggered her setback, he decided, and recalled Michael's similar reaction when he learned Kiri was injured in Yemen.

He returned to the living room, phone in hand. "I'll call in a repair of the window, put the towels in the laundry, and sweep up the mess above. Then you can help get Kiri to bed and call off the others for the night. I'll stay with her. You guys deserve a break. Let's say you start watch again about 6 a.m."

Gus nodded. "I'll clean up the yard on my way."

With a new windowpane in place and Kiri tucked in, Gus took his leave. Henry secured all doors and examined them for Michael's security system, but he could not find the magic switch. He wondered, too, where Michael kept his firearms. Probably not safe to have them in the house with Kiri's current state of mind, but he was unsuccessful uncovering those as well. He turned on water for tea, checked for adequate food stocks, and sat in the nook to write a note. *This new phone is untraceable. Use it. 1-Henry,*

2-Doyle, 3-Frank, 4-Devin, 5-Gus, 6-Doc. He wanted to write more but did not know what. Every phrase he considered seemed so trite. *Henry.*

He turned off the water and set the tea to brewing. He spied a jar on the counter that sparked an idea, picked it up and left the house with the door ajar. He crossed the road and knocked on Paddy's door. The older man came out, a pair of binoculars around his neck.

"Henry Callaghan." He extended his hand. "I'm a friend of Michael's... and Kiri's. I understand you keep an eye on their house."

"Pleased to meet you, sir. The name's Paddy." The older man took his hand. "Yes, I've been on watch. I write everything down like she asked. Quite a lot of activity over there of late."

"I hope my men... her friends... haven't concerned you."

"No. After the first day, I recognized them... and you... as the ones what carried Michael's coffin from the house. Decided you must be dear friends to have that honor."

"Yes, it was an honor. Have you seen any others around?"

"Sure. The same black SUV and the same man with the funny eyes... sometimes two or three times in a day when he thinks you fellas aren't watching. If he stops way down there and gets out of his car, I walk to the road and put these binocs to my eyes and stare him down like I did this morning. That chases him right away." He demonstrated, then patted the glasses fondly. "Kiri gave me these, you know. They were Michael's."

Henry smiled. "She wants you to have this too." He handed the faithful watchman the jar of jam. "She's not feeling well, but when she's better, I'm sure she'll be over to thank you for standing guard. May I ask you to continue to keep an eye out until she's back on her feet?"

"My pleasure, and tell her the jam is much appreciated. My Maureen loves a spot with her muffin in the morning."

"Could I leave my number with you?"

"No need. I'm sure it's one she already give to me."

Henry shook hands again with the kindly neighbor and returned to Kiri's house, reassured that Patrick did not intrude on her... yet.

With tea on the bedside table, the rocker in place by the bed, and lights dimmed, Henry settled in to keep watch over Kiri. He could have done so from the living room downstairs or from the sitting room the other side of the wall, but he wanted to be close in case she woke up frightened. He gazed on her curled into a ball clutching a hoodie, once so strong and sure of herself allowing no obstacle to stop her. Now she seemed small and vulnerable in their huge bed, like a tiny acorn adrift on a vast sea of grass. He wanted to touch her... smooth her hair from her face... plump the pillows and pull the covers up to her ears... rub her shoulders gently... but he was afraid she might awaken... and afraid of what he might say to her if she did. He leaned back into the rocker content to have twelve undisturbed hours in her presence... to imagine what months and years might be.

Day One...again:
One sun salutation; one downward dog
One well-balanced meal—check the freezer
One constructive chore...

Kiri looked down at her cup of tea and saw a phone on the kitchen table... with a note nearby. Thoughtful of Henry. He sensed she did not want to use her own. She could not face all the messages. Not yet. She looked down at her hands... and arms... with a few tiny scabs on them. Where did those come from? She propped her head in her hand and tried to remember yesterday. What happened yesterday? She gazed out the window at Aurora... bare of several lower branches! The memory came flooding back and remorse followed. Why did she take her desperation out on Aurora? On a tree that had only been a comfort to her? She grabbed a jacket and flip-flops and walked outside to examine the damage. She rubbed her hand against the worst of the scars—one above the other. "I'm so sorry," she said to the tree. "I won't harm you again." She reentered the house to plan for the day.

One constructive chore—not today
One half-hour of outdoor exercise

She returned to the back garden, her jacket pulled tight against the morning's chill, and started walking around the perimeter of the yard. Each time she flip-flopped past Aurora, she brushed her hand against its needles and forced a positive thought. At the end of her rounds, she stopped at the tree to tenderly pat its scars, now oozing pitch to heal itself. Caught in the goo of each scar was a feather... a small black feather. She removed the two pinnas and returned to the house to place them alongside the others. Now there were four. Did they come on a breeze? Did a little bird sit too close and get stuck? Did Michael...? No matter. They gave her the tiniest pinpoint of hope that she would find her way out of her despair... someday.

Day Two:
Two sun salutations; two downward dogs
Two meals
Two chores—no thank you's yet; no bills; no phone calls
Two half-hours of outside exercise   inside the yard
Two waves through the window to the guys on duty today

Day Five:
Yoga and meals as usual
Chores—call Mom? Not yet, still too emotional. Maybe tomorrow
Wave—oh, the guys are switching shifts. Shorter shifts. Improving?
Exercise—outside the fence! Ask Devin to walk to the main road and back with me. Must be really boring to sit in a car and wait for me to go ballistic. Sorry to disappoint!

Day Seven:
Yoga, exercise and healthy diet on track thanks to Frank who brings
fresh food
Chores—yuck. I sleep a lot
Make one decision.

Deciding on a decision to make was a decision in itself. Kiri finally determined to call their solicitor. He mentioned three times—at the vigil, the funeral and the gathering—that business items must be dealt with. Good place to start—nothing personal.

When the well-meaning receptionist answered with, "Mrs. O'Connell, we're so sorry for your loss," Kiri nearly burst into tears. *Does everyone read from the same script? If I hear those words one more time, I will SCREAM!* She responded graciously to hundreds, maybe thousands, of guests at the vigil—condolences from people she did not know and could not take seriously. She did not need the pity of strangers. After all, her own mother hardly exchanged sentiments with her.

When the solicitor asked her to come to the office, she made a second decision: she refused. She was not yet ready to go out in public and look people in the eyes. Any business could be handled by phone, FAX, and email. The most urgent was the West House. Automatic payments to the family stopped with October's. November's was now five days late, since the bank required annual renewal for their unusual arrangement—if she intended to keep the property. If not, he needed to see a copy of the contract to determine her options now that Michael was....

Keep the house? She already had two. Their dreams for the third died with Michael. Major decision—not yet. Buy time. She agreed to call the bank and continue the payments for another year. She could not believe the solicitor had no copy of the contract, but that was not worth contesting. Yes, she informed him. She would search their safe and FAX a copy. She suddenly realized she *had* made a major decision after all—to open the safe. She climbed in bed and pulled the covers over her head.

Day Eight:
Yoga, food and exercise to clear my mind before unlocking all the
hopes, dreams and memories in the safe

The safe in the floor of the mudroom contained three 12 by 18 inch plastic boxes, one for work, one labeled Michael and the third for Kiri. She had not opened the work box since they returned from Yemen, and she never opened her husband's out of respect for his privacy. When she secreted items for safekeeping before an assignment, she always put them on her box. Its lid had ridges to prevent phones, passports and rings from sliding off. Kiri planned to attack the middle box first—the most likely location for legal documents—Michael's. She decided necessity trumped respect in this case.

Kiri lifted the safe's door with no problem. Shocked, she stared down at a large white envelope bearing her name in Michael's handwriting. Impossible! She was the last to open the safe to secure their rings before the Syrian mission and the first and only to open it after, to retrieve them. The envelope was not there either time. She was certain.

She raised the right edge to reveal the passports and two family phones on top of her box—proof positive that the envelope came after Syria even if she were confused about the rings. She lifted the white paper cover gingerly, its weight scarcely that of a feather. She sliced its seal with her finger and allowed the contents to drift to the floor—a tissue-wrapped lacy medallion, as thin and delicate as the wing of a fairy. She fingered the three-inch airy ornament, afraid its gossamer threads would dissolve in her hand like a tuft of cotton candy. Barely discernible words, again in Michael's hand, covered the tissue.

Dearest Kirin,

This Celtic Circle is as ancient as my ancestors. The Celtic world turned on circles, from the shape of the earth, sun and moon, to time measuring seasons in a continuous cycle of days following on days, to natural rhythms like the tides or human breath moving in and out only to move in and out again. The three intersection points on the circle represent many triads.

First, the three worlds in the Celtic belief system: The underworld beneath the surface of the landscape where the fairy people dwell; the human world; and the supersensual world of the heavens where a warrior might walk again fully clad and pass through the thin space that separates his domain to spend time in either of the others.

Second, the phases of our existence through time—our states of being which cannot be imagined until one arrives there: the unknown, in the womb; the known, on earth; and the unknown, beyond our life on earth.

Third, the Celtic Trinity knot, so named by Christians to represent Father, Son, and Holy Spirit in their religion.

Fourth, the connection of one generation to the next from grandmother to mother to daughter. Pick your point on the circle. Another for your mother and the last for our daughter. Trace your path to Paula. That was your life as a sentient being in her belly. Trace the other path to our daughter. Your essence flows from your mother, through you to her and then to her daughter—our granddaughter who will then inhabit the space of her great-grandmother, and so on, until generation layered on generation continues around the circle. A father may pass his name to his descendants, but mothers provide a seamless passage to complete and continue a circle.

Finally, a Celtic Circle can represent the promises of a man to his wife: to love, honor, and protect her eternally as she weaves their thread through a complex knotwork of experience to connect them through all time. I promise to protect and guide you on your journey from this phase of your life to the next. Listen to the good fairies whispering from their world. Reach toward the heavenly world when you birth and baptize our children, assured that our souls entwined to shelter you now and will bring us together again.

Grá anois agus go deo, mo anam čara.
Michael

Impossible! Ridiculous! Surely, this was a cruel joke. She and Michael did not have a daughter... and now, never would. Whose hurtful consolation could this be? She stalked out of the house toward Frank's car, her ponytail bobbing behind barely able to keep pace with her. She thrust the crinkly tissue between his nose and his book. "Which one of you did this?" she shouted.

"Calm down so I can see what you're flapping in my face." He smoothed the thin paper on his thigh and tried to read it. "Looks like a note from Michael, but I can't make out all the words. Why is this a problem?"

"It wasn't in the safe before we left, and no one else wandered around my house after we returned except you guys and my brother. He doesn't know squat about Celtic culture, so one of you wrote this note and put it in the safe. Who?"

"Hold on. Don't accuse your friends until you've thought this out. None of us has a home safe. Why would we imagine Michael did? How would we know its location or how to get into it? We can't even bypass his security system to get into your house. There must be a logical explanation. Was the note loose?"

"No. It came in a light envelope with this." She opened her hand to reveal the ancient circle.

"Whoa! I've never seen one of these for real. Only heard stories about them. If authentic, that little trinket is quite valuable. None of us could come by one, for sure—proof that your letter is from Michael."

"But how? When? It wasn't there when we left for Syria."

"It had to be. Think science. Physics. Maybe static electricity held the envelope to the door and you didn't notice. Or when you broke the vacuum seal, even a slight rush of air moved it to the side. Or..."

"Stop. I agree. There could be many explanations, but not one would account for his message. He refers to our future... my future without him... as if he knew I would be alone... and confused. He could only write those words after..."

"Not true. Before we left on any assignment, Michael encouraged all of us to have our affairs in order. Even you know how uneasy he was about our latest mission. It would be like him to plan ahead... for the worst... hoping it would not come. You..."

Kiri grabbed the note and ornament from his hand and was back across the road and through the door before he could finish. She ran to the safe and opened her box. Michael wrote her another such letter before a similar mission, and she forgot about it once they returned from Yemen. Before he died, he said that everything she needed was in the safe. Maybe there was a clue in that missive.

The letter, being small, was near the top with folders of documents below. She flipped through them to remind herself what they contained and found a new one labeled contracts—one for West House and one for Paddy's. How strange, she thought. No, logical. Michael knew where he put them. In an emergency, she would go for the will and Quincy deed and stumble across the others. She removed the one the solicitor wanted and set it aside.

She opened the old letter and perused it quickly. *...everything you need to know in the event I do not return to you whole.* Check. *Do not trust Patrick Murphy.* Double check. *Work as closely with Henry as you can.* Check. *Deed is in our safe place.* Check. *Will is in our safe place.* Check. *... deposit at Eternity Sperm Security...* Oh my God!

She dropped the letter into her box, tossed the Celtic Circle in after it, and snapped the lid shut. Closing the safe door with a bang, she twirled the combination's dial, replaced the flooring and sat on top. She clutched her arms across her chest and rocked back and forth, back and forth, as if she could grind everything beneath her into a deeper chasm and her body too. She started to shiver so violently she could hardly hold onto herself. How could he? How could Michael even suggest? If he returned half a man, she would not question his wishes. But *no* man? What fantasy world did he inhabit to imagine he could puppet her through life?

Despair turned to anger, then to despair again as she prayed for the earth to stop spinning... in Celtic circles... long enough to make sense of Michael's death and her life. Her life without him. But the world would not stop. It banged on her kitchen door. Over and over. It called out, "Kiri, are you in there? It's Frank. Let me hear your voice so I know you're okay."

"Go away and leave me alone!"

"Right. That's all I need. I'll check back in a bit."

In that moment Kiri could care less if Frank or anyone else—even Michael—ever came again. She pulled her knees to her chest, wrapped her arms around them, and rocked harder and faster... harder and faster....

Day Ten:
Yoga, Exercise, FAX and food

After satisfying her obligations to physical exertion and the solicitor, Kiri felt her first hunger pangs since... she could not remember. Food. She opened the frig and found... nothing. No fresh fruits or veggies. No milk. No eggs. No fresh bread. Strange. Frank kept her well stocked, but he had not come in for a couple of days. Apparently he decided she should buck up and run her own errands.

She began salivating, craving an apple—the perfect apple. She dressed and left the house for the grocery shop she and Devin discovered on a walk up to the top of the road and two over—a neighborhood where she was not recognized. She gestured for Devin to come with, but he waved her off. She was on her own. He aimed to wean her from dependence also. She entered the shop and headed straight for the apples. Only moments later she ran out the door and all the way home, tears streaming from her eyes.

"How foolish I am," she cried, "to think I could find a perfect apple or anything else. Apples aren't perfect; they have worms. Flowers aren't perfect; they wilt. Men aren't perfect; they die. Life isn't perfect; it explodes without warning and rains down rubble. And I'm not perfect; I forgot to take money! I couldn't even buy a wormy apple with only a tissue in my pocket!"

Devin called the office. "Heavy crying going on. Should I go in?"
"Not yet. Give her an hour to work through whatever triggered her."

Short of an hour, Kiri stopped her sobbing, wiped her face and stared at the skylight. What went wrong? What would Michael do? Analyze the problem, then fix it. The problem: her mind was a jumble. She could not remember a thing for more than two minutes. The fix: reminders. She wrote three sticky notes and affixed them inside the doors. *Keys, money, phone.* She put keys and phone in her pocket but could not find enough change to count, so she reluctantly searched for her credit card. To avert writing her name in the shop, she decided to find an ATM in the unfamiliar neighborhood first. She marched out the door and locked it this time. She was absolutely starved for a wormy apple.

*   *   *

Thomas stared blankly at the words swarming on the newsprint in front of his bleary eyes. A physical newspaper rustling in his hands was one of the pleasures he clung to in advancing age, particularly when accompanied by a cup or two of tea in the morning. The texture and smell could not be replicated by an online version of the world's latest events. Staring at a screen watching his son's life flash by did not satisfy his need to linger with the words and memories that described his boy. More than two weeks after the funeral, the grieving father still struggled daily to find focus.

Paula pattered back and forth past the kitchen nook, distracting him further. Her sudden burst of activity was uncharacteristic given her mood of the last few weeks. Kiri cut off all communication with her mother, and Paula was frantic with worry and the unsatisfied longing to comfort her child. Henry contacted them regularly to assure them that his men looked after Kiri, but he did not elaborate. When asked of her condition, he replied that she could not handle the emotional stress of a face-to-face. She would be in touch in good time. Thomas wondered if there ever would be a "good time" in their lives again, and Paula's bustle did not help.

"You're full of energy this morning. Have a good sleep?" he asked.

"Hardly, as you well know. We both tossed and turned most of the night and finally had to synchronize to keep from injuring one another. I'm putting together snacks for the grandchildren. They'll be here within the hour."

Pages of Thomas' paper fluttered to the floor. "They'll what!"

"Today is the November Saturday we scheduled with them, and they'll be here shortly."

"Surely we can't be expected to…"

"No, we can't be expected to, but we will. The grandchildren have their own problems adjusting to Michael's death and they need the consistency of a normal routine. I've already had calls from the young ones who ask if we remember the date. Grace and Caitlín offered to help if we would host the little ones who look forward to the day."

"An afternoon of songs and games at a time like this? You must be crazy!"

"No games. Borrowing from Emily's fine idea, we're making picture pages for a scrapbook about Michael. Scissors and sticky fingers will be involved."

"You can't do that!"

"Why not? The whole family has gone quiet, as if loss lasts for a predetermined number of days and then is tucked deep inside and spoken of no more. We cannot allow their parents to erase Michael from the grandchildren's lives like words on a tablet." She hurried off and returned with bags from the freezer. "This will do. Frozen grapes… and we'll make ants on a log, a favorite. You can help."

"I will not!"

"Then go upstairs to the suite, lock the door and sit in the dark—alone. Your grandchildren need an activity to channel the pain they feel from losing their favorite uncle. There is a time for gloom, but we also honor a person's memory by sharing some of the joys he brought into our lives." She turned from him and busied herself at the sink cutting celery into two-inch pieces. Thomas grumbled and picked up his paper.

"Do you remember the last words you heard Michael speak, Thomas? Kiri echoed them in her charge for the funeral. Your son stared out of our television screen at you, his father, and asked, 'What do we want our children to learn from us?' You think long and hard about your reply."

She searched a drawer for a handful of butter knives. "I will hold myself together long enough to demonstrate that a grownup can laugh and cry at the same time and that children are allowed to do the same. When the afternoon is finally over and the last little foot is out the door, I will take refuge in my tub and weep my sadness into the water. You are not invited!"

Thomas capitulated in a move to return to Paula's good graces. He participated as fully as his fumbling fingers allowed but lacked the eptitude to guide gooey peanut butter along a narrow groove of celery stalk, and the raisin ants did not want to stick to anything but his digits. Ronan took pity on him and offered to help. "Maybe you're more suited to be a holder," he suggested. Soon Thomas was the favored holder, balancing four short stalks at once while the little ones giggled. A production line ensued with every child wanting a turn with the grumpy grandfather.

Connor spoke without thinking. "Remember when we made these on the Boyne Valley picnic with Uncle Michael?" Silence fell on the nook. "He shoved two pieces of celery up his nose and said, 'Don't ever do this! It's bad manners and dangerous! You'll look like a goof and we'll have to tie you to a tree and shake you until they fall out.' Then he tried to eat a log, but the stalks in his nose were in the way and he kept making funny faces to snag it with his tongue and we all laughed." The grandchildren broke into the same laughter at the silly memory, and Paula did too. Even Thomas allowed a half-grin to creep onto his face.

Once everyone settled at the big table in the playroom—even Thomas, uncomfortable on a child-sized chair—Paula explained the project. One picture page, both sides, per child. Scissors, glue sticks, crayons and markers, a box of tissues and a box of pictures were at their disposal. Thomas gave her a disapproving look, but Paula explained, "These photos are from all the fun times we've shared with your uncle over the last four years. Pick a few, mount them on the page, and write some words to remind you where you were and what you were doing that day. Your older cousins can help with the writing. We'll keep the book here, and anytime you come to play, you can look at it and remind yourselves what fun times you had with Uncle Michael."

The colorful pictures sparked memories the young children were eager to share. The decorating and storytelling began in earnest. One little voice piped up, "I'm sad Uncle Michael died and can't play with us anymore." "Me too," Paula replied and reached for a tissue to dab at her eyes. Two of the older grandchildren did the same, feeling comfortable now to use the words "Michael," "died," and "sad" all in the same sentence.

"Why can't we take this book home with us?" Fíona asked.

"We only have one book to share. It will be fun to look at the pictures together when you come—anytime you want."

"I wish I could take one home with me." Her eyes dropped to the scraps on the table.

"Let me count and see if I have enough for everyone." Paula tried to smooth over the girl's disappointment.

Thomas rolled his eyes, then disappeared. Paula assumed he had his fill of sentiment for the day and started to call an end to the activity, when he returned with a ragged file box hiding a bonanza of memories. "These might be of interest," Thomas told the grandchildren. "They are old pictures of Uncle Michael and your mothers and father when they were about your ages. Perhaps you'd each like to take one of these with you."

Wide-eyed, they dove into the family collection and urged their grandfather to tell them about this photo and that event, this funny face and that holiday, relishing his stories and grasping at the tiny thread of history that held them together. When each grandchild had his selection labeled with names and ages, an exhausted Thomas assured them they could do this again sometime.

"When?" their high-pitched voices chorused.

Meggie studied the picture in her hand, then looked at Paula. "Did Aunt Kiri die too?"

Startled at the suggestion, Paula asked, "Why would you think that?"

"Because she doesn't answer our calls or come to play anymore."

"She will again… when she feels better."

"If she would play with us, maybe some of her sad would go away."

Out of the mouths of babes, Paula thought, dabbing at her eyes again.

Chapter 13

Day Fourteen:

The loud rumble of heavy equipment brought Kiri bolt upright. Collection day! With no friendly vehicles parked outside for the last few days, the responsibility of taking the rubbish to the road returned to her. She slipped into sweats, gathered refuse along the way, and ran for the bin in the garage. She pushed it out to the road just in time. When she retraced her steps, she noticed something unusual in the garage—the Lotus.

A careful examination of Michael's racer revealed no evidence of her ill-fated drive—no scratch, no dent, and no permanent scar; only a fine polish. She opened its door and found the keys on the seat, climbed in and turned the ignition. A powerful purr filled the garage. No trouble with the motor, thank goodness. *I'm sorry, Michael. I didn't mean for your pride and joy to be harmed. I wasn't thinking straight.* She shifted into reverse and let the clutch out slowly. No movement. She shifted to neutral and back to reverse again. A slight lurch, but no movement. Don't cry, she told herself. Tears cannot fix a transmission. She turned off the motor and stepped out, patting the door affectionately. *I've ruined your car. Forgive me.* She cast her eyes downward and spotted the culprit—a boot on the wheel. The car was fine. Apparently, the guys judged, she was *not*—yet.

Kiri returned to the house to call in her thanks to them. #2—Doyle. *Message box full.* #3—Frank: *Leave a message.* #4—Devin: *Not available at this time.* #5—Gus: *Leave a text.* A familiar foreboding washed over her. She phoned Henry and waited nervously through several rings before he answered. "Hi, Henry. The guys returned the Lotus in tip-top shape, and I wanted to call and thank each one personally but can't seem to reach them. In fact, I haven't seen any car here except yours for a few days. Where is everybody?" She tried to sound cheerful.

"Sorry I can't help you, Kiri. I have no idea where they are at the moment. They'll get in touch when they can, I'm sure."

"Are they still in town?" she asked casually.

"I really couldn't say where they are right now," Henry answered soberly. "They were pleased to find you functioning more fully on your own recently and will be happy to receive your appreciation when they do get in touch. Remember, the doc and I are here in an emergency. Feel free to call."

"Thanks, Henry. Message received. I won't bother you again." Her shaking hands could barely turn off the phone. She heard these words before and knew the drill well. The guys left on an assignment—no warning, no contact, no goodbye. But this time, she did not go with them. *Go soirbhi Dia dhuit.* Godspeed, guys.

In stress, go to water. She ran for the bathtub and turned on the faucet. She set the waves to gentle and the heat to moderate. She was responsible for her own welfare now. She sank deep beneath the surface and welcomed the soothing undulations. She sat up to take a breath and smooth wet curls from her face. *Help myself... help myself,* raced through her mind. *I'm out of the loop now.* She inhaled deeply and submerged again. When she came up, she expelled a long, slow breath. *This isn't about me. Michael's friends... my friends... are in harm's way and I am in a safe place. The guys helped me reclaim my sanctuary, probably juggling their time between me and planning their mission. This is about them, and I can't help them from here—not until they come home.*

She laid her head beneath the water again, and emerged moments later. *Where is home for them? None of the guys are married. Where do they go when they aren't working on an assignment or babysitting me? Who do they talk to when they return? Michael and I had each other, but who are their confidants?* A spurt of laughter escaped her. *Gus has his eight sisters, but he wouldn't dare share secrets with that many women.* She leaned against the end of the tub and slid to its bottom, blowing bubbles. When she reemerged, an idea came to her like a fair.... *As a certified counselor, I have knowledge and experience on my side, more so than most of them. Use it! Heal myself by helping them.*

She sprang from the tub, wrapped a towel around and was still dripping when Henry answered her call. "Henry, I..."

"Is this an emergency?"

"Quite the opposite. This is an invitation. When the guys ret... when you all gather at Ryan's..."

"You want to come?"

"No. I had my celebration with Michael, and I've contributed nothing to this... venture. I might stunt your conversation. I want you all to come for dinner after."

"Do you think that wise? You may not feel ready for..."

"If not now, when?" I may not be ready. I may have to have a meal delivered, and you may have to pour your own drinks, but I want you to come and I'll try to be worthy of your company."

"We could meet someplace else, maybe, so you won't have to bother with..."

"No. Quincy Street. I insist. You men helped me reclaim my sanity and my sanctuary, and I want to share it. I want you to feel welcome here when you need a safe place to gather and talk about... issues you are not free to discuss elsewhere... a warm and comfortable environment where you will not have to guard every word you say. If you want to discuss specifics, I can make myself scarce. I'm good at that. What do you say?"

Silence. "We'll be delighted. I'll send a warning."

"I eagerly await your call."

*   *   *

Thomas scuffed into the suite and set a tea tray on the end table nearest his wife who stared without blinking at the mountain photos on the wall. The cathartic experience of the grandchildren's visit perked him up enough to become the caretaker to Paula's depression. Meggie's comment toppled her over the edge, so he assumed the role of hand-holder, shoulder-rubber, back-scrubber and reason. "Have some hot tea, love. It will take the chill off this rainy day."

"I'm sorry. I can't seem to shake off the coldness inside me. 'Did Aunt Kiri die too?' keeps running through my mind. I am certain that is not true, but we have no evidence to the contrary—no voice message, no email, no sighting—other than Henry's few reports, and even he stopped taking your calls. I can't get the picture out of my head—Kiri lying on the bed, like Michael, drowning in her sorrow with no one to help her. I don't understand why she won't get in touch."

"I say we've waited long enough. We should take the first step. How about a short jaunt before Mass?"

Thomas pulled into the drive at the Quincy Street house. He did not know how to refer to the home now that Michael did not live there anymore. He rang the front bell and when there was no answer, went to the back. No answer. He tried the door. Locked up tight. He looked for an open window to shout. No luck. He stumbled through the bushes around the exterior to have a peek inside, but saw nothing to indicate habitation. He started to return to the car with the disappointing news when he was surprised from behind.

"Nobody home, sir. Can I help you?"

Thomas recognized the older man with a fringe of white hair showing beneath his cap. He wore a pair of binoculars. "We were looking for Kirin. Do you know where she is?"

"Couldn't say."

"Where she might have gone?"

"Couldn't say."

"When she might be back?"

"Couldn't say."

"Perhaps I'll leave her a note so she'll know we stopped by."

"No need. I do that. I push one through the mail slot every time someone comes 'round. I watch out for her. That's my job now." He patted the binoculars against his chest.

Thomas realized it was useless to press the point with the stubble-chinned man. "I'm sure she appreciates your help. We'll be back tomorrow." He returned to the car to give Paula the frustrating news. "Paddy won't give an inch. We'll try again tomorrow. Spend the afternoon in her drive if we have to."

Paula watched the raindrops slide down the windshield. "I've been thinking. Thanksgiving is barely a week away. Would it be so terrible if we broke with tradition and stayed here this year? I know it would be healthy for us to try to celebrate as usual, but I don't think I can summon the enthusiasm for a trip to Colorado."

"What about Kurt? Won't he be disappointed? After all, Thanksgiving is the only family holiday we spend with him. He and Tanya and Kiri and Michael loved to go skiing and return to your fabulous turkey dinner. Oh…" He halted, realizing what he said, and squelched a tear. "A good meal doesn't make up for absent members."

"I talk to Kurt almost every day, and he hasn't heard from Kiri either. I'm sure he'll understand if we change our plans this year, and I have the feeling that she'll want to skip the holiday altogether. Maybe by then we can convince her to come to our house, even if just for an hour or two and even if the best I can do is pull a chicken lasagna out of the freezer."

"I think that would be perfect. I don't feel much like making a major trip right now either and was secretly hoping we might stay home. Truth be told, I'd like to sleep through the entire holiday season. Family occasions change forever when there's an empty chair at the table. We'll find a different joy as the years go by, but now is too soon. Do you think we could skip Chr…?"

She shook her head. "We can't disappoint the grandchildren. No matter how wretched we feel, we cannot disappoint them."

* * *

Kiri squiggled from her tunnel of bed pillows and blankets to peek at the morning. She discovered that she slept better in a small space. Her large bed was too barren, so she stuffed pillows under the covers along the sides. When her nightmares returned and her feet and hands reached out frantically for Michael, at least they found something to pull close to assuage her loneliness. She remained thusly planning her day in her mind until it was safe to get up.

Day Twenty-One:
Exercise and food routine as usual
Chores—thank you notes done, finally! Call Mom today, maybe.
Bake lemon bars.

Unable to reach her by phone, Meghan mailed Kiri a list of names and addresses of those who would expect acknowledgement for their acts of condolence. Had it come from Anne, she would have thrown the list away, suspicious of its validity, but Kiri trusted Meghan's judgement and ticked off names from top to bottom in one's and two's and for the last couple of days, a marathon. Done!

She sniffed out a stationer near the grocery shop who was happy to fill her order for cards and postage stamps paid with cash. She dealt only in cash, still uneasy about revealing her identity. She functioned fairly well incognito now and wanted to avoid an inadvertent, "Aren't you Michael O'Connell's widow?" to send her into a tailspin in public. She expressed the same to Paddy who caught her on the way out one day to question her hurrying up the road with her head down and not speaking to neighbors.

"Folks think they've crossed you in some way." When Kiri explained her inability to deal with people at present, he spread the word quickly up and down the road. "She's still in a tender way just yet. A friendly smile and a wave will do more to buck her up than chit-chat and pitying glances."

When faced with preparing ahead for her dinner party, Kiri found the modest grocery shop lacking in variety. Her mother's recipe for chicken lasagna required free-range chicken, two unusual cheeses, costly mushrooms and fine wine. Likewise, her red salad called for specific lettuces and other garden vegetables. She brokered a deal with the grocer for the items she wanted. She brought in a list one day. He found sources the next, to be delivered fresh to his store the following morning. She appeared early afternoon to pick up her supplies and hand over a new list, since she preferred fresh fruit, vegetables and bread daily. If a supplier only sold in large quantities—five pounds of beets or a full wheel of cheese—she bought the full order, took what she wanted and left the remainder for the grocer to resell. Given the harsh economic times, he was more than willing to accommodate this unusual customer.

On her return home she hung small bags of goodies on her elder neighbors' fence posts—a head of lettuce, a wedge of cheese, a couple of oranges or beets, a tin of biscuits—in thanks for their respecting her privacy. They smiled and waved from their windows or front stoops in appreciation and understanding. Kiri sighed with relief when she opened the door to her kitchen, having survived another walk into the real world and avoiding Thomas and Paula's drive-by while she was out. Paddy's notes through the mail slot revealed their pattern so she could safely be away when they stopped by.

Paddy's notes also began each day for her. She kept to the upstairs, thinking and tidying herself as she was this morning, until she heard the mail slot open and clap shut. That signaled Patrick's departure from his regular drive-by before work. The watchman's curt notes revealed the pattern: *sly guy 8:35; sg 8:28....* When she heard the clap this morning, she smoothed her quilt and headed for the stairs.

A second slap of metal against metal sounded. Odd, she thought, and approached the door cautiously. Two articles were on the floor in front of it: a newspaper and a note. She did not order *The Times.* She opened the note first. *Sly stuffed it through before I could stop him. 8:22.* She opened the daily paper and read the scrawl above the headline: *I AM sorry—truly. Must talk to you about the American.* She began to tremble. Why would Patrick do such a cruel thing? Another false apology served no purpose, no matter what words he used or why. Her eyes focused on the date: *November 19,* the one-month anniversary of Michael's death!

Nausea flooded her stomach and the welling up of anguish rose in her chest. She ran up the stairs and dove headfirst beneath the bedcovers, pulling the pillows close around her body. She nearly passed out from hyperventilation in an effort to block her tears from breaking through. *Please, no. Don't fall into that abyss again. Hold on.* She fought with herself for control but felt it slipping away. *...more than you can bear... call for help.* "Michael, I need you!" she called out.

She crawled to the head of the bed and reached out for her phone. She could not dial the guys; they were far away. Nor Henry; he was busy helping them. Her mother? No. She wanted to be fully in control when she talked to her mother. The only one left was the doc. She could hardly steady her finger enough to press 6.

"Kiri. What's up?"

"I need help."

"Emergency?"

"Sort of. I'm slipping into a dark place. I don't want to go there, and I don't know how to stop myself."

"Have you called Henry?"

"No. Please don't you either. The guys are... away, so he's very busy now. If he finds out I'm having trouble, he'll call off our dinner. Planning for the meal has been therapeutic. I don't want another disappointment on top of this setback."

"Your secret is safe... for the time being. Describe your physical reaction. Remember, crying is natural."

"I'm nauseated. My chest is tight. My limbs are so heavy I can't control them."

"Do you know what brought this bout on?"

She hesitated. "Michael died a month ago today."

"Anniversary grief?"

"Yes. I don't know how to help myself out of it. The counselor inside me locked the door and left."

"Where are you?"

"In bed, hiding under the covers."

"Get out now and lie on the floor."

"What?"

"You heard me. You must get out of your hiding place for a different perspective. Take a blanket and something for your head. Don't trust yourself to walk. Crawl near the fireplace and lie down." He heard her rustle the bedclothes. "Swaddle yourself like Gus did."

"Gus did what?"

"Never mind. Roll yourself up in the blanket tightly. The pressure should have a calming effect like it does for a baby. Place the pillow under the skylight and spread the blanket open to one side. Once you swaddle yourself, you won't be able to reach your phone, so place it on the pillow to allow us to communicate. With your arms at your sides, grab the blanket and roll yourself up, just like rolling down a grassy hill when you were a kid."

He listened to her thud across the floor. "Are you warm and cozy?"

"Yes, but…"

"Try to breathe normally. I'll leave this line connected to you so I can listen to your breath. I'll check in every fifteen minutes or so to see how you're doing. Be patient. While you wait for me, concentrate on your surroundings—the kaleidoscope of glass above you, every grain in the wood, every thread in the drapes. Become one with your environment and allow your melancholy to fade away as you press yourself into the floor. Talk to you in a few."

Kiri attempted to follow doctor's orders. She watched the light change and a small bug clear a winding path on the misted glass. Leaves played twirling games against the panes until a wisp of breeze carried them away.

A voice interrupted her reverie. "Kiri, how are you?"

"Better, I think. I'm not crying so much. What time is it?"

"You don't need to know. Keep at it."

Birds flew overhead. A small black one lit on the skylight allowing her to examine the patterns on the underside of its toes and claws.

"How now?"

"Much better I think. I'm not trembly or nauseated anymore. Doc, why can't I pull myself out of my depression?"

"The process of grieving is not linear. You know that as well as I. You can't say, 'today I'll begin, work my way through, and finish in two weeks or months or years.' You will probably never heal completely. You are like a bead of oil on a slinky, sliding along a spiral, around and around, high and low, back and forth, and you are not in control of the constantly shifting toy. Rest a little longer. I'll be back in a few."

When rain pattered against the windowpanes, she tried to recall pieces of music with the same rhythms.

"Kiri, are you still with me?"

"I almost fell asleep."

"Good girl. Is there anything on your schedule that must be taken care of today?"

"Lemons."

"Lemons?"

"I ordered a bag of lemons special for the dinner party. If I don't show up on time, the grocer will think something is wrong or that I abandoned him. Maybe I can pull myself together enough to…"

"Not on your life. I'll give him a call. What's the name of the shop?"

"I don't know. It's up the road west, then two over. I've never noticed the name."

"That's okay. I'll google it."

"Don't use my name. They don't know who I am in that neighborhood, and that's how I want to keep it."

"I won't. I'll call you the crazy lady who buys lemons by the bag. There could be only one."

"Thanks. Tell the owner I'll be in tomorrow for sure and ask him to order the usual lettuces and bread. He'll know."

"No problem. I want you to get up now... slowly. Unroll yourself little by little and crawl into your tub. Water barely above body temperature. Waves gentle. Hydrate. Take your phone with you and leave it on. You there yet?"

"Almost." Sounds of running water filtered over the line. "Okay."

"I want you to visualize a peaceful scene—sand shifting, waves lapping, breezes blowing grass. I'll check in after I contact your grocer."

"Doc... thanks."

At a break between clinic patients, the doctor found the grocer's number and called. "I'm a friend of the crazy lady who buys lemons by the bag. She can't pick them up today, but she'll be in tomorrow if you'll be kind enough to save them for her."

"Mrs. O'Connell? Sure I will. She's likely feeling a bit down."

"You know who she is?"

"Since the first day she walked in without a cent in her pocket. Everybody hereabouts knows, but word is she likes to keep to herself so we let her be. Anything I can send down to her?"

"Not today. But she did want to order the usual lettuces and bread."

"I'll have them for her day after tomorrow. Nice lady, that. She always buys more than she needs to share with the less fortunate folks in her neighborhood."

The grocer's remark rankled the doctor. How could anyone be less fortunate than Kiri at this moment? "Pardon me, but the lady in question is in mourning—certainly not a fortunate state!"

"Excuse, sir. I didn't mean any harm. She's bearing a great sadness, we all know, but she is lucky to have so many who care about her such as yourself. I'll look for her tomorrow."

"Thank you. She appreciates your accommodation." He decided not to inform Kiri that her identity was discovered. One jolt at a time was enough.

"Kiri, how you feeling?"

"Mellow."

"Good. All set with the grocer. Time for you to get out. If you think you can make it downstairs, some soup would be in order. Lots of water, for sure, and then to bed with you."

"But I just woke up a while ago."

"Well, it's evening now, so you can crawl back in bed if you want."

"You mean, I've wasted the whole day?"

"Do you feel better?"

"Yes."

"Then your time was not wasted."

"Doc, where did you learn this technique?"

"I didn't. It popped into my head like… If it works, we'll write a paper and publish."

*   *   *

Day One…again…again:
Yoga—one sun salutation; one downward dog
Food—at least one healthy meal; up water intake
Exercise—walk to grocery shop; pick up lemons; walk back

Day Two:
Yoga
Food—two small meals
Exercise—walk to shop for lettuces and bread
Chore—bake lemon bars

Day Three:
Routine on hold. Henry called last night. The guys will come late afternoon!
Prioritize. Keep it simple. Vacuum and dust (haven't in over a month)—living room only. Set table. Defrost lasagna. Make salad. Set out snacks and drinks. Yikes! I completely forgot! Check the pantry. Michael always kept that shelf well stocked. If not, water—with lemon.

*   *   *

The guys' laughter preceded their knock. A small sign taped to the door dispelled any misgivings about Kiri's state of mind and ability to host them for dinner.

Counselor K. O'C. Post-Mission Let-Down Specialist.
Open for Business.

The young professional welcomed them into her home, thoughtfully arranged for their comfort. A fire warmed the many hues of green that graced the walls. Ottomans from the upstairs sitting room added more choices for feet or seats. Cards for a game of 25, a cribbage board for Irish Don, and a sheepskin game board for *fidchell* replaced delicate curios on side tables. A photo album from trips to Colorado—long on landscapes and wildlife but short on two-footed intruders—invited limited personal comment. Traditional Irish music played softly.

"You're like a rose in winter—a beautiful sight to see," Gus said as he pulled Kiri in for a hug.

Doyle embraced her as well. "You look good, girl, with color in your cheeks."

Frank took both of her hands in his. "I'm looking forward to *your* cooking for a change."

Devin stroked her right arm. "I'm grateful for this invitation to your home. Gathering at the pub gets to be old—too raucous for me. I want to sit quietly with my feet to the fire."

"It's good of you to have us over. The guys could hardly wait to see you once they returned. This was the first time a sudden departure with no goodbyes really bothered them." Henry rubbed his hand across her shoulders. "Give me a nod when you've had your fill. We don't want to overstay our welcome or you won't invite us back."

Kiri smiled at the men grouped around her. "You have no idea what a relief it is to see you all safely home." She dabbed an eye with one of the many tissues she stashed in her sleeves and pockets for the emotional moments she knew would arise. "I want to say that I hope we never do this again—gather at the end of a mission." They nodded solemnly. "But I know that is not realistic, so welcome... anytime, and every time."

She ushered them toward the kitchen. "Drinks and snacks are in here. Help yourselves. I'll put dinner in the oven for about forty-five minutes while you relax and do whatever guys do when they don't know what to do. I'll be upstairs for a while finishing up some business."

They understood from Henry that she intended this time for them to speak freely and privately. They made their choices and wandered back to the fireplace while Henry walked with her to the stairs. "I don't want to upset you, but we have some news. We've identified the van driver. We know his village and where his family lives. He has not returned there... yet. We're going to try to trace a money transaction to him. That should be enough to nail Patrick, but we'll also try to find the driver, to cement our case."

"Thank you, Henry. And the guys, too. I want to know what you find out even if unsettling."

"I also want to apologize for springing the whole crew on you tonight. I didn't realize that this is your American Thanksgiving. You should have put us off to be with your family tonight, especially this year."

"I am with my family, now that all you are here." She disappeared up the stairs, leaving the men to their informal post-mission debriefing.

* * *

For the second time in their short life together, Thomas and Paula found it necessary to alternate doldrum days with one of them acting as supporter while the other fell to pieces. Thomas was the despondent one the previous day—off his feed, in a foul mood, and weepy. Paula remained calm, trying to anticipate his every need to avoid his bark. The interminable hours ended with a long hot bath, a short restorative yoga session and a massage before he finally fell asleep.

Good thing, Thomas thought as he listened to the clatter of pots banging against pans in the kitchen. He looked up from his newspaper cautiously, but she caught him. "What's the matter? Not fast enough for you? Why don't you make your own tea for a change? I'm not a slave, you know!" Then she stormed out of the kitchen and left him wondering what set her off.

He decided to give her some calming time before he brewed the tea and took her a cup. He pattered around the kitchen fixing a tray and happened to glance at the calendar hanging in the pantry. He read the entry in the space for the day: *Thanksgiving. All Koyles together in Colorado. Whoopee!*— obviously written weeks ago. Drat! He should have prepared for her reaction. Although Thanksgiving meant nothing but a good meal on a snowy day to him, he realized it was important to his wife—one of the few days both of her children were together in the Koyle family home on the hill. He wondered how he could help her endure this horrible time away from them.

Thomas found her at her desk in the suite, peering out at the gray day with tissues in her hands. He set the tray down to rub her back. "Go on, love. Have a good cry. It's your turn today."

"I'm sorry. I didn't mean to snap. I thought that if we weren't in Colorado, being without both kids this holiday wouldn't hurt so much, but it does. I cannot understand why Kiri won't even talk to us. She's out every time we drive over, almost as if she anticipated our coming and arranged to be away from the house. Today is a day I should be mindful of all I am thankful for, but with everything we've experienced over the last few weeks, I'm finding it very hard to feel grateful."

"Ah, but I am. I'm thankful for you every day. I could not bear these last weeks without you." He kissed her gently on the cheek. "I have an idea."

That idea brought them to Quincy Street early evening. Thomas pulled the car up opposite Kiri's house. He planned to park in the drive where he could go to her door quickly before she had a chance to turn out lights and pretend she was not home, but he was foiled by a string of cars parked in front. "She's home, for sure, but there is a crowd here with her. Let's watch for a bit." Thomas took Paula's hand and gave it a light kiss. "Maybe we can catch her when they leave."

Warm light radiated from windows upstairs and down. They observed Kiri on the second floor at her computer with men below gathered around the fire. Henry they recognized; the others, vaguely. She turned off the light upstairs and in a moment, joined them. The men moved to the table where she placed a steaming dish in the center and sat down. They all bowed heads while the big burly guy mouthed a prayer. Thomas did too.

The group was not jovial, but pleasant and content as each filled his plate with hot dish, salad and bread. One left to refill drinks, and Kiri appeared embarrassed that she did not think to do that. The man patted her on the head and said something that brought laughter from the others. Thomas lowered the car windows and stuck his head out. After a sniff or two he said, "I think that's your chicken lasagna they're having, love. I'd recognize the aroma anywhere." He squeezed her hand. "Maybe we should leave and try another time."

"Please, no. I want to watch a little longer. Look how the men comfort her by patting her hand, touching her arm and rubbing her shoulders. Kiri seems relaxed and enjoying herself—a very satisfying image."

The older couple observed through two—and for some, three—helpings. The two slighter men cleared. Kiri set dessert on the table, then put her hands over her embarrassed face. Henry left for the kitchen and returned a few minutes later with teapot and mugs in hand. Dessert disappeared, bar by lemon bar, until one man stood up and pointed at her. She shook her head. Heated discussion ensued with every man offering an opinion. They all looked to Henry who shrugged and seemed to agree with the rest of the men. Kiri still shook her head. Another of the guys took his phone from his pocket, looked at Henry and entered a number. Then he shoved the device into Kiri's hand.

Paula's phone rang, startling both occupants of the car across the road.

"Happy Thanksgiving, Mom."

"And to you, Kiri. I'm so delighted to hear from you—especially today."

"You in Colorado?"

"No. We couldn't face the trip this year."

"Me either. I'm with friends."

"How are you feeling?"

"Good and bad. Up and down. You?"

"The same. We miss you."

"I'm not ready to talk yet. I'll try to call again soon. Love you. Bye."

Thomas and Paula watched the men crowd around her emotionally shaken daughter to cheer her up with pats and encouraging words. The burly fellow folded her close and whispered into her ear while she wiped her eyes. The group then moved to the living room, pulled up the game boards and settled in for a companionable evening by the fire.

"Best not to wait around, don't you think?" Thomas asked his wife who wiped her own eyes.

Paula nodded as he pulled away from the curb. "If those few words are the only 'happy' in this Thanksgiving, I'm grateful for them."

Chapter 14

A familiar early morning rumble along the road signaled collection day, and on this day Kiri had lots of rubbish for collection. The guys gathered at her house for a second time the previous day, creating enough refuse for two bins. They hauled the trash to the garage before they left, but she needed to push it to the road... quickly. On her return to the garage, she noticed something amiss—the wheel boot on her car. They removed it! Their way of saying, "You're well enough to drive on your own now," but since they left the Lotus immobilized, the message was, "just not too far or too fast."

Frank proposed the gathering. "Did you really mean 'anytime and every time'? We sure could use a few hours without... someone looking over our shoulders."

"Absolutely. Open for business. Name the date and time."

"Tomorrow. Mid-afternoon?"

"Done. I know most of you have a key if I'm out. I'll disengage security. See you then." She checked her larder and decided on buffalo chili and cornbread—a hearty man's hearty meal. Decisions came more easily now. She added a couple of items to her list, visited the grocery shop, and had the dish assembled and in a crock pot early the next morning. The only adjustments she made to her décor were opening out the nook table, clearing off the dining table, providing a spare laptop and furnishing pads of paper and pens. Michael tended to revert to old-style when he planned. They might do the same.

The guys arrived by one's and two's at the appointed time. Kiri welcomed them in, then left for her daily trek to the shops for fresh fruit and veggies. She noticed how brightly decorated the windows were with red and green lights, a sure sign of a holiday season in full swing. Christmas! Her stomach knotted and her breath came hard and fast. She ducked through the nearest door to find a chair.

The proprietress of the teashop brought her a soothing cup without being asked. Soon Kiri felt calm enough to continue her errands. She wanted to drop a few coins on the table and leave but that would seem impolite, so she browsed the variety of cakes and confections sold at the shop. The owner offered her a sample of a traditional holiday one, very much in demand but difficult to find in small portions. "Families aren't the size they used to be, and young working women don't have the time these fine cakes require—a full two and a half hours in the oven. I have to order from the south and hope I'll get a few in. I could sell five times what I receive."

Kiri kindly complimented the flavors and texture and inquired about the ingredients. The woman found not only a list but an old recipe. "If you'd like to try your hand at a bit of baking, we have the sweetmeats here.

The rest you'd have to get from the grocer." Kiri purchased four containers of the candied fruits and nuts. She stopped at the grocers for the rest of the items in the recipe including the magic one—Guinness. She wrote a short note and delivered all to the fences along her road, confident that within a few days the teashop would overflow with the prized, individual holiday cakes.

The grocer was surprised to see her again so soon. She explained she had a second list to fill since she could only carry a little at a time. He offered to deliver. "Don't bother," she said. "The exercise is good for me. I might come a third time or more for beverages." Her slight smile hinted at a secret. She deposited her loads near the gate to take them into the house at the end of her treks. She did not want to disturb her hard-working guests.

At the end of the afternoon she walked into her kitchen, arms loaded, to find the guys had taste-tested the chili and eaten their way through the bread, cheese and apples she left out for them. Empty bottles told the rest of the story. When they arrived, they said they would be gone by dinner, but the spicy smells from the pot changed their minds. They straightened up and fixed salad to speed a light supper along. Afterwards, they settled around the fire for a few hands of 25. Then the conversation turned serious.

"Have you talked to your mother since we last saw you?" Doyle asked.

Kiri shook her head.

"Oh, Kiri. You must. You know she's longing for her daughter. You owe her a meeting." Gus was insistent.

"I will. Soon. But I'm not ready yet."

"Don't tarry too long. Opportunities have a way of vanishing before you realize they slipped by," Frank cautioned.

"Please, Kiri. Put our minds to rest, hmm? Talk with your mother before we… before another week goes by." Gus' appeal made her uneasy.

"No promises, but I will try."

Gus motioned to Devin and Henry, deep in discussion by the merlot wall—the photo gallery of landmark moments in Michael and Kiri's short life together: *For Better, For Worse and Forever.* "Let's be on our way. Our little lady needs a good sleep tonight. She's going to see her mother tomorrow!"

All their goodbye hugs were especially long and lingering, proof of Kiri's suspicions. The guys were due to leave on another assignment soon.

Kiri left the garage happy that she had wheels again. She had no plans to drive, but knowing her guardians trusted her was a major breakthrough. She had no idea when her friends would leave, where they were going, or when they would return, but she owed it to them to ease their minds. Worry about anything other than the job might divert their attention for an instant—a fatal instant.

*   *   *

Paula found an intermittent shaft of sunlight in the suite and moved her laptop into it to edit a draft of her latest book. "Oh, no!" she moaned. "Where did this come from? And this one? And this one?"

Thomas was at her side in a twinkle. "What is it, dear? Trouble with your computer?"

"No. Look!"

Thomas did look but could see nothing spidery or sticky within her immediate reach.

"Here. On my arms. These brown spots. What's happening!"

He tried not to smile. "They are signs of your graceful aging—just like mine. Haven't you noticed when we're in the bath?"

She shook her head. "They weren't there yesterday. I'm sure."

"They've arrived daily over the last several months, and I welcome every one." He began a series of light kisses up her arm to demonstrate his delight.

"Look! That's new!"

"I'll get there. Be patient."

"Not a spot. This email from Kiri. Her first since…"

"Well, open it!" He was as excited as Paula to receive contact. The three weeks since Thanksgiving seemed months or years when his wife hoped daily for a message. "What does she say?"

Paula read: *Mom. Meet me today on the bridge in the Green. 3 p.m. Come alone. K.*

"What does she mean by 'alone'?"

"You're not invited."

"But we go to Mass together at 3. You'll have to…" He started to bluster his way through alternatives—Mass earlier, Mass later, invite Kiri to tea.

"Drop me by on your way, and pick me up when you return. I won't risk losing this chance with my daughter because you feel slighted. You can continue welcoming my brown spots when we return home."

Paula spied her daughter standing alone on the stone humpback bridge over the ornamental lake in the city's center. Her hair hung down past her face as she bobbed her head over the edge to commune with the ducks. Paula approached slowly and touched her shoulder. "Kiri?"

The young woman turned and hugged her mother warmly. "Hi, Mom. Glad you could come."

Paula took her two hands and stepped back to gaze at her. "You look good… healthy… considering…"

"Considering what?" Kiri snapped.

Her mother bit her tongue. Tread cautiously. "I have brown spots."

"What?"

Paula noticed the confusion on her daughter's face. "Those small golden medallions that herald my advanced age."

"Mom, I never thought you were vain."

"I wasn't until I looked in the mirror one morning and saw great-aunt Ella looking back at me. She was the only relative with green eyes like mine... and your brother's. Have you talked to Kurt?"

"No. I hardly talk to anyone. No point. When I'm asked, 'how are you?' I don't know how to respond. I can't say 'fine' because I'm not. If I say 'I feel like jumping off a bridge,' both parties will be uncomfortable. What's the point? I have nothing to add to a conversation."

"Perhaps you and Kurt can have a long talk when he and Tanya come for the holidays. I'm sure he would understand."

"He can't understand, nor can you. You both wake up next to your partners every morning. Besides, I thought they were going to her folks' this year."

"Kurt... uh... reconsidered. Thomas wanted the whole family together."

Kiri rolled her eyes. "That's impossible."

Paula tried a different tack. "Tell me how you spend your days."

"Trying to get through them."

She tried again. "The grandchildren are coming to decorate cookies this Saturday. Can you help?"

"No. I'm sorry, Mom. Can't you see I'm in no condition to be sociable? If cookies are important to you, ask Thomas to help. They are his grandkids. If the kids want to do the cookie thing, a couple of them are old enough to help. I can't even help myself." Kiri felt tears well up.

Paula took her daughter in her arms and felt her flood of emotion. "My dear girl, how can I help? Come home with me and let me take care of you."

Kiri shook her head.

"Then let me come to you. Have you cleared out Michael's things yet? I could help."

"Mother! How can you suggest such a thing? I'm not ready. Just leave me be!"

"I don't understand. I thought you wanted to talk. Why are we here?"

"Because they made... I thought that's what you wanted, but I realize I'm not ready. I need more time alone."

"Surely you'll come for the holiday."

"I could not possibly spend Christmas in the same house as Thomas and Anne! I won't be judged by them or anyone. I don't meet the O'Connell standard of behavior—never have, never will. No exceptions for grieving widows in their circle."

"You can't blame all your despair on Thomas."

"I don't," she said with narrowed brows.

"The truth, Kiri. Why do you insist on separating yourself from the rest of the family?"

"The truth will hurt you. I can't."

"If I survived these last weeks without a word from my dear daughter, I think I can handle the truth."

Kiri hesitated, then stared into her mother's deep green eyes. "You chose your husband over your daughter. I understand that because Michael chose me over his father. But I'm not ready to accept that when I stood in front of you at the gathering, defenseless and vulnerable like a three-year-old covered in mud in the middle of a clean kitchen floor and needing my mother desperately, you couldn't find love enough to support me." She glimpsed the sadness in Paula's eyes. "I'm working toward acceptance, but I'm being selfish and taking care of myself first. I need to accept life without Michael before I can work my way back to you. Please be patient with me."

Paula nodded and wiped her nose.

"I have an idea." Kiri pulled her phone from her pocket. "Let's take a picture to send to Kurt. Let him know we're at least speaking again. Call this my symbolic gesture to you—to talk again soon. For now, remember... Christmas is whenever we're together."

Paula wrapped an arm around her daughter in a near choke hold and forced a smile while Kiri snapped the shot. She took a quick look and said, "Oops, Mom. We need a do-over. Your brown spots were showing!"

When Paula laughed, Kiri snapped another with her own arm around her mother. She sent the photo through cyberspace to her brother and the other important men in her life before she walked away.

Patrick Murphy heard a collective cheer through the situation room door. He wondered what could possibly raise the spirits of men on their way to war-torn Syria.

Chapter 15

Paddy settled his Maureen in the rocker in front of the window to enjoy the sun on this bright Christmas afternoon. He went back to the kitchen for tea and the small holiday cake Kiri brought them from the teashop. He fed his wife a bite, then took one himself—tasty, like the ones she made for him in their early years together. Her second bite was on its way to her mouth when a familiar vehicle with a stranger driving pulled up across the road. He grabbed the binoculars and went to investigate.

A tall, skinny fellow with sandy hair knocked hard on the door. "Kiri, it's Kurt. Let me in, please." He banged harder. "Kiri, open the door." And harder. "Open this door, or I'll break through a window!"

"It's been my experience, young man, that threatening damage doesn't usually win one an invite. Just who would you be?"

Kurt jumped at hearing words so close to his ear. "I'm Kiri's brother Kurt, from Colorado. I'm picking her up for the family dinner at Thomas' house."

"Did she know you were coming?"

"Not exactly. Is she home today?"

"Couldn't say."

"Do you know where she might have gone?"

"Couldn't say."

"Have you seen her at all today?"

"Couldn't say."

Frustrated, Kurt snapped back, "Well, what *could* you say!"

"That you're quite an upstart of a lad to be related to that nice young woman. I'll see if I can raise her." Paddy bent to the mail slot and banged the metal door three times, then shouted through it. "You might want to answer this one. Says he's your brother, but he doesn't act like it. Got green eyes." He straightened up and glared at Kurt. "You treat her tender, now. She's been in a bad way the last few days." He turned for his home and that tasty cake.

Kurt winced at the disheveled appearance of his sister when she finally opened the door. He stepped through and gave her a hug. "Glad to see you." She did not reply. "Who is that old guy?"

"My watchdog."

"Well, he's a good one! I've come to deliver you to dinner at Thomas' and I won't take 'no' for an answer."

"You may not take 'no' but you won't take me either."

"Everyone is there, and the grandkids keep asking for you. Mom tries to make excuses but is really upset. She wants you there. She needs you there, and you should be. She's your mom."

"I told Mom I would not come. I will not spend one minute in that house with those people. I don't need to be insulted and kicked in the stomach again by them. Do I look like I can defend myself?"

"You look like you should clean yourself up, then maybe you would feel better."

"Impossible."

"On a scale of one to ten?"

"Negative one hundred."

"Whew. You're down there all right. Look, if you feel that low, you can only go up. Maybe one positive thing will happen—one kind word, one smile from a kid, one hug from Mom. Negative ninety-nine is a step in the right direction."

"You don't understand. I'm sliding on a spiral. If I fall much deeper, I won't be able to pull myself up. I cannot predict what I might do. Here in my house, upstairs in my room, I'm safe. I feel protected. I don't want to slide out of control again."

"I'll stay right by you all night, I promise. Tanya's here. She's anxious to see you. She can be your 'plus one.' After all, she was your best friend."

"We have nothing in common anymore."

"Why so bitter?"

Kiri spit back. "She has a husband!"

"That's a low blow, so right back at you. What would Michael say? What would *he* want you to do?"

Kiri could not speak, but she knew exactly. *What do we want our children to learn from us?* Michael would want her to be a positive model for the nieces and nephews.

Kurt started in on her again. "You are talking crazy. No more nice brother. This morning there was nothing in my stocking from you—no Christmas pledge. You owe me one, and I want it now! I want you to come to dinner with me. You can't refuse. Now get upstairs and clean yourself. I'll bet there's a mess in the kitchen I can tackle as my symbolic gesture to you. Thirty minutes. Go!"

Meggie spotted her favorite aunt first. "You came! I wished and wished that you would." She hugged as high as she could reach. Kiri found a gentle smile for her and patted the little girl on the head. The rest of the cousins crowded in to receive their greetings in turn. Paula was last in line and held her daughter long and tight. "I'm delighted you came. Surprised... but delighted. What changed your mind?"

"Kurt made a pretty strong case, but don't send him after me again, please."

"I didn't send Kurt. I was convinced you meant to stay away."

"Then who?"

Paula glanced over Kiri's shoulder at Thomas standing near the fireplace with a twinkle in his eye she had not seen for several weeks.

"Doesn't matter. Come help me get dinner on the table and leave these little tykes behind."

Kiri placed her arm around her mother's waist to walk with her. "Do you really think I'm capable of putting the *proper* dishes in their *proper* places in my state of mind?"

Paula chuckled. "I hope you don't!"

All adult eyes scrutinized Kiri for any signs of vulnerability. Was she thin from not eating? Heavy from overeating? Pallid? Flushed and nervous? Weepy? Hair unkempt? Clothes wrinkled? They found nothing more telling than her vacant eyes absent of their sparkle. "What meds do you think she's on?" Anne asked Meghan.

For the past two years, Paula hosted Christmas dinner at Thomas' house. She insisted. His daughters deserved more time with their growing families during the hectic holiday season. With the economic downturn and cutbacks in house help, less time in the kitchen proved an added bonus. Each family brought one favorite dish, potluck style. She, with Thomas' help, provided the rest. Thomas issued an edict. Everyone agreed except... Initially, Anne pretended offense but was secretly relieved. Her beautiful holiday décor featured prominently in social gatherings with chosen invitees—not necessarily *all* family.

Thomas called dinner. Brendan made a quick pass through the dining room to switch place cards enabling him to sit by Kiri. Then he stationed himself at the door to remind his cousins to leave all their exciting new electronic devices on the hall console table, arranged by family and birth order. He tried so hard to emulate his uncle.

Kiri was surprised to find herself sandwiched between Kurt and Brendan with Tanya one over, since her brother and wife agreed to insulate her from the stepsibs. The young man took her hand under the table. "Thank you for coming, Aunt Kiri. All the cousins miss you. You look very nice tonight. Uncle Michael would be proud of you."

She allowed herself a sniffle as he withdrew his hand. "Thank you. I miss you too." Thomas' call for the blessing saved her from further uncomfortable conversation but not from emotion. The family patriarch cleared his throat and stumbled through words he had repeated a million times, stopping to wipe his nose once or twice. The collective 'Amen' was less hearty than usual; its primary vocalist, absent

The sons-in-law attempted amiable chatter that died from lack of participation by others. The grandchildren's eyes shifted from one adult to another to gauge the atypical atmosphere. Silver clinked against china. Thomas sighed deeply and often. Paula patted his thigh. Brendan's silver dropped with a clank onto his plate. "This is crap!"

Thomas startled upright. The aunts and uncles glared. His mother Meghan cautioned, "Watch your manners, young man!"

"That's all we *are* doing, Mother—watching *your* manners. Crap! You grownups are trying to pretend this holiday is normal, and it is not.

Uncle Michael died. He's not here. All us kids are sad, but we're afraid to admit it—afraid to say something that might upset you—and you aren't helping. You act like a smile is sinful now, but you can't explain why and you hardly mention Uncle Michael's name out loud. Crap!"

"Your language, Brendan. What would your uncle say?" Meghan scolded her son.

"He'd tell me to 'choose an appropriate synonym,' then laugh behind his hand while I stuttered around because I didn't know what that meant. I know what 'crap' is. It's stupid or foolish, and that's what you're being. Well, I don't feel stupid or foolish when I cry at night because I miss him, and I don't feel stupid or foolish... or guilty when I'm having fun with my friends. He'd like that. He'd want us to remember the fun times. Paula and Grandfather are old and they understand how kids feel. Why can't you?"

All eyes turned on Meghan, then on Thomas who shook his head to indicate the boy should not be stopped but allowed to vent his frustration.

"Uncle Michael would let us be sad. He'd help us be sad, and then he'd make us laugh again, like telling a story to make us cry, and then he'd tell us to cry harder and harder, and then he'd suddenly shout 'Hands over your mouths!' and we'd all clap our mouths shut, and then we'd try to cry some more, and snot would go all over. We'd laugh so hard that we'd cry again and then we'd feel better. That's what Uncle Michael would do at a time like this, and it's *not* stupid or foolish."

The cousins tittered behind their hands. The young boy picked up his fork and began shoveling food into his mouth. Kiri leaned toward him and whispered in his ear. "That was quite a speech, Brendan. Where did all those words come from?"

"I have no idea. They popped into my brain like a..." A knowing smile escaped Kiri's lips.

Thomas wiped his nose again, cleared his throat and began to speak. His audience expected a harsh reprimand for Brendan's outburst. "I cannot understand why young adolescent boys find humor in normal bodily functions... but Michael was certainly no exception. One Christmas... when he was about ten..." He proceeded to tell a short but relevant story that had all the young ones giggling by the end. He dabbed at his eyes. "I miss that young boy very much... and the man he became."

Hesitantly, Michael's brother and sisters shared similar memories as the meal continued. A few of the older grandchildren added theirs. Meggie exclaimed, "I have so many favorite times, I can't choose just one!" Kurt shared a skiing adventure, and Tanya told of Michael's "Sweet Molly Malone" monologue in lieu of karaoke. Kiri passed.

Brendan's turn arrived. He put down his fork and announced, "My best time with Uncle Michael was this past September when we compared wee-wees." Thomas' head dropped onto his hands. The men flushed. Anne was aghast. Emily covered her eyes and giggled. Meghan shouted at her son. "Brendan Thomas Daly! Your behavior is absolutely inappropriate!"

"Why, Mother? You always tell me to talk to people I trust. When I ask you about personal stuff, you say to talk to my father. He says 'later,' and changes the subject. Am I supposed to ask my friends or look it up on YouTube? Grandfather is too old for that stuff..."

Thomas and Paula blushed but did not stop him.

"...so I went to the person I trust and admire most in the world, Uncle Michael. He didn't treat me like a kid. He made me feel like I *could* grow up to be a man just like him someday. He talked about respect and boundaries and consent and how I would want my cousins to be treated. He gave me what he called a 'physiology lesson' and explained 'no' and 'stop' to me. Then he said I could ask him questions, and he showed me what I was curious about. Don't worry. I won't even think about girls until I'm maybe thirty. But I have to say, Aunt Kiri. You're a brave woman. I can't believe you survived... IT!"

All the adults erupted in laughter. Their napkins dabbed more eyes than mouths. A good laugh being contagious, the bewildered little ones joined in. Even Kiri doubled over, tears dripping from her eyes but with a smile on her face. Mystified by the mirthful reaction to his matter-of-fact account, Brendan asked, "Is there any dessert tonight?"

Tears and laughter put to rest, dessert devoured, and small children squirming in their seats prompted Thomas to suggest a move to the living room for coffee, conversation and music. Grace grabbed her new device, downloaded an app for Christmas sing-alongs, and engaged the younger cousins in less cathartic activity.

The doorbell sounded. Thomas answered wondering who would interrupt a family Christmas, but true to the Celtic tradition of hospitality he opened the door with a smile. Henry Callaghan stood on the stoop with a manila envelope in one hand and a crudely wrapped package in the other. "Henry, come in. Share a drink with us."

"Thank you, but I can't stay. News from the Middle East doesn't stop for a particular date on the calendar, as you well know." He held the envelope out to Thomas. "If memory serves, Michael used to leave final reports of his assignments abroad with you for safekeeping in case... in case a question ever came up. He kept his most recent ones at home where Kiri would have access, but we... Michael's team and I... feel she should be spared the details for a while yet. We'll give her one later, but we agreed someone in the family should guard this information for the time being. If an occasion should arise that warrants opening it, we trust you will remember the contents are classified, and you are honor-bound not to share them with anyone... not even your wife."

Thomas was quick to reply so the 'occasion' could 'arise' immediately on Henry's departure. "Understood. Thank you." He took the envelope apprehensively.

"I stopped by Quincy Street to leave this package for Kiri. We would have kept her company tonight, knowing it would be a difficult one for her, but the guys are... very busy at the moment. It is a comfort to find her with family. I'd like to speak with her personally."

"Of course. I'll say goodbye and lock this away upstairs. Thank you again. Kiri will see you out." Thomas motioned to Paula who alerted her daughter to Henry's visit while he climbed the stairs to their suite.

"Henry!" Kiri brightened at his unexpected appearance. "Thank goodness for a friendly face."

"You look great. How are you holding up?"

"As long as I don't open my mouth I'll probably survive, but I'd rather be home. Isn't that where you should be on this holiday evening?"

"Duty calls. I've wanted to stop by several times, but..."

"I know. I may be out of the loop, but I do know how to read the signs. I hope all is well with the guys."

"Actually, that's why I've come. Before they... they wanted you to have this. We checked with the doc and he approved. Devin worked his digital magic to create something for your wine-red wall... someday." He watched her face carefully for any signs of distress as she unwrapped the photo.

Her eyes filled with tears but her face remained calm as she ran her fingers tenderly over the image in the frame. "This was Michael's last breath... his passing breath to me. How did Devin...?"

"Doyle's phone. When we started to put your mission's final reports together, we decided to include footage from it. Devin worked his wonders to spruce it up a bit. The report you sent in—which, by the way, we didn't expect—convinced us that this photo would be more comforting than disturbing. We wanted you to find peace in the memory of this last, beautiful moment."

Kiri threw her arm around Henry. "This picture is very precious. Thank you. When you see them... soon, I hope, please tell the guys how meaningful it is to me." She left a few tears on his jacket.

He folded an arm around her. "Anything for you, Kiri. Anything. Merry Christmas." He released his hold, then took her hand. "I must get back to the office. Take care. I'll be in touch soon." He left her standing alone, clutching the photo to her chest.

Anne and Meghan watched the scene from across the room. "We now know where Kiri finds her comfort," Anne said with a cunning smile.

"Stop it! She certainly didn't get any from us."

Kiri returned to her place next to Tanya on the sofa nearest the Christmas tree. She held the photo tightly as if she thought it would evaporate as quickly as her life with Michael had. Meggie broke away from the singing and came to her wearing a broad smile. "Is that a present?" Kiri nodded. "Can I see?"

Reluctantly, Kiri laid the frame in her lap, exposing the image.

"That's you and Uncle Michael! Is he dead?"

Her innocent question shocked Paula and the others nearby, fearful of its effect. "No," Kiri smiled. "He was very much alive at that moment. That was our last kiss."

"It looks like you are in the clouds."

Kiri did not know how to explain that the aura Devin enhanced around their faces was really dust settling from the explosion and the frenzy of Michael's soul searching frantically to unite with her own before he departed. "It was misty that day."

"That's good. Clouds are too high up for kissing. Oh, that's my favorite song." She bounced away to dance with the others to an upbeat version of "Jingle Bell Rock."

Tommy sauntered nearby and examined the photo as closely as he dared while Kiri protected it on her lap. His discerning newsman's eyes made out enough detail to realize that his little brother was *not* alone at the moment of his death, as the family lamented. Kiri was in Syria with him and guarded that secret despite the pressures of the last few weeks. Only he and Thomas could comprehend the value of her silence, but he did not dare tell his father.

In his second-floor suite, Thomas sat at his desk with trembling hands. His head warned him that he would break confidence when he broke the seal on the envelope, but his heart yearned to know the details of his son's death. Was that knowledge worth the loss of his integrity? His finger slid beneath the seal, and the contents spilled out in front of him.

He bypassed the USB drives, digital photo cards, and maps for an examination of the written word. He thumbed through the stack of reports from agents involved in the operation: Henry, Doyle, Frank, Devin, Gus, realizing that even their names and duties were classified. The last was shorter than the others and displayed two names at the top: Michael K. O'Connell, agent deceased, by Kirin A. O'Connell and Kirin A. O'Connell, agent. *I submit this report on behalf of my deceased husband as well as myself since we were at almost all times in the presence of one another. Details herein refer to the actions and movements of both agents.*

The report dropped to his lap. Kirin was there! With Michael every minute! *Even unto death!* He retrieved the papers and toiled meticulously through every detail. He learned with anguish that Kirin partnered with Michael in harm's way for the last two years, that long-time acquaintance Patrick Murphy betrayed them both, and that his son sacrificed his own life to save a young boy's.

Henry was right. Paula should *not* learn of this. Both he and his wife accepted the dangers of Michael's job after the Yemen operation, but they never suspected that her daughter continued her affiliation with the agency other than for an occasional counseling assignment. Kirin camouflaged her movements carefully to spare her mother two years of frantic waiting and worrying. What a strong and loyal woman she was!

Thomas read Kirin's final recommendation several times: *In regard to Patrick Murphy: while some sanctions against his responsibilities within the company should be considered, to jeopardize the integrity of the network and the important work of this division because of one man's unlawful actions would not advance the cause for which Michael gave his life—to assure truth in journalism and to make the world a better place.*

The letter from the US State Department slipped onto the desk. Thomas found it curious since the network never dealt with foreign governments. When he read the contents, his fist pounded the stack of papers, scattering them. How could that scoundrel Patrick be such a self-serving schemer! And doom his son in the process! Kirin had every right to ban him from the funeral and to denounce him at the gathering—if she realized his motive. If she did not, Thomas could not be the one to tell her. He folded away one more toxic secret to hide from his family.

Mindful that he must replace the envelope's contents exactly as he found them, he methodically layered report on report until he came to Kirin's. He noted the date: December 19, the two-month anniversary of Michael's death. He wondered how she forced herself to relive the tragedy of those horrible days to fulfill an obligation no one expected of her.

Kirin's actions—or nonactions—over the last several weeks began to make sense, from her cool and unemotional responses during the days immediately following Michael's death to her placid exchanges with her mother. He recalled how she sought refuge in his boat to heal herself when she was worried about his son in Yemen and could tell no one. Her Thanksgiving with the guys made sense now, too. They were the only ones she could talk to, the only ones who shared her story. Stoicism became her coping mechanism... until her justifiable outburst at the gathering.

A wave of remorse washed over Thomas as he recalled his part in that confrontation. At a time Kirin needed family most, he scolded her like a child and turned not only the family, but her own mother, against her—and that, after questioning her every decision. Apology was too hollow a word for the atonement he owed his son's widow.

"'Tis a stickery bush I've jumped into," he said aloud as he locked the reports away. "This is not a time for public confession—not with the grandchildren present—or for asking Kirin's forgiveness. To do so would reveal I've broken confidence with Henry, with Kirin and with everything my son stood for." He took a few anxious moments to consider a plan. "I'll go to early Mass—alone—and after, have a chat with Bishop Byrne who constantly counsels me now about 'God's plan.' He'll be happy for a change of topic. He'll know how to reconcile my transgressions with Kirin. That's it. Ask for forgiveness from the top down on St. Stephen's Day—a good day for absolution."

By the time Thomas returned to the party, the grandchildren donned coats and caps for the trip home. He patted each one on the head as they said their goodbyes and hustled to their cars with their fathers. The daughters lingered, giving polite thanks to Paula and waiting for a final embrace from their father.

Anne approached Kiri. "You look very nice tonight... almost as fetching as you did in those widow's weeds you shopped for on the day Michael was killed."

Kiri bristled but held her tongue.

"I understand why Henry was so anxious to stop by for his Christmas hug. He certainly cheered you up!"

Kiri spit back. "You understand nothing! How dare you suggest..."

At that moment Thomas witnessed the girls grouped and angry. "What is going on here? Have you no respect? You disgrace this house!"

When Kiri heard those words, she turned on her heel and ran out. Kurt followed. Paula froze, dumbfounded. Meghan and Emily flushed, and Thomas... Thomas was horrified that everyone, including Kirin, misinterpreted his reprimand directed at Anne.

He rushed after her to apologize and ran smack into Kurt. "This may be your house, and you may be married to my mother, but that does not give you the right to verbally abuse my sister."

"I didn't. I meant Anne and didn't realize I was misunderstood. I must apologize. I cannot let Kirin believe she has no one..."

"With all due respect, sir, keep your distance from my sister. This evening was emotional for the entire family, I know, and for you in particular. I'm sorry for you, but you pulled her trigger tonight—intentional or not—and this is no time for apology. I know my sister. Kiri will tell you when she's ready to try the family thing again." He stood his ground in the doorway to the dining room.

"Kurt. Let me see her." Paula tried to push past.

"No, Mom. She needs to be alone to handle this in her own way. You know that. Leave her alone. Don't force her to take a step before she's ready. Say goodbye to the girls, lock up, and go to bed. I'll take Kiri home when she calms down."

Visibly shaken, Thomas and Paula retreated to the hallway where his daughters looked on with curiosity. He sent them off abruptly, and the older couple climbed the stairs more slowly than usual.

Kurt found his sister in the kitchen, face down in a sink full of cold water. He picked up a towel, soaked it, and applied it to the back of her neck. "Forget it, Kiri. Forget everything Thomas said. He didn't mean it—truly. He tried to scold Anne and his words got away from him. Don't give that man another thought."

She came up for air. "I can't do this, Kurt. I cannot be forced into situations with this family that I am not ready to handle. I have to get away from here."

He helped her wrap a towel around her head and slide into the nook. "You're not going anywhere until you calm down." She placed her forearms on the table and her forehead on her fists while he wrung out another compress for her neck. "Let me see if there's anything in this kitchen as American as hot cocoa and marshmallows."

"I don't know why I can't get along with Anne. There must be good inside her. After all, she *is* Michael's sister. They came from the same parents. He loved her, so she can't be all bad." He applied a new compress while the milk heated. "I don't have the energy now to figure her out. I can't even guarantee two good days in a row for myself. I have to be functional before I can deal with anyone else. I'm selfish, I know, but I have to take care of me first right now."

"Stop your babbling and try this." He set down a mug with white domes bobbing on top, then slid in beside her. "Just like old times, hmm? A dark, quiet house. The two of us talking and licking the goo off our fingers." He tried to cheer her with a few memories, but her responses lacked spirit. "I have an idea. Come with me." He led her to the living room where the Christmas tree and fire provided the only light. "We're going to lie down under the tree together."

She started to protest, but he pulled throws from the sofas and made a nest on the floor. "You don't have so much as a holly berry in that house of yours and I understand why, so let's do this for a few minutes. The lights will give you a lift." He threw her a pillow, then lay down beside her. "I stopped doing this when I was what… ten or twelve?"

"Twelve. You decided it wasn't 'cool' anymore."

"Did you and Michael ever sleep under your own tree after that first Christmas?"

"At least twice a year, but our tree is outside in the back so weather is always a factor."

"You're weird."

She punched him and sighed deeply. "I guess it will be as lonely outside now as it is inside."

"I know, Sis." He took her hand. "Do you remember when we…?" They reminisced until Kurt squiggled out from under. "How can you stand this? The floor is ten times harder than when we go camping. I'm moving to a sofa. Let me know when you're ready to go home." He dragged his blanket and pillow to the closest one and fell asleep within minutes.

Kiri gazed up through the brightly-lit branches of the Christmas tree. Since she maimed their tribal tree Aurora, she wondered if a branch remained with her name on it. Which path, if any, was left for her to follow? She listened as Kurt drifted off, comforted by the sounds of a man's deep breathing close by. Her eyelids drooped for just a second….

She awoke with a start, disoriented. Then she remembered. Kiri was in *Thomas'* house, on *his* floor, under *his* tree. She felt like an intruder and could not escape fast enough. She grimaced at a strange sensation on her cheek. She brushed her hand against it and pulled away a feather... a small black feather. Spooked at first, she tried to think logically. It could have been caught in the tree and not fallen to the floor until now. Just a coincidence—but enough of one to prompt her into action. She twisted her compass ring, and Michael's, around her finger. She knew her direction now. She grabbed her shoes, coat and photo, gave her brother a pat on the shoulder, and walked out the door into the thick fog of a Dublin night.

Chapter 16

St. Stephen's Day. 5 a.m. Karys Kolton, Welsh medic volunteer, presented herself at the Air Lingus ticket counter in Dublin Airport. She bought a one-way ticket to London, paid cash in euros and checked two large bags. At Heathrow, she collected her bags, passed through customs with no problem, bought a one-way ticket to Denver with U.S. dollars, checked her bags again and was on her way… home.

During the sleepless transatlantic flight, she ticked off her list of preparations for closing the house and leaving Ireland. Establish a new email account for business with the solicitor only. Duplicate files on all USB drives to leave them in the safe. Pack originals in carryon. Put one laptop in the safe and pack the other. Leave all phones. Write a note to Paddy re hasty departure and indefinite absence and slip it through *his* mail slot. Turn off gas. Lock garage. Collect and store all personals and valuables in safe. Pack. Remember cords and cables for electronics. Double-check security systems—both of them!

Satisfied that she remembered all major responsibilities, she began to consider the minor ones and wondered if she were obligated to follow through. First, Paddy. He would worry about his monthly payments. Reassure him they would continue and add some funds for watching the house and running a few errands for her. Second, the grocer. He counted on her "generous" business to augment his meager one. Third, the cake ladies. They found renewed hope for their economic situation with increased demand for their baking talents. And of course, Charles. He still expected her to reconcile his finances monthly—despite recent events.

Communication was key, and that required a means. She decided to purchase a prepaid disposable phone as soon as she arrived in the States. She could then call Paddy and the grocer. Either one would pass on a message to the ladies. Charles was the problem. A second new email account would take care of him and online banking. He would not know—or care—where in the world she was as long as she released his quarterly allowances.

She did not want to be traced—not yet. After the previous night's flare up, the family would not expect any contact from her for some time. Time was what she needed to readjust to a new life. Henry would not be a problem until the guys returned and wanted to visit her. Using her Welsh passport made tracking difficult but not impossible. Devin would discover her ruse and be so pleased with himself. Yes, she might be able to buy two or three weeks, maybe a month if she were careful. Thank goodness she and Michael kept lots of cash—both currencies—on hand for emergencies. No need to use credit cards for a while. Minor responsibilities: covered.

Karys Kolton, Welsh medic volunteer, looked up at the signs welcoming her to the United States of America. She received a hearty "enjoy your visit" from customs and immigration. She ducked into an alcove, stripped the pages from her passport and tossed them, her glasses and mouthpiece into a dumpster. Kirin A. Koyle emerged from Denver International Airport to forge a new life. St. Stephen's Day—a good day for absolution, she thought. "Forgive me, Michael. I cannot live in Dublin without you."

*   *   *

Kiri winced with each hazelnut brown curl that fell into a pile on the bathroom floor of Paula's house on the hill. She cropped her hair short, then shorter and shorter still into a near pixie cut. A new life demanded a new look. She did not recognize herself when she gazed in the mirror. She saw only her prominent cheekbones, sunken cheeks and vacant blue eyes—no curls to hide behind. Task #1—complete.

Tasks #2 and #3 were job and housing. She decided to secure a job first, then search for housing nearby to cut transportation costs. She knew she could live at her mother's but it was located far from prospective employment opportunities. She could bunk with Kurt and Tanya for a week or two, but that was not a permanent solution either, so she opted to find a place to rent near the job—whatever that turned out to be. She needed to prove she could support herself independently again.

A job search required a résumé. For starters, Kiri listed all the education and experience she acquired over the past four years: foreign currency exchange, proficiency in Welsh dialect and conversational Arabic, medical relief work, firearms training, surveillance video analysis, detailed project planning, financial advising, aquatic therapy for the disabled, trauma psychotherapy with an emphasis on women and children, official document evaluation and procurement, water rescue, trauma triage, and repatriation of the dead.

She glanced at the list, disheartened. She was overqualified for a role in a fictional movie thriller, but she had no transferable skills to a job in the real world. No references, no recommendations. The only documentation she possessed was her work at the bank—the years before and a few months after her leave of absence—a certification in counseling, and another in water therapy. She had no record of gainful employment for the previous three years. Her life with Michael was a black hole.

A tear slipped down her cheek. Kiri realized her secret life with Michael could never be revealed if she were committed to honor his memory. The network would disavow any connection with her other than as his spouse. Her earnings were probably deposited to her account in cash so they could not be traced. Until she rebuilt an employment record and established credit, she had few alternatives. Trying to talk her way into a job with her old bank was the most likely. Applying to a recreation center as a water aerobics instructor ran a distant second. Approaching the BBC bureau in Denver was a cop-out, definitely off the table.

She spent hours creating an impressive résumé with little on it; then she showered and fell into bed. She missed her curls. She missed Michael. She missed the security of knowing someone always watched out for her. The syllables of "a...lone" resounded in her ears as she hugged the photo of their last kiss and cried herself to sleep.

Kiri spent two weeks preparing for this day—job interviews. First impressions made the difference. She took extra care with her appearance for the first time in three months. While bathing she reviewed her minor responsibilities to her Dublin neighborhood.

Paddy was on board to keep watch and to convey messages. She did not reveal her name or whereabouts when she called the grocer. She referred to herself only as the crazy lady who bought lemons by the bag. He agreed to supply the cake ladies at cost. She agreed to reimburse him the difference monthly. Paddy was happy to whisper in their ears. "Have a word with the teashop. Offer to bake specialty cakes for holidays year 'round like Easter and such. I expect the grocer will give you a very good price on supplies."

Charles received his quarterly allotment by the 15th of the month, as usual. Kurt and Tanya had not discovered her hiding out at Paula's, and her mother had not tried to contact her as far as she could tell. She would contact both when she had a job and new digs.

She blow-dried what was left of her hair and slipped into her professional outfit—white blouse, black skirt and sweater, sensible shoes and no accessories or makeup. She looked herself up and down in the full-length mirror and saw nothing but drab. What was expected in Dublin for a post-mission debriefing was out of place in Denver. The only things that sparkled were her rings. They shouted WIDOW!

You're on a mission, Kiri. Look and act the part. Put on a show. Convince the checkpoint guards. She zippered her rings into a suitcase, looped one of Paula's bright scarves around her neck for color, borrowed a bracelet with bangles, and applied shadow and blush. She took a deep breath, picked up her briefcase and departed for her interviews. At night she could mourn her husband, but during the day she must be *Ms.* Kiri Koyle, single mid-thirties professional, confidant in her ability to do the job—any job.

*   *   *

Thomas and Paula parted ways in Kiri's drive. She tried the back door out of habit, then let herself through the gate. He made his way to the front door to slip a note through the mail slot. "No point. Nobody's home" startled him to standing.

"Paddy!" He exhaled slowly. "We haven't seen Kirin in a few days, so we thought to stop by."

"No point. She hasn't been home for most of a month."

"Do you know where she's gone?"

"Couldn't say."

Thomas did not have enough patience to play that game again, so he tried a different tack. "Have you talked to her?"

"Couple o' times."

"What did she say?"

"Tell anyone who asks that she is on holiday."

"When she calls again, please tell her how anxious we are to speak with her. Can you do that for us?"

"Couldn't say."

Thomas jammed the note back into his pocket and left to search for his wife without a proper goodbye to the neighbor. He found Paula gazing at the mutilated evergreen tree. She heard his steps squish in the wet grass and turned to face him. The two spoke in unison. "Kirin's gone." Then, "How do you know?"

"The gas meter isn't running,"

"Paddy says she left almost a month ago." He rubbed his fingers across his eyes. "My fault, I suppose."

"Don't go there again. We all act without thinking sometimes—an O'Connell family trait, it seems." She took his hand. "Let's sit for a minute. I wonder what happened to this tree?" The pungent scent of damp fir wafted through the air.

He picked up two lawn chairs by the fence and set them in the empty space on the evergreen's bare side. "Another O'Connell acting without thinking, probably." They both laughed, sat and patted one another's knees. "Let's go to your house in February, after all." He traced circles around her kneecap. "I know I said I wanted to skip our trip this winter, but I have a feeling Kirin is there."

"How so?"

"When she seeks solitude, she finds a safe, familiar place. The only one left to her now is your house on the hill."

"Won't the trip be too difficult for you... emotionally?"

"Of course. Every trip to Colorado is a trial, as it should be. How can we ever forget the loss of *our* child, or count *his* less meaningful than the loss of another? I'll mourn them both for the rest of my days. Not in quite the same way. We never knew our son his promise. His life unfolds in my imagination. I've shared thirty-four years with Michael and have memories to comfort me, but he does not hold a dearer place in my heart than our own son."

He clasped her hand, brought it to his lips for a kiss and guided it to stroke his beard. "Call me crazy, but I pray that their two souls find one another in their world and hold close as family... until we see them again— our wee, innocent babe ten years older than his hulk of a brother. A strange sight to envision, for sure," he said with a tearful smile.

Paula agreed with a chuckle until she felt her phone vibrate. She opened it to find a text from Kiri. When it dropped to her lap, Thomas leaned over to stare at the message: *Mom. Thanks for the hospitality! I'm hiding out at your house. Move into my own place the end of the month. See you when you come in Feb. Love, Kiri.* He glanced at the date: *Jan 19,* the three-month anniversary of Michael's death.

"This is a sign, Paula! My sons sent a sign. God, forgive my doubts. Only on this date could these events converge to bring a moment of happiness to such a mournful man."

He sprang from the chair and waded ankle-deep into the muddy garden. He tumbled to his knees and grubbed in the soggy earth with bare hands. "I have an idea!" He hoisted two dormant bulbs high into the air, then slipped and fell to his rear, laughing. "If we can't propagate children, we'll settle for flowers! One bulb for each son lost. We'll plant them at your place, not near the house where little people will trample on them, but down by the stream in a peaceful, sunny spot we can view from your deck. In a year or two, they'll reproduce and so on and on until they become a field... a whole hillside... generations of sons!"

"You *are* crazy! Even if we can get them to the States, they won't transplant in February. We'll never be in Colorado when they bloom. We don't even know what type you've dug up. Have you lost your senses?" Paula tried to grab his hands to help him to his feet, but he would not let go of the bulbs.

"Don't try to discourage me from this. What's the harm if my fantasies bring me comfort? Allow me to hope that these symbols of eternal life are a sign from my sons that they are together."

"I give up." She plopped down beside him and cupped his hands in hers. " I knew you were crazy the first time you proposed over forty years ago. I shouldn't be surprised now, but where did this ridiculous plan come from?"

"I have no idea. It just flashed through my mind."

* * *

Henry entered Ryan's Pub with a longer face than usual. The guys returned from a month in Syria and expected an up-to-date on their favorite female friend. He did not know how to break the news that she was gone. He could not convince himself that she left without a word of warning. He became accustomed to hearing her voice when he called and being welcomed warmly when he stopped by. He believed a pleasant familiarity grew between them. Then she escaped with their secrets. He did not know how to explain to the guys what he could not accept himself.

"How's our little lady? When can we see her?" Gus shouted the minute Henry walked through the door.

"She's... uh... gone," he said as he pulled a chair up to their table.

"What do you mean 'gone'? Gone how?" Doyle asked.

"She disappeared before dawn on St. Stephen's Day. Left a note for the neighbor saying she'd call, but no other details. I lost my temper with Patrick when I caught him driving by. 'You've run Kiri out of town! Happy with yourself, Patrick? Don't come here again or I'll call the authorities!' Scared the neighbor enough to drop his binoculars in the grass."

"Did you give her the photo? I bet that's what spooked her," Frank said.

Henry nodded. "She loved it. She seemed happy and appreciative—not upset at all."

"I disagree with Frank," Devin said, signaling for more drinks. "I think the photo emboldened Kiri. Gave her the courage to do what she's been trying to for some time—wean herself from dependence on us."

"I agree," said Gus. "Almost every one of my eight sisters slammed the door on the rest of the family at one time or another to work through troubles on her own. If we can't talk to Kiri, we should write her a note. Tell her how much we miss her and hope she hurries back."

"I have to disagree again," Devin said. "If we do that, we'll make her feel guilty for leaving to take care of herself instead of playing hostess to us. What she needs is a kind of 'proof of life' to show her we made it back safely. Something like this." He grabbed a napkin and began to draw a caricature of himself with shaggy hair, big eyes, narrow face and his nose in a book. Beneath the figure he wrote, *Safe. Healthy. Happy. Devin.*

The other guys followed suit, and soon a pile of messages lay in front of Henry awaiting his. "I can't send these. We don't know where Kiri is."

"I'll check airline passenger lists."

"I'll take the banks."

"I'll talk with all the neighbors and the grocer."

"I'll check Facebook."

They all stared at Gus. "Facebook?"

"Why not? Her brother might let a clue slip."

"Agreed," said Henry. "I'll contact Thomas and Paula in case they've heard from her. I doubt it. Now, let's discuss the refugee situation."

To a one, the guys finished their drinks, pushed in their chairs and walked toward the door. "Later, boss. We've got work to do," they chorused.

"But you have a couple of days off to rest up after we finish here."

"We'll sleep after we've found Kiri," Gus said with a wave.

Henry thumbed through the guys' messages: Doyle's pirate cartoon, Frank with darting eyes pointing in opposite directions, and bushy-haired and bearded Gus showing off his strongman physique. To his knowledge, Henry displayed no outstanding characteristics so he had no idea what to sketch. He did not look at himself much in the mirror. He depended on dress and manner to define him.

Reduced to words, he mulled over breaking the rules to tell Kiri that he missed her very much and hoped she would hurry back—a feeling new to him. He tested several phrases. Word choice was important—not too pleading or demanding—if vs. when, need vs. want, with a hint of expectation. He finally settled on: *Call me when you want a lift from the airport. Henry.*

Chapter 17

Paula glanced over the menu at a small café in Arvada, a suburb north of Denver. She sensed an impatient figure standing next to her. "Tea, please, for now. I'll wait to order until my daughter arrives."

The figure did not move. "Your daughter *has* arrived, Mom."

Paula jumped from her seat in the hope of an embrace, but halted. "Kiri! I hardly recognize you. You look so different."

"But I am still huggable, I hope," she smiled and reached out to her mother.

"Absolutely! I've waited for this moment for months—a chance for us to be alone together."

"Thomas?"

"He refused to stay home, of course, so I left him in the bookstore in the mall. I'm sure he'll call... several times."

Kiri chuckled and welcomed her mother's tight, lingering hold. The two sat, ordered and clasped hands while awaiting their meal. Paula's green eyes sparkled with excitement and her cheeks danced in uncontrollable smiles. "Tell me everything. Where do you live? Do you work?"

"Not far from here on both counts." Kiri explained her job search, glossing over the problem of limited experience. She did approach her old supervisor first and was told the expected—no openings at present but if something came up, he would get in touch. She asked for references to other banks and he seemed happy to give them. Her pursuit of a financial position proved fruitless, however, and she was about to canvass recreation centers when her former supervisor called.

"The strangest thing," he said. "The husband of the assistant manager at the Arvada branch received a sudden transfer to Oklahoma. He wants his family on the road with him by the end of the week. We have no one in the pipeline to replace her and no time for a job search. Are you interested?"

Kiri jumped at the offer. Arvada, Longmont, Platteville—the location was inconsequential, and the job title too, as long as she could support herself. She began to search for affordable housing nearby.

"Surely you're not in trouble financially!" Paula exclaimed. "Michael's..."

"Don't go there, Mom." Kiri's jaw tightened and her lips pursed. "I will NOT use Michael's death to support my life!"

To avoid further antagonism, Paula reached in her bag for an envelope. "Henry asked me to deliver this."

One corner of Kiri's mouth turned up in amusement at the pile of hand-decorated napkins in front of her. She breathed a sigh of relief at their perfect means of conveying a message she never expected to receive. *The guys are safe at home!* She tucked the notes in her bag to enjoy again in private.

"Anything you can share?"

The arrival of lunch saved Kiri an evasive explanation. The women examined their salads and exchanged wistful looks. Their plates held none of the Irish reds, greens and array of vegetables they so enjoyed; the bread, not dense and dark as they preferred.

"Tell me about your new place."

Between bites, Kiri described her small, modest townhouse. Paula read the melancholy in her daughter's eyes. She missed her home in Dublin. "Finding an older house to rent was impossible, so I settled for a newer development where people and buildings are crushed together. Not ideal, but close enough to walk or bike to work when the weather turns nice. I did buy a second-hand Volvo, but I've been so busy at the bank that I haven't had a chance to get out much."

Paula arched an eyebrow, so Kiri explained. On her third day, she was asked to assume additional responsibility—in foreign exchange. "We have a program, of course," the manager said, "but none of us can interpret it. We must watch fluctuations in the euro, and we're beginning to see exchanges in Middle Eastern currencies. Could you keep on top of those markets for us?" Kiri considered: translate technical drivel into common English, analyze financial activity in the Middle East, search Arabic websites for clues—all no-brainers. "Happy to," she replied. "Thanks," the man said with no hint of additional compensation.

Her mother arched the other eyebrow. "No big deal, Mom. I'm set for now. I'll ask for more when I've proven myself."

The ring tone on Paula's phone halted her protest. "Yes, Thomas. No. Not yet. Not until we've finished. Be patient. No, I won't. I'll call when I'm ready to leave." She looked at her daughter and shook her head.

"No explanation needed, Mom. I understand. Do you want to leave now?"

"Not a chance." When the plates were cleared, Paula took her daughter's hand again. "You haven't told me how *you* are... how you feel inside."

Kiri forced a smile. "I have good days and bad. Today is a good one because I'm with you. I won't know about tomorrow until I wake up. Learning to function in a new environment helps. Thomas?"

"Much the same. I try to maintain a routine, keep him active with *tai chi*, long walks and visits with the grandchildren, but despair snakes its way into his thoughts. Good days and bad. Today is a very bad day. He cannot understand why you refuse to speak with him... to allow him to apologize."

"Apology will not erase the humiliation I endured every time he opened his mouth. I'm sorry I can't help him feel better, but seeing him will make me feel worse. I won't put myself in that position when I'm grappling so hard to crawl out of the hole I'm in."

"He acted before thinking, Kiri. He didn't mean a word, and he needs to tell you that."

"Yeah, the famous O'Connell proclivity that cost Michael his life," she let slip with downcast eyes, then tried to recover. "Thomas will have to be patient with me. I'm not ready to see him."

Paula studied her daughter for the real culprit. "The truth, Kiri. You wouldn't hang onto resentment this long over a few angry words."

Kiri promised herself she would not cry in front of her mother, no matter what. Honesty challenged that vow. "You said it yourself... in the canoe on the lake that April. You said Michael was 'loving, generous and so like his father.' For the rest of my life, whenever I look at Thomas I will see Michael in him. They share the same bearing—the same gestures and mannerisms, the cock of their heads and inflections in their speech. The flashes in their deep-set blue eyes are similar when they think they've caught someone in a game or a trick. Thomas is more conservative and volatile. Michael had a stubborn streak too, but I don't want to believe he would ever treat me with such disrespect.

"Generous and loving. Michael doted on the nieces and nephews as much as his father. Witnessing Thomas' relationship with the grandchildren is a constant reminder of what I will never have. I don't need more reminders. I'm alone every night. Oh, Mom," Kiri cried. "I miss Michael so much." Her flood of tears jumped its banks. She dissolved in her mother's arms.

Paula tried to comfort her, holding her tight and stroking her hair while staving off the café's waitstaff. She rocked her slowly while murmuring, "My dear, dear girl. I'm so sorry tragedy visited you this early in your young life. You mustn't lose hope that..."

Kiri pushed her mother away, tears still streaming down her blotchy red cheeks. "Don't tell me what I mustn't do, and don't tell me that I'm unreasonable or irrational. I'm grieving! And for heaven's sake, don't repeat anything I've said to Thomas. If you do, I'll say you lied to make him feel better." She gulped back her tears. "Promise me you won't tell Thomas!"

Paula nodded, knowing her daughter asked the impossible. "I promise." She folded her arms around Kiri and watched her weep until the young widow could no more.

*   *   *

Kurt convinced his sister that a weekend on the ski slopes would perk her up. "You cannot avoid every place and every pastime you shared with Michael. That will relegate you to life as a pill bug. Pack a bag. You can rent gear when we get up there."

Kiri tried to refuse, but when she considered her options she decided her brother had a point. The long Presidents' Day weekend loomed before her. Three days alone with her thoughts in a house she did not particularly like in a place she really did not want to be versus three days of fresh air and exercise in a place she loved was not a fair contest. She steeled herself to have a good time.

She found her rhythm after a couple of easy runs and decided to take the lift to the summit—mistake #1. She skied cross-country along the ridge—mistake #2. She jumped trail at the near-fatal draw—mistake #3— and headed, full speed, for the cliff—mistake #4. As her skis reached the edge, she felt them lift her higher and higher until she soared through the air, arms outstretched, hoping to touch Michael one more time. She landed in the only clear spot in Boulder Canyon and maneuvered frantically at racing speed through the giant stone obstacle course. She arrived exhausted at the base of the mountain and ran smack into a gray unisuited older man with a cowboy hat atop his salt-and-pepper hair.

"What the hell you tryin' to do jumpin' off-trail like that and hot-shotting it through the boulder field! Yer lucky ye didn't start an avalanche roaring down the canyon to swallow ye up. You tryin' to kill yerself!"

Kiri did not answer her old friend and instructor Rick.

"You git over here and look me straight in the eye and tell me you weren't tryin' to kill yerself, Kiri."

She did not budge.

"Well, I'll be damned! That's exactly what you were aiming for—a quick one-way ticket out of this world. Thought you'd take the good Lord's will into yer own hands and do His job for Him, huh? Thought you'd arrange a rendezvous with that dead husband of yers?"

A tear loosed itself from Kiri's eye and slid slowly over her frosted cheek.

"I'm sorry as I can be he got himself blowed up. All yer friends here are. We all shed more'n one tear for that crazy runt of a guy whose heart was bigger than our two heads put together. But let me tell you somethin', gal. Yer not the only one ever to lose somebody they loved. Everybody here has lost—and some more than once—to accident, disease, divorce, abandonment, and some of us had daddies who got shot over in Vietnam and never made it back to tuck their boys in at night and give 'em a hug."

Rick scratched through his mottled chin whiskers and softened his tone. "You think yer the only one who's ever felt pain? Then you've got a pretty small mind thinkin' the world revolves around you and yer sorrow. You do that fine man you called a husband no honor by selfishly tryin' to take yer own life. What you 'tempted is an insult...an abomination to Michael's memory. You should be ashamed of yerself fer tryin' to rob this Earth of another fine soul."

Tears streamed down Kiri's face, too many for her to catch with her tongue so she gave up trying.

The old pro became emotional and started shouting again. "No one's dyin' on my mountain, not on my watch! You git yer pitiful self outta here an don't come back 'til yer ready to fall on those knees of yers and ask forgiveness from the Lord for actin' like such a fool today. And while yer at it, you might thank Him for given' you such a good life and the years you had and the memories you made with that damn fine man of yers. And double while yer at it, you might give thanks for the family and friends who love you and for this beautiful place yer in where you can be at peace with yer thoughts and as close to heaven and the stars as yer ever gonna git in this life."

Kiri dropped to her knees, her shoulders heaving with her sobs.

"And triple while yer at it, you might be thinkin' of what *you* can do to make this world a better place instead of wastin' all yer energy feelin' sorry for yerself. Think of a way you can honor Michael's memory with action more worthy of him than throwin' yerself off a cliff. You've got to live for two now...work twice as hard to get the things done he thought needed doin'. It's high time you got started."

With that, Rick skied away planting his poles hard and deep with each stride, leaving Kiri to her sobs and her anguish. She had no idea how long she remained crumpled in the snow. She returned to the condo and hit the hot tub. Since she rode up with Kurt and Tanya, she saw no escape to the safety of her house. She was stuck. Let the warm water wash all the scary things away, she remembered.

Kurt found her floating in the hot tub just before dark. He scoured the village for her after the story of her near-suicidal run down Boulder Canyon made the rounds.

"Thank God I've found you!" he exclaimed. "The whole village is out looking for you after word got around of your confrontation with Rick. He's worried sick about you, Kiri. I'll give him a call."

"Rick can go to hell!"

"Kiri!"

"Well, he can! He had no right to talk to me that way. What I do with my body is my business!"

"He doesn't think of it that way. He thinks of you like a daughter and he reacted the only way he knew how. You should be happy someone cares enough to help you screw your head back on straight."

"Shut up and go away!"

"Nope. You are coming with me. Get yourself cleaned up. We're going to the karaoke bar. Rick has something special planned."

"If you think I'll go within twenty feet of that man, you don't know your sister."

"I know Rick, and if you don't show up with me, he'll come get you and drag you there himself. Now, get out of that tub and let's get this shindig over with."

When Kiri entered with Kurt on one side and Tanya on the other, the place hushed. Rick, who was at the bar, turned to face Kiri and pushed his hat back on his forehead. "I owe this little lady an apology, and now is as good a time as any. I apologize, Kiri, fer the way I ranted at you this afternoon. I had no call to be that hard on you... but, damn it, girl, you had me scared to death! I thought you were gonna end up a pile o' bones on the side of my mountain. But you didn't. I musta taught you better than I thought for you to make yer way through that boulder field without a scratch. Or maybe that good man of yers held you in the palm of his hand and eased you down.

"Doesn't matter. Yer here with us now and we're happy for that. So happy, in fact, that I'm throwin' a party—a western wake—fer yer dear departed Michael whose spirit is here with us this evenin' fer sure. We're gonna spend some time rememberin' him with pictures and stories. I even brought me a clean handkerchief in case we cry a tear or two. Then we're everyone, to a man and woman, gonna lift a glass of *warm* beer to that crazy Irishman of yers an' toast him on his way."

Stories commenced and videos followed pieced together from iphones and racecam footage, from Michael's first performance of "Molly Malone" to his last race the previous year. The American mourners lifted their glasses in a tearful toast, and Rick followed with an unusual announcement.

"Weep as you want tonight. Tomorrow we're gonna have a Tribute Run down Racer's Hill. Anyone who wants, the lift will be open at 9. We'll ride up and race down. The timer will be on, but we're all racing against Michael's best time. He beat most of us down that hill...some of us, more than once. And then to rub salt in the wound, he beat us all through those pearly gates. Damn him, anyway! So this is our last chance to say 'in yer face, Michael O'Connell!' I'm goin' first in the right lane, with the spirit of Michael in the left, and I'm gonna ski full bore shoutin' at him all the way down. And I hope I beat him and beat him good!

"Kurt and Kiri go down next, and the rest of you pair yerselves up and have the best run of yer sorry lives tryin' to beat that man who never should have tried to strap that burly body of his onto a pair of skis in the first place some four years ago. When everybody's given his best shot, we'll post all the times along with Michael's to see who's shown him what fer. Now, git yerselves to bed so you'll be ready to go at nine in the mornin'. God bless you all... and God bless Michael, may he rest in peace... after we've all had our chance at him tomorrow, that is!"

Even a few who did not know Michael but had heard of him—the crazy Irishman with the orangutan stance—showed up to try to be spoilers of his record. But at the end of the morning, none succeeded. Rick came closest at five hundredths of a second, with Kurt, Jason and Kiri close behind. The rest followed. But no one bested Michael once again. In fact, they were sure they could hear him laughing as he glanced at the time board and skied through those pearly gates, his poles pumping the air in triumph.

Kiri did not wait around to see the results. She fled to the condo and caught a shuttle for the city. When she finally reached home, she rolled herself tightly into a blanket on the floor and cried herself to sleep.

Chapter 18

Anxious to hear the latest, Henry hurried to Ryan's Pub to meet the guys. Devin discovered Kiri's surrogate identity ruse within a couple of days and placed her in Denver. Frank ascertained from her Dublin bank that there was no activity in her accounts except for prearranged electronic fund transfers to locals. The locals informed Doyle that no one knew her phone number or where she was, but she paid her obligations on time. Henry reported that their messages were well received but Paula did not know where Kiri lived or worked—somewhere near Arvada. Gus finally made contact with her brother but could not comment on the breakthrough until after the guys returned from another short trip to Syria. Tonight was that night!

"What's the good word?" Henry asked, nearly out of breath.

"I finally got Kurt to friend me," Gus said as he opened his laptop. "I had to set up a dummy page. He wouldn't let me in as an old college chum of Kiri's, but when I asked him as 'Raceleigh Guy from Dublin,' he wrote back right away. Good thing I posted a bunch of racecar photos. Anyway, as soon as we got back, I found this from a couple of weeks ago." He read, *Sis almost bought it in Boulder Canyon but rallied to finish fifth in Tribute Race. Way to go, Sis!*

Devin opened his laptop. "Let's google that canyon." He zoomed in on the ski area. "Whoa! I don't like the looks of that. How did Kiri get caught in there?"

The guys crowded around and studied the images on the screen. "The only access is from above," Doyle said, then voiced what the others were thinking. "She didn't end up in the canyon by accident. She jumped!"

"Our little lady has gone fool crazy again," Gus said. "We've got to go help her... but where is she?"

"I think I know where she works," Frank said. "I checked with the bank on the way here. No withdrawals from any of her accounts to date, but she deposited *to* one yesterday from a bank in Arvada. Here's the address and phone. Should we ask one of the reporters from the Denver bureau to have a look?"

"No!" shouted Gus. "We'll jump on a plane tonight and be there to greet her when she walks in the door tomorrow. That's what we'll do!"

"Hold on, guys. She'll run the other way the minute she sees a gang of mad Irishmen waiting for her. She mustn't realize we're spying," Henry said. "I'll think of a reason—job related—and fly over tomorrow. You have plenty to do here to prepare for your next trip. Look busy and cover me if Patrick should ask. I'll be back the day after."

Disappointed, the men closed their laptops and shifted their pints on the table. "Will you at least let us send Kiri another proof of life," Gus asked.

At Henry's nod, he grouped the team with glasses raised to her. They broke out in toothy smiles while their boss snapped a photo.

*   *   *

Kiri jumped when the receptionist buzzed her. No one at the bank ever buzzed her; they shouted through the door. "There's a man with a sexy accent on Line 2 looking for a Kirin O'Connell. He insists she works here. Your name is closest, so would you mind taking the call? If you aren't the person he's looking for, ask him if he's free for a drink after work with a stranger."

Unmasked at last, Kiri thought. *After more than two months of freedom, I'm caught in the web again.* She smoothed her hair and straightened her neck scarf to calm herself. "Kiri Koyle speaking. How may I help you?"

"By acknowledging who you are. This is Henry."

"I guessed. To what do I owe this call?"

"To some clever men who are very good at what they do—finding people and helping them."

"Are you in a position to help?"

"No, but you are. I hope you can rescue me from unrelenting boredom while I wait at the Denver airport for a late flight to a UN conference in San Francisco. I'm desperate for a friendly face and conversation. Do you have time to meet me for a drink?"

"The receptionist will be so disappointed. *She* wanted the invite from the man with the mysterious accent. Of course I'll meet you, Henry. Be outside door #506 in forty-five minutes."

Kiri pulled up to the curb at 4:43 p.m. and recognized Henry's tall, dignified figure immediately. No one traveled on a transatlantic flight in suit and tie anymore. She motioned to him, but he stared right past her. She stepped out of her car and waved, but he turned to look the other way. She walked up and tapped him on the shoulder. He jerked away, startled by the unfamiliar figure. "I rather expected a hug," she said.

"Kiri? I didn't recognize you. You look so... chic American."

"Goes with my new life. Do you have a bag we should pick up, or is it checked?"

He shook his head. "I'm traveling light this trip—carryon only."

"Then hop in. You're about to experience some of the Wild West."

"I thought we'd stay here for a couple of hours. Have a drink or two before my flight to the conference."

"Don't be ridiculous! You are very clever at dancing around the truth, but you are a terrible liar. Planes from Ireland aren't routed through Denver to San Francisco, and you would never attend a conference in only the suit you are wearing." She directed a sly smile at him. "You came all this way to see if I'm cracking up and likely to expose your unit. I'm surprised there aren't half a dozen Irishmen with enchanting accents climbing in my little car right now. You can't go home without a tale to tell them, and you won't get one in two hours over drinks."

Chastened, Henry threw his small bag in the back and climbed in the passenger seat on the wrong side of a car. "Can I at least buy you dinner?"

"Tomorrow night, maybe. Tonight, I'll cook and you'll stay at my place. We can't have a discrete conversation in public." He gave her one of his severe looks. "No argument!" She pulled away from the curb and headed toward the freeway north.

Henry settled back uncomfortably and attempted polite conversation. "The guys all send greetings. Gus told me to ask if Michael's lingering soul is happy here in Colorado—whatever that means—and Doyle wants to know..."

At Kiri's piercing glare, he swallowed the rest of his words. After several minutes of silence and studying the strange surroundings, Henry dared ask, "How are you, Kiri... really?"

"Lousy most of the time, but I know how to put on a good show—part of my new life."

*   *   *

Henry stared up at the ceiling of the small room that served as Kiri's office, art studio and guestroom. For the second night in a row he had trouble settling his mind after long, serious discussions. He mulled over what to tell the guys when he returned to Dublin the following day. Should he take a clinical approach, telling them that they witnessed her best and her worst, and that she was now somewhere in between—functional, but still unable to experience momentary joy, even in her painting? Or should he go further and describe the comfortable, yet revealing time they spent together?

Those hours together were not all serious and maudlin. She complained about her humdrum job, then excitedly told him of a scam she uncovered with a Middle East connection. He told her they traced a monetary transaction from Patrick to the van driver but wanted more evidence before they made a case against the rogue to management. She registered neither concern nor elation.

Henry then complained about her poorly appointed kitchen with only one pot, one pan, a couple of plates, bowls and mugs and no teapot. "How can you operate without a proper kitchen?" he asked. To spite his criticism, she prepared a delectable one-pot meal, served it to him in a bowl with a spoon and poured his cold beer in a cup. They both laughed, but her eyes did not dance.

The following morning—barely twelve hours earlier—they drove to Paula's house on the hill to pick up boxes of cookware, dishes and linens she left in storage. That is where he discovered her paintings—colorful, fanciful pieces—so unlike the moody ones she recently produced and hung in the guestroom. "These are from my sunny period," she said. "I'm going through my gray period now—therapy, I hope."

Conversation flowed freely between them. Kiri seemed to find relief when her words spilled onto the bare floor to be rearranged into emotions, actions and consequences. Trained counselor that she was, she recognized that she could not seek professional help because she could not reveal the truth about her life with Michael or his death. Still bound to secrecy, she could not communicate her needs to her mother or brother or any of Thomas' family, for sure. They, in turn, had no way to truly understand her despair and comfort her.

"I have no one but you, Henry, and the other four guys to share my story with, and you have lives and responsibilities of your own. I can't remain Gus' ninth sister forever, so I ran. I thought I could separate myself from the memories enough to start a new life—like painting on a fresh canvas—but the tragedy of losing Michael seeps through and discolors any vision I attempt to create. I want to paint in daisy yellow again and not watch vibrant hues fade to gray."

By evening, sitting on her second-hand couch in her tiny living room in the light of a few stubby candles, they trusted each other enough to share their guilts. "I never should have pressured Michael to accept Patrick's change of plan, and I certainly should not have allowed you to go with him. When I think of you witnessing and enduring such horror, I'm sickened inside and break out shaking and in sweats. If only I could take back that morning…"

Kiri refuted his argument. "*You* are not to blame. Michael made his own decision. I made mine. None of us could predict that a well-planned mission would spin so out of control because Patrick schemed to betray us. If our vehicle were not blown to bits, we would have crossed the border safely right behind the others. *Patrick* is at fault, not you."

Henry rested his head in his hands and closed his eyes, relieved—not because she absolved him of guilt but because she allowed him to confess it. Sharing pent-up emotion was foreign to him.

She touched his shoulder. "Somehow I, too, must find peace with the part I played in my husband's death." He blinked and turned to her wide-eyed. "Patrick put us in the predicament, and the boy tossed the bomb, but *I* could have prevented Michael from being in the wrong spot at the wrong time." His jaw dropped and he shook his head, incredulous.

"Oh, yes, Henry. We settled down to rest for a while. Michael wanted to… I needed a few private moments, so he walked out of our hovel to talk with Doyle who spoke with you on the phone. If I held onto him longer, he never would have left me… and we would be safe together in our home on Quincy Street tonight. That guilt torments me every time I close my eyes." Hers glistened from tears gathering to fall.

Henry grasped both her shoulders and pulled her close to reassure her. "Patrick's and the boy's actions were matters of choice. We could not control them, nor can we control matters of chance—a foot right or left, a minute this way or that. Don't allow the 'could haves' in your life to paralyze you. Michael died doing the work he loved in the arms of the woman he loved most in the world. Not many men are lucky enough to pass their final moments in such bliss."

Despite his avoidance of intimate encounters, Henry rocked Kiri gently and was not embarrassed to cry with her, shedding more of the agony he ignored for so long. He suddenly realized that the two of them were closer in experience—tragedy, disillusion, and despair—than anyone could imagine and that unknowingly in her own self-analysis, she uncovered emotions haunting him too.

His mind still a muddle, Henry rolled to his side and inched the heavy blankets closer to his nose against the chill. He tried to recall his earliest disillusionment—that fathers who say they will play with you when they come home, do not... come home, that is. He was about three when harsh knocking on the door of their modest home in northwestern County Leitrim interrupted his bedtime story. Two men burst in and spoke with his mother who screamed, drew up her apron and started to wail. One of them wrapped him in a blanket, ran outside and shoved him into the back seat of a car. The other helped her gather their belongings and pushed her and their one suitcase next to him. They speeded down the bumpy road, his mother crying into his blanket.

"Where's Papa?" he asked. "How will he find us in the dark? He promised to play with me when he came home."

"Your papa is not coming home... ever again," his mother choked through her tears. Henry remembered the sting of abandonment even now and rubbed his chest to make it go away.

The men dropped mother and child at a home in a heavily Catholic town in the Midlands. The family there spoke in a language he did not understand yet. A couple of days later, he and his mother were moved to a small house near the church where she began work as a cook—where she trusted her son would be safe. No one spoke his father's name again.

The truth of his family history was foremost in his mind. When he questioned his mother over the years, she shared only the barest facts. "The rest I'll keep secret 'til the day I die." After his graduation from Trinity College, Henry's mother packed one suitcase to return to her village in the northwest. "I miss my home and family. I've been away for 'most twenty years, and need to be near kin. The Troubles in the North are settling now, so no harm will come to me."

She placed her hand tenderly on his cheek and stroked it. "Don't be paralyzed by your past, Son. I've tried to give you a running start on a new life. How tall and straight you stand now makes your mother very proud. Follow your passion... but keep yourself safe."

Henry eased himself from the bed and crept across the hall to peek into Kiri's room. He stared at her through the crack in the doorway, much as he had at his mother years before. She lay on her side, her left hand above the covers touching the framed photo of Michael's last breath. Her finger was bare during daylight hours, but that night she wore her rings. He could not remember if he ever saw his mother wear a ring. He listened to Kiri's deep, steady breathing—a peaceful sound belying her torment inside.

A surge of guilt swept over him. He was responsible for Kiri's fragile condition in the big-picture sense—he and Michael and the guys. They lured her into a life she did not ask for, coaxed her to partner in their secrets, and once snared, barred her escape—like a little blackbird following a trail of crumbs, totally unaware of the consequences. In her new life, how could she ever forge friendships... or a relationship with another man... when a chunk of the history that molded her into this new woman could never be revealed?

Henry slipped back into his bed. If Kiri were to move forward with her life, he must entice her to return to Dublin and a circle of empathetic friends. Her inability to share her story impeded her recovery... and, he had to admit, the same was true for him.

* * *

"We demand proof of life! We demand proof of life!" the four men chorused, pounding their pints on the table at Ryan's Pub.

Henry laughed, pulled up a chair and opened his phone. "Kiri and I took this one after I showed her yours. She loved it. Said it was the perfect way to communicate." He passed his phone around so the guys could see her smiling with her arms around his neck.

"What happened to her? She looks like a bloody internee," Doyle said.

"Not a curl on her head," Frank added.

"Lifeless eyes and sunken cheeks," Devin observed.

"I could scoop that little lady up with one hand and bring her home." Gus wiped his eyes.

"No scooping. Kiri will balk if we force a return. If she does come back, it will be of her own free will and when she feels safe here. She is healthier than she looks but more dispirited than she appears. She is depressed but lucky for us, feels she can't talk to anyone about her feelings."

Henry shifted in his chair and fiddled with his tie. "I don't think she intended to ski off that cliff," he said. "When she's upset, she soaks in warm water or swaddles herself, but if she is out where she can't do that, she loses control and frankly has no idea what she does. We need to nudge her our way... give her a reason to come back... but she must think it's her idea." The other guys nodded agreement.

"For the time being we'll watch for any other risky behavior. Gus, that's your job. The rest of you work on tying up the case against Patrick. She as much as said she wouldn't come near this place until he was out of

the way. She did make one concession. She gave me her phone number…
to be used only in an emergency or for proof of life each time you return.
Don't ask. She said if I call for any other reason, she'll throw that phone
away. We all know she will. So we'll play by her rules until we have more
cause for concern."

*   *   *

*April 20: Sis had a close call. A bunch of us stopped at the Hot
Springs after a hike. She wasn't hungry so went straight for the water. A
stranger came by the lodge to tell us he found her face down in the stream.
He pulled her out and performed CPR. Said she probably slipped on moss
and hit her head. Then he disappeared. She seems OK now.*

"Lots of slippery rocks in a warm stream," Devin said.

*June 8: Annual bike race near Steamboat. The wife and I finished in
the middle of the pack. Sis dragged in near the end. Broke a brake cable on
a steep downhill and nearly did a header into a tree. Some guy saw her go
off-road and fixed her up enough to make it to the end. Bumps and bruises.
Nothing broken but spokes on the bike.*

"Chains break. Cables break. Doesn't prove a thing." Frank rubbed his
chin with a fist.

*July 5: Had a great BBQ out at Mom's! Fireworks terrific!! Sis went
kayaking instead. Still on the outs with the fam. River too low, so she had
trouble in the rapids. Boat made it to the take-out before she did. Lost her
helmet along the way too. No permanent damage. Some guy gave her a
ride down to pick up her craft.*

"She's a great swimmer. Michael taught her how to handle herself in
the water, but she should have checked levels before she left." Doyle shook
his head.

*August 2: Sis did it again! Skydiving! Her parachute didn't open, so
her instructor had a heck of a time catching up. Caught her at about 1,200
ft. She hobbled away from the dive with a sprained ankle and a great video
from his helmetcam. Click the link for one scary ride!!*

"Michael's birthday! We trained her to extricate herself from any
ticklish situation, but we never taught her to fly. The video is plain as day.
She didn't even *try* to pull the cord!" Gus ran his thick fingers through his
bushy hair.
    "That's it. I'm on my way!" Doyle drove Henry directly to the airport
without a word exchanged between them.

Chapter 19

Kiri pulled up to the curb at the Denver airport, and this time Henry jumped right in and tossed his bag into the back seat. "Don't pretend you are on your way to a conference in San Francisco, Henry. Your face tells me you have something else on your mind. So, what's up?"

"You... until you nearly plunged to your death. What the hell were you doing jumping out of a perfectly good airplane!"

"Spying on me now, are you?" she snapped in defense.

"The video of the crazy lady who didn't pull the cord on her parachute made the rounds faster than you made it to the ground!" He stepped back onto the curb. "Get out of the car. Now!"

"Who are you to give me orders?"

"I'm the man who will not ride in a vehicle with a woman who is dangerous to herself and others... a woman who doesn't value her own life. Now move! I'm driving."

He took her place behind the wheel and peeled away before Kiri securely fastened her seat belt, then he immediately got caught up in airport traffic. After two circuits through "Arrivals" and "Departures," he pounded the heel of his hand against the steering wheel and pulled over to a traffic island, fuming.

"What's the matter, Henry... Embarrassed by your uncharacteristic fit of temper and ready to catch the first flight home?"

"No!" He slammed his hand against the wheel again. "I'm embarrassed that I can't drive us out of this bloody maze. I keep pulling to the left!" He turned to her, flushed. "How can I expect you to take my 'life's path' advice seriously when I can't even follow a simple road sign?"

Kiri burst out laughing. "I guess we'll have to help each other. I'll be your GPS." She patted his hand. "Don't worry. I have no self-destructive tendencies today. I'm having too much fun watching my unflappable friend... flounder."

Henry convinced Kiri to call in at work for a couple of personal days. "We need to talk," he said. "We pay a high price for staying silent about our psychic injuries."

"'We?' Do you suffer from mental torment too?"

He stammered to recover. "I meant the editorial 'we.' People... many people are afraid to express how they truly feel and that takes a toll on their health and their relationships. You said that I was the only person you could talk to... so you talk. I'm here to listen."

They spent a day talking while they walked the labyrinth of trails through designated open space, skirting towns and neighborhoods. First stop along their trek was a mini mall. "You won't last four late summer days in Colorado in a suit and tie." Further on, an ice cream parlor beckoned them in. "Don't be so self-conscious about a little dribble on your chin," she chuckled. "Your dignity is still in tact."

Later, they took advantage of a shady bench along a stream teeming with ducks. "Patrick is gone."

"How? Where?" Kiri grew tense, almost frightened.

"We finally found the van driver and 'persuaded' him to give a statement to a UN rep. That, along with the money trail, our eyewitness reports and video from the bombed-out vehicle convinced management we had a good case for complicity in attempted murder. They agreed with you that going public with a trial would damage the network irrevocably and shut our unit down, so we settled on a compromise. He's been promoted..."

"Promoted!" Kiri sprang from the bench with fists clenched and jaw drawn tight.

"...to Bureau Chief in the Falklands. He has a staff of one and a chip in his passport that prevents his leaving the islands except for two weeks late June, early July when you, Thomas and Paula are usually here in Colorado and for two weeks during the holidays. When in Dublin, he must wear a tracker set to alarm if he comes within a half-mile of your home or theirs. You are now safe."

"Perfect!" Kiri threw her arms around his neck. "Napoleonic exile on an island! How did you ever come up with that?"

Surprised by her sudden reaction, he held her long enough to smile slyly down at her. "Cunning is in our job description... and we're very good at it." Relieved that Patrick's banishment brought closure for Kiri, Henry determined not to reveal the whole truth—the Alice connection—now, or ever.

After hours along the trail, she asked if Henry had any idea where they were.

"Wyoming?" he replied, using his handkerchief to wipe his sweaty forehead.

Kiri pointed beyond a two-lane road and a large alfalfa field to a cluster of housing complexes. "Home is over there. We walked about a twelve-mile circuit, but first I want to show you this." She grabbed his hand and pulled him up a grassy slope toward a large building with lots of windows. "I discovered this rec center not too long ago. I like its layout and the variety of water programs it offers. Look here." She pointed to specific listings on a schedule board. "I could teach this... this... and this one. I'm hoping to get a foot in the door soon... until I can finance a place of my own."

Her face beamed. "Michael..." Then her enthusiasm waned. She recovered and with a sigh of resignation, continued. "Michael and I planned to remodel the house and yard next door into a water therapy center— smaller of course—and were set to break ground this past January. What can I do with that house now?"

Henry opted for a day of rest following their long trek. "I haven't walked that far since… I can't remember. And in heat!"

"The altitude probably got to you." Kiri finished cleaning up the breakfast dishes in her compact, one-person kitchen. "Either that or you're out of shape. Too much time behind a desk?" she asked with a glint in her eye.

"If I could find someone to spell me when all the guys are gone, I might be able to get out more. Could we stay in today… at least for a while?"

"In Colorado, one doesn't 'stay in' on a bright summer day unless one is deeply depressed. Are you depressed today, Henry? I'm not. In fact, I feel better than I have in ages. Must be your dapper presence." She gazed at the tall, slim figure of the staid professional nearly eight years her senior who had far more consequential ways to spend his time than flying five thousand miles to help her feel good. "Your pleasure," she smiled. "What would you like to do?"

"I'd like to watch you paint." She shot him a quirky look, so he explained. "I want to know what you use."

She tilted her head and shrugged. "Canvas, brushes and acrylics."

He laughed gently. "I mean your process. How do you decide what to paint and what colors to use? Do you just begin and see what happens, or do you have a specific idea or emotion that causes you to pick up a brush, or do you look out the window and try to depict what you see in your own way?"

Kiri stared deeply into his mysterious gray eyes, then scanned him from head to toe until he grew restless. "What will you do while I paint?"

"Sit on your lumpy hide-a-bed and watch an artist's process unfold."

Henry followed her to the small studio and watched her tie back the curtains and open the window to let in more light and air, clear the table and move a tall stool near it for more height and perspective, stretch and staple a canvas around a paper-sized frame, assemble water, rags, brushes and small smearing tools, and finally squish globs of color onto an old plate and mix them. He scrutinized every stroke, splash and splotch of pigment that flowed in an exciting rhythm from her fingers: fireweed and chokecherry reds, glacier lily and butterfly yellows, pine and moss greens, deep lake and columbine blues, high mountain and lupin purples, and all their shades in between.

After a couple of hours she left the room abruptly without a word to Henry. She fixed herself a sandwich and ate in silence, leaving him to fend for himself. She stepped outside and turned her face upward as if sniffing the air for scents to translate into color. She returned to alter a tint here, a spot there and to add only a few fine, black curves—hints of a petal, leaf or vine—to hold the composition together. Henry could discern no distinct forms or figures.

Kiri then began a perfect rendering of a human thumb—long and slender—near the lower left corner. Soon the silhouette of the side of a left hand emerged, including knuckle and index finger disappearing behind all the color. She took pains to include every crease, wrinkle and vein on the digit, and the sheen of the nail. By mid afternoon she emitted a satisfied sigh and asked, "What do you think?"

"I love the colors. I'm guessing this is an abstract, so I don't understand the thumb."

"That is *your* hand, Henry, holding a picture of all the vibrant colors you hope I will see again someday." She left the house and jogged out of sight along the path.

Henry did not follow. He held the painting with his left hand and studied the two carefully. Every detail was exact, every shadow and nuance of fleshy tone correct. He placed his left hand on top of its image and found them identical in size and shape. Touched by how accurately she depicted him and how intimately she seemed to know him, he felt a welling up inside he had not experienced in years.

Kiri returned shortly and in good spirits. "Don't look so worried. Your reaction—or lack thereof—didn't offend me. I often walk away after I've finished a piece. I hate to clean up… to second-guess myself. When I finish with a project, I'm done!" She smiled. "Of course I have to eventually, so I can start fresh again… but I can do that anytime."

After supper, Henry cleaned the studio… to prepare it for her next burst of color.

The two spent another day at a mountain lake, canoeing. "As long as you don't plan to shoot rapids. I'm not in the mood for a water rescue."

Kiri arched an eyebrow. "You know about that, too?"

"Remember, my men are very good at what they do, and watching over people they care about is what they do best." He let that thought settle for a few minutes, then used it as an opening for him to talk and her to listen.

"Syria is frantic right now, and we are shorthanded with two men out of the picture. We can never replace Michael, of course, but we do need extra hands at home base… for detail work and to spell me with communication… so all four guys can be gone at once. Worst of all, we've had to let counseling services go… when we need them more than ever. We have no time for background checks on prospective employees." He paused to let his seed of an idea sink in. "Now, tell me what else you do besides crash your bike."

On Henry's last day, he played tourist with Kiri as his guide. They drove a road along the foothills to tour a brewery or two. By the last taste-testing he did not even mind the samples' cold temperature. "Ah," he sighed. "The best yet. I'll have a pint of this one." He nodded to the young man behind the bar and then to her. "You haven't touched a drop all day. Please join me, or do you still hold to your two-fingers rule?"

"My miserable life hasn't pushed me over the edge yet, and I don't intend to let it. But for you, I'll take a sample size of your favorite." She secured a small table across the room by the windows overlooking the hills.

He arrived with their drinks and took great pains to rearrange the table setting, placing utensils and condiments in a row along the room-side edge like a barrier between them and the rest of the guests. He fiddled with the laminated menu, propping it upright, then sideways and finally on the window ledge. At her quizzical look, he used his hands to demonstrate. "This is my office. The menu is my shingle and our toast, 'the counselor is in.' This is your last chance to avail yourself of my services." He clinked her small glass and leaned back in his chair with uncharacteristic ease and a relaxed smile. "So tell me, Kirin O'Connell. What burning questions are still unanswered?"

She bristled. "I'm *Ms.* Kiri *Koyle* now. Remember that! Kirin O'Connell does not exist. Her past cannot be documented. She has no professional record. She has nothing in common with anyone around her. Her best friends—even her brother—moved on with their lives. She has no one to carry on her name. She cannot share her narrative with any new acquaintance. Like so many others damaged by severe mental trauma, there *is* no social class for people like Kirin O'Connell!" She tilted her head back and downed her sampler in one gulp.

Henry sobered up fast enough to catch her glass as it flew across the table. "I'm sorry. I didn't realize I'd hit a sore spot."

"No. I'm sorry. I didn't realize I was bubbling up inside. You just popped the cork. I'm glad you're here, Henry. No other soul in this room could understand a word I just said." She took a deep breath, dropped her head into her hands and shook it. "Why, Henry? I don't understand why?"

He tried to console her. "The pain of loss never really goes away. I expect you'll experience outbursts like this frequently and shouldn't apologize when you do—especially to me." He handed her a napkin.

She dabbed her eyes. "I don't understand why Michael had to die and not me. If anyone were sitting here enjoying a drink with you, it should be he. He was a good man and had so much yet to contribute. As I stated emphatically earlier, I'm no one without him. Why didn't *I* die instead?" She looked at Henry, pleading for an answer.

He took both her hands. "There is no logical explanation, Kiri. You know that, but you will not accept it yet. For analytical types such as we are, we want some proof that there was not an alternative—that your death couldn't substitute for his. After all, a body is a body. Right?"

She nodded and removed one hand to dab at her eyes again, then let it find its way back to his.

"So, supposing we look at your situation systematically... pit you against Michael on paper... compare your skills and attributes to see if you possess any critical quality Michael did not. Michael was a stronger swimmer; you, a biker. He had a lightening sprint; you, greater endurance over distance. Both of you were crack shots. When Michael envisioned a grand scheme, you fleshed out the flaws. Both of your minds fed on puzzles and problem solving. You adapted Michael's lofty goal to 'make a difference in the world' into a plan to rebuild a small corner of it by helping your neighbors help themselves. Both of you had beautiful eyes and good teeth. I would hand you the win on hair alone, but I'm still getting used to your new look."

Kiri's eyelids fell as a bashful smile crept across her face

"So, on balance you contributed equally to this sphere we inhabit. When it comes to equipment, however, you are uniquely qualified to fulfill an essential survival task."

She stared at him, not grasping his meaning.

"Other than to spend the rest of his life with you, what did Michael want more than anything else in this world... something only you could give him?"

Her eyes grew wide and she tried to pull her hands from his, but he gripped them firmly.

"Hear me out. You have days, months, years ahead of you to live... whether you choose to or not. You can find fulfillment doing something that makes a difference, or you can waste your unique gifts. If you seek a profession that won't tie you down, your skills are in demand all over the globe. Pick your location and any NGO or relief agency. If it's a business you want, find a piece of ground and build it. You have the means, and Michael would be the last one to hold you back from following the tattered remains of that dream. If it's a house full of children you want, go after it! But look around you carefully. There's not a man here worthy of you... or one that you could tolerate in your home for longer than it takes to make a baby... and never a baby called O'Connell!"

Kiri jumped up, jerked away from him and stormed to the rest room. Henry did not follow. He wiped a hand across his face, shook his head and ordered another pint. With each swallow, he cursed himself. He pushed her too hard. She was not ready.

He stood at the window gazing out at the vast and varied landscape and kept one eye on the car. He did not want Kiri to run away from him again. He toyed with the idea of taking a cab to her house and then the airport, but he could not get in to retrieve his passport. Besides, that would make him the runner.

Henry prepared for this conversation. He studied the video of Michael's last minutes until he could repeat every word and vouch for his friend's intent, but Kiri refused to entertain that option. The guys would hang him by his heels for botching the opportunity to persuade her to return. In simple terms, he blew it and would never have another chance to play that card... even if Kiri did speak to him again with less than fury.

No live music played on a Sunday evening at the brewery, so guests plunked quarters into an old fashioned jukebox converted to play CD's. Henry could not remember a time he hung around a pub listening to music like this. Must be an American thing. A lively "Achy Breaky Heart" gave way to a softer number—one he remembered from his youth—and he hummed with it. *I... can't... help... falling....* He felt a tap on his shoulder and shifted out of the way.

"Dance with me, Henry?" Kiri took his hand to coax him onto the floor.

He followed reluctantly. "I'm so sorry. I didn't mean to..."

"Don't apologize for the truth. Someone needs to tell me when I behave like an adolescent. Now, please? As I remember, you move very well on a ballroom floor." She tugged and this time he followed her willingly.

He twirled her into his arms and held her close. "I do owe you the end of a dance, don't I." He smiled down at her and welcomed her melt into his chest.

She felt comfortable there, close to a man who cared for her. "I wish you were my therapist, Henry. You make a very good one."

He rested his chin on the top of her head. "My pleasure. Anytime. If you don't mind the flight over the water, that is. Rather a long distance to come for a simple office visit."

*   *   *

"You're in T-shirt and shorts paddling a canoe. I don't believe it!" Doyle said as he studied the proof of life on Henry's phone. Polo shirt and khakis were the most casual dress their boss ever wore, even when training.

"I had no choice. Kiri locked up my suit until it was time to leave for the airport." Henry smiled, recalling the laid-back few days he spent in Colorado.

"You look like you're on a bloody holiday, not a mission!" Gus passed the smartphone along to Frank, then ordered another round of pints for the small group gathered at Ryan's Pub.

"Both of you look mighty fine in that craft, but I'd like to hear the outcome... of the mission, I mean." Frank handed off to Devin.

"Kiri appears healthier... full cheeks, but her eyes are still lost. What's the verdict? Good news or bad?"

Henry squirmed in his seat and put his phone away. "Short answer? A little of both. She knows we're watching. I threatened to force her into a doctor's care if we learn of any further risky behavior. We analyzed the triggers and brainstormed techniques to avoid them, so that's a positive. She released a lot of anger... especially at me for interfering, so that's a negative. Hearing that Patrick is permanently out of the picture gave her great relief, but I'm not sure that's enough to bring her home."

"Tell us more. No holding back. We want every detail." Gus placed his brawny forearms on the table and leaned toward Henry, staring at his boss earnestly.

Henry pushed himself away from the table and crossed his arms. "Sorry, guys. I'm not going to do that. Not now." They stared wide-eyed at his refusal. "You leave in a couple of days. Your minds must be spot on your job. If any of you are the least bit distracted, you will jeopardize the safety of all. Kirin O'Connell does not exist for you until you return."

Gus started to protest, but Henry stopped him. "If harm should come to any of you, Kiri will assume it's her fault. She cannot carry any more guilt, and she won't survive another loss." He leaned back and steepled his fingers. "I will make two concessions. While you are gone, I will prepare a detailed report of our every conversation and have a copy ready for each of you on your return. Secondly, if I should hear anything *positive* from Kiri, I will communicate that to you." Henry emptied his pint in unison with the guys. "Be safe. And watch out for each other."

*　　*　　*

A month passed without a word from Kiri. The guys were of one mind and one voice when they returned from their mission, but Henry disappointed them. "Nothing yet." They met in the network's office building—their old haunt on the lower level. "With Patrick gone, we don't have to meet secretly anymore, so we'll use this space for both our official and unofficial duties... unless you have a better idea."

"I liked meeting at Kiri's," Doyle said. The others nodded in agreement.

"Not an option," Henry replied as he snapped an impromptu proof of life. "Now, let's get to business. Word came down from the top that your recent mission was your last... to Syria, that is. The situation there is too dicey—the use of chemical weapons and the kidnap of a Red Cross van carrying medics and supplies near the northern border. We have until after the holidays to come up with plans to do what you do without crossing the border. Here is an outline of basic services any scheme should support. Each of you take one, put your heads together and make some recommendations."

The guys did not turn one page. "You said you would prepare a report on Kiri while we were gone," Frank reminded his supervisor. The others nodded again.

Henry threw a pile of thick files—one for each—onto the table, pretending nonchalance. "In your spare time, flip through these for any insight on how we might welcome Kiri if she does come back."

To a man, they placed the fat files on top and left. "Later, boss. Work to do."

*　　*　　*

A week later, the men assembled again. "Nothing yet," Henry said. "I hear you have a plan."

"We do. Several, in fact," Devin said and began to enumerate.

"I don't hear one mention of Syria."

"We'll work on that later," Frank said. "For the moment, we have five options for Kiri's return. Plan A: Holding Pattern—everything we can do outside, since we don't have access inside the garage or house. We'll work over there on Saturdays. Plan B: No warning—we discover her home and have to weasel our way in to clean up a bit. Plan C: Little warning—a call that she is in the air, so we'll meet her on the doorstep. Plan D: Adequate warning—two or more days, giving us time to collect our gear before she arrives. Plan E: Great Expectations—the best of all worlds. She gives us a couple of weeks' warning, wants to have a party, and sends us a key!"

Henry shot them a skeptical glance. "How did you come up with these harebrained schemes?"

"They just popped into our heads like ..." Doyle said.

Their serious boss grinned and shook his head. "Now, about Syria..."

*   *   *

Henry looked over a list of suggestions for operating outside of Syria or any other Middle Eastern or African country that prohibited journalists from entering. The men submitted their ideas a few days after they settled the Kiri question. When his phone rang, he answered without checking the caller. "Callaghan here."

"If your offer to give me a lift from the airport is still open, I arrive Sunday at two."

He smiled at hearing the familiar voice. "I'll be waiting."

"I need to schedule an office visit with my therapist. Can that be arranged for Wednesday or Thursday?"

"I'm sure."

"Don't tell Mom and Thomas. I need a few days to myself."

"Understood. Anxious to see you."

"Thanks, Henry."

The instant the call ended, he texted the guys who were spread throughout the city. *Shift from Plan A to Plan D. Sunday at 2. Mission accomplished!*

Chapter 20

Henry pulled into the drive at Quincy Street. He watched Kiri scrutinize her home and the area surrounding it for anything out of place or unexpected. With a deep sigh, she opened the car door and stepped out. "Are you okay?" he asked.

"I will be. Give me a minute to disarm the security system. I'll come through the house to let you in." She smiled softly. "Don't peek."

"Promise," Henry chuckled and watched her disappear through the gate to the back garden.

Within minutes she heard the heavy bars release to let her in. She walked through the kitchen and noticed what a mess she left—a result of her hurried departure; the living room, likewise. She started upstairs to survey the damage but imagined it a worse disaster than the kitchen. So much for a clean canvas and a fresh start, she thought—the first snag in an otherwise perfect plan for her evening's agenda. She briefly considered rushing to the garage, jumping in her car and speeding back to the airport for a quick getaway to Colorado, but her car probably would not run after sitting for almost a year.

Face your demons, Kiri. That's what you came here to do. Better release Henry from his chauffeur's duties first. She inhaled deeply and opened the front door.

A crowd of manly men pushed its way in. Gus was first to scoop her up. He tousled her thick brown hair just beginning to wave on the ends, then tilted her chin upward and smiled. "You're the prettiest little thing I've seen in months," he said, giving her a wet smooch on the cheek.

Doyle hugged her tightly. "You've finally got some meat on you. Very becoming."

"I've missed my favorite chess opponent," Devin said and put his arm around her shoulders to steer her toward the kitchen door while Frank deftly picked up the set of keys she dropped onto the console table by habit and slipped them into his pocket. Henry brought up the rear.

"We don't mean to stay long, just time enough for a quick drink and a welcome," Gus assured her. "You make yourself comfortable under this tree while we unload the car and pour a few." Henry faced her chair away from the house and pulled one up for himself nearby. Gus disappeared, purportedly to find those drinks, and Devin followed. Frank and Doyle veered toward the garage and hoisted a thumbs up when they were able to unlock it.

Henry engaged Kiri in conversation, keeping her focus on the perimeter garden. "I'm surprised at how well-tended it is," Kiri said.

"Thomas and Paula come every week or so to work on it, he tells me. He calls often to ask if I've heard from you. So far, I haven't had to bend the truth."

Devin came with two bottles and a small glass. After a few minutes, Gus replaced him. Kiri was vaguely aware of the sounds of motors, but dismissed them as passing traffic. Frank gave a wink as he sat and Gus left. Doyle took his turn with a nod and a smile. Henry suggested Kiri give him a tour around the yard of the property next door where she might someday build her business. He led her through a gate she did not remember being there. Michael built it before they left for Syria, she decided. None of the other men followed.

Paddy watched the curious goings on through his binoculars from his house across the road. He described every movement to his Maureen. Seated beside him near the window with her head lolling to the side and her jaw slack, she did not share his excitement. For the past two days, the same cars and group of men came to work at Kiri's house. They climbed ladders to wash windows outside, trimmed bushes, and cleaned the walks and the yard at the house next door.

That solemn friend, Mr. Callaghan, came across the road to tell him Kiri was expected back soon. "Please don't bother her for at least a week," the man said. "Spread the word to the other neighbors. She still needs time to herself. Can I count on you?"

Paddy nodded enthusiastically. "I won't let a soul near the place. My Maureen and I are happy to keep watch." Watch he did, surprised that this day all the activity took place inside where he could only grasp snatches of the bustle to report to the neighbors.

Totally unaware of how much time elapsed, Kiri chatted with Henry about the plans she and Michael had for the yard and vacant house as they sat on its back stoop. She paced out the pool area, amazed at how trim the yard looked after nearly a year of neglect. She asked Henry's advice on placement of the water system's controls. He questioned parking space, and the two peered over the back fence to see if moving it forward would provide adequate area with access from the alleyway behind. Next thing Kiri knew, the other four men joined them, bottles in hand, and gave their opinions freely.

Gus suggested they go for another round of drinks, but Frank cut him short. "We think we have all your bags in the right rooms, but there is a large, skinny carton we're not sure about. Come tell us where you want it." On entering the house, the men blocked her view to the kitchen and ushered her to the fireplace in the living room. "That looks to be a four-hand job we'd like to help you with before we leave. Maybe even a six-hander. What are you hiding in there... a metal shield?" he joked.

"Of sorts." She glanced at Henry who nodded back and smiled. "Open it, if you like, but gently, please."

Gus and Doyle pried the front panel off and watched it fall to the floor revealing a framed 24" by 30" portrait of Michael from the waist up, his muscular physique evident through the tight T-shirt in a light shade of green that blended with the other tones in the room. His powerful arms crossed his chest as if daring anyone to trespass against those under his roof. A two-fingers-length haircut surrounded his square face with one copper curl left to bounce above his right eye. He smiled out from his typical half-grin, also to the right—the one that, when coupled with a crafty gleam in his deep-set blue eyes, conveyed his ability to outsmart any opponent. Clusters of bright colors encircled the confident figure.

"The artist captured his look exactly. Whose fine work is this?" Frank asked.

Kiri's timid voice replied, "My therapist suggested I try adding color and familiarity to my life."

"Well, you've sure done it!" Gus squeezed her. "Once we hang this painting above the fireplace there will be no question that Michael O'Connell is master of this house and that, true to his saint, he will protect the souls of all those dear to him who reside within its walls. You need never feel afraid... or abandoned... again. His spirit dances among us even now." He twirled her with an awkward two-step to the jeers of the others.

"Why don't you run upstairs and make sure we haven't misplaced any of your bags," Devin said.

Even before she reached the landing, she heard mutterings of "left... no, right... left corner up a dash," and pounding on the wall. She scanned the sitting room and noticed her laptop set up and running on her desk beneath the north window, the papers surrounding it neatly organized. The lemony scent of fresh furniture polish filled the air all the way to the doorway of the bathroom that glistened from a recent scrubbing. The thrum of the dryer in the utility room below indicated the whereabouts of missing piles of towels she knew littered the floor before she departed.

All the windows there and in the bedroom opened wide to the kelly green sights, sounds and smells of the familiar setting. Gone were the heaps of clothes she left on the window seats, now neatly arranged in the closet. Crisp corners of the wildflower spread drew her focus to the bed and two peculiar objects lying on its pillows: a black feather and the delicate Celtic Circle. She shook off an uneasy feeling. With so many wide-open windows, an entire flock of birds could have flown through, she reasoned. She thought she locked the delicate ornament in the safe, but she might have left it on her bedside table. It could have dropped to the floor where one of the guys found it while cleaning and set it on the bed. Do not read a double meaning into everything you see, she reminded herself.

She chuckled at the image of three grown men drawing straws to determine who would dust, hoover the floors, and scour the bathroom fixtures. Devin, no doubt, set up her computer. How loyal and caring they were to provide her with a clean canvas... a fresh start. She tripped lightly down the stairs to thank them for just that but found the living room empty of male bodies. Thinking they must be under the tree enjoying their second pints, she peered out the back but saw not a person. She ran to the front but found not a car. The whole lot of them disappeared without a word, even

Henry. She laughed out loud when she finally grasped their intent. They were Michael's team—the quiet and on the sly guys—on a mission: steal in, get a job done, and leave without a trace. Their leader taught them well.

Kiri returned to the living area and noticed her keys, along with one for each car, lined up on the console table on top of a note with the name and phone number of Michael's construction crew. She did not need to fear that her cars would not run; she trusted they would. She looked in on the kitchen and found the table set for one and a meal ready to heat and eat. She chuckled again, admitting that those guys would make wonderful husbands… someday.

Michael's eyes followed every step she took through the living area. His sparkle and grin defied her to feel unhappy now that she was home… that they both were home again. She flopped onto the sofa and stared at his portrait, unwilling to admit that some outside force guided the paintbrush in her hand and the resolve in her heart to return.

"Here we are, Michael, you and I. Not quite as we imagined a year ago, but I am determined to do my best to fulfill my promises. You know I can't do this alone, so I expect a sign now and then that I'm on the right track. You owe me that if I'm doing all the grunt work!" She stood up abruptly and headed for the kitchen. "Stop staring at me!" she shot over her shoulder.

*   *   *

"Tonight—our fourth anniversary," she said as she pushed food around her plate. "I must eat so I won't wake up hungry in the night." She tried again and finished all but the first bite, then shoved the plate aside and picked up tacks, hammer and the framed photo Henry gave her of Michael's last breath. She carried them to the rogue's gallery of reality on the merlot wall in the living room and relocated some of the pictures.

The one on the bottom titled "Forever" of the scruffy couple in the photo booth on their secret wedding day found a new spot beside them as prince and princess dressed for the Ball under the heading "For Better." "For Worse" remained the same—desert photos of their agonizing experience in Yemen. She toyed with placing Syria's tragic night next to them but the title did not tell the whole story. Their Dublin home—absent Michael's physical presence but filled with riffles of his soul—remained her sanctuary. She placed the photo of their last living moment together—the moment filled with her promises to him—under the heading "Forever."

That task completed, she went to the pantry for their ceremonial vessels and water. The piece of Irish linen was in tatters now—she made the bag for his grave soil from it—so she left the remnants behind. She gathered all the items onto a tray, added pencil, paper, matches and a knife hidden near the back door, and hunted for their double sleeping bag.

She carried it out to their tree Aurora and remembered the exuberance of their last anniversary night. How different this one—and every one after—would be. She sighed and rolled the bag out beneath the limbless spot to cushion her against the cold ground. Lying in its large, empty space would make her loneliness unbearable, so she folded it in half. She returned to the house for the tray, set it beside her bag, and sat cross-legged on top.

"I have no idea how to conduct a one-sided ceremony but here goes," she announced to the branches and the birds nestled in them. "I missed giving my pledge this morning, so I'll do it now." She scribbled *I'll do my best* onto the strip of paper, lit it and watched the smoke curl its way to the top of the tree and beyond. She poured a small amount of their respective waters into each small vessel and began to recite their vows, *...my love... first bite of meat... sip from my cup... cry your name... honor you...* pouring alternately from each cup into the glass bowl. When she reached the line, *our love is never-ending like a Celtic Circle*, the phrase took on added significance for her, as did the ornament she left upstairs on the bed. Did Michael have some premonition of the fate that awaited them?

She ran her fingers around the rim of the bowl, swallowed four sips of their mixed waters, and sprinkled the rest around the base of the tree. She pleaded with Michael to send a sign. "Anything. Please. The night song of a blackbird. A breeze that suddenly swirls around my shoulders, then dissipates as quickly as it came. The voice of a fairy whispering in my ear. Please, Michael." She watched and listened until the sky turned midnight black. Disheartened when no sign appeared, she snuggled deep into her bag and cried herself to sleep.

Bone-chilling cold awakened her sometime in the night. She shivered until she could not stand it any longer and ran for the house. She stopped in the kitchen just long enough to pop a cup of tea in the microwave and noticed that her dinner plate was clean. Michael! was her first thought. Mice! soon followed. One more obstacle to overcome.

Still shivering, she climbed the stairs to the bedroom and cursed herself for not dressing warmly now that she had no man to snuggle against. She pulled a pair of Michael's sweats from a drawer and yanked them tight around her waist. She looked for his hoodie and realized that she forgot to take it to Colorado. She searched frantically around the bed, hoping the guys did not find it and throw it in the laundry to suds away Michael's scent. Her fingers finally found the familiar top lodged between the mattress and headboard on his side. When she jerked the sweatshirt free, her elbow knocked against his bedside table, toppling everything to the floor.

She nestled into the hoodie, then bent to clean up the mess. The last item she picked up was Michael's Bible—the one he kept in his drawer— the drawer that was still closed. The cherished book fell open in her hand to Job 39: 12: *...(the unicorn) will bring home thy seed, and gather it into thy barn.* Coincidence, probably, but she took it for a long-awaited sign that he *was* lingering near. Her eyes darted around the room hoping to find him, but instead they found the Celtic Circle she left there earlier. She fingered it and found the nub of a new whorl near her vertex. A message? She slipped the disk into the hoodie's pocket to hold in the night. Signs or not, she felt better now and returned to her nest under the tree with a hot cup of tea in her hand, encouraged… inspired… for the arduous pilgrimage ahead.

*   *   *

Sounds of voices and footsteps near the gate woke her. Kiri slithered deep into her bag and pulled it tightly over her head leaving a tiny crack to spy on the intruders. She gripped the knife, ready to defend herself if they came near. Then she recognized the voices.

"The sun is up as are we, but it is freezing out here. I don't understand why we have to tend your garden at such an early hour. The hose will spurt nothing but icicles."

"Stop your complaining, Thomas, and drag it over here. This patch of mums needs a drink, and I'd like to dig some carrots for soup. I'm filled with nervous energy this morning and should put it to good use. You can nap later."

Kiri watched her mother bend to attack some weeds while she waited for Thomas to turn on the hose. They were her only clue, now, to what old age might have been with Michael. Thomas had to keep busy—to do something toward resolution. Paula was calm and centered as she tried to reason with him while cutting back spent blooms which did not need trimming yet and gathering the end of the season's produce she nursed through the summer on her own.

Even though they were only sixty-eight and seventy, they looked as if they aged ten years in the last one. Grief took its toll on them. Thomas shuffled with a slight stoop, and the little hair left on the top of his head was stark white as was the fringe from ear to ear. His face was lined and jowly. Kiri was afraid to witness a similar change in her mother, so she slunk deeper into her bag.

Thomas noticed the movement and turned the hose on her, shouting, "Vagrant! Get out of here! I'll teach you to lie your despicable body down in my son's garden. Get out before I call the Guarda!" He aimed the cold stream of water directly at the bag until a sopping figure emerged.

"Thomas! It's Kirin… Kirin O'Connell. I've come home!"

She smiled and flung her arms around the shocked patriarch, causing both of them to topple into a soggy pile beneath the evergreen tree. Water from the hose shot up through its branches to the height of a blackbird perched near the top and rained down on the Celtic Circle glistening in a puddle at the foot of their Christmas tree Aurora.

Chapter 21

Depending on one's point of view, Michael Thomas O'Connell began life fifteen months after his father's violent death in Syria. The little baby inhaled his first breath nine months later, right on schedule, the day after his mother and father would have celebrated their fifth secret wedding anniversary with pledges to one another. His mother Kirin finally fulfilled hers—made shortly before their fated mission together two years earlier—to bear her husband Michael's children.

Kirin Aurora O'Connell, independent woman of thirty-six years, a widow for two of them and a mother for a day, gazed up through the branches of her tribal evergreen tree. From her vantage point on the grass beneath it, she marveled at how readily she and her tree adapted to the new course their lives had taken, both of them badly scarred but producing new growth. With a baby in her arms, a burgeoning counseling practice and her aquacenter in constant use, she knew she should feel blessed, but...

After a year of emotional whiplash, she returned to Dublin and defied convention to incubate the child she promised Michael—a child Thomas vehemently opposed from the moment he learned of its conception. Strict doctrinal interpretation demanded it. She struggled to convince him to welcome his son's child. Her commitment to Michael demanded it.

She thought she had her head on straight. She thought that all the puzzle pieces—fairy whispers, feathers, and the Celtic Circle—fell into place and that she understood Michael's intent. But when she delivered a son instead of the daughter he predicted, only two possibilities seemed plausible—either her mind played tricks on her or Michael did.

If she based her decision to create Michael's vision of a future on figments of her imagination fed by deep longing or coincidence, she was a fool. If his puppeting her life were real, he showed his hand by sending her a son to carry on the family name—family first—and she was merely the vessel to fulfill Thomas' and his fondest wish. Either way she could not rescind that decision.

Dripping with love for the innocent babe at her breast, she faced the uneasy truth. "We're in this together, little pea pod," she said. "You and I are alone. No father. No family. No options. I give you my pledge. I'll do my best... to raise you as Michael wanted."

Kiri studied the branches above her. Instead of choices, each one now bore a question. She cuddled the decision that could not be undone and wondered, when is a promise fulfilled? What is the life span of a commitment? How long is forever?

A tiny black feather tinted with iridescent blue fluttered on a breeze and came to rest on the infant shoulder of Michael Thomas O'Connell.

AUTHOR SHERRY SCHUBERT, named 2012 Writer of the Year by Idaho Writer's League, is a graduate of the University of California at Berkeley, Class of 1967. Subsequently, she spent two years hitchhiking abroad, gathering grist for stories and a packful of dreams. "Life" called her back to her home state of Idaho where she raised a family and taught teenagers to solve quadratic equations.

Ms. Schubert's yen to write fiction during retirement is precipitated by her daughter's observation, "I have no idea who you were before you were Mom." The author specializes in fiction appealing to contemporary women from Baby Boomers to Thirty-Somethings.

Puffin Island relates how the historical events and social issues of the Sixties shaped the author and still reverberate in her children's lives today. ***Celtic Compass, Part 1,*** applies her experience in a "blended family" of the Sixties—before that term was coined—to present-day realities. ***Celtic Compass, Part II***, explores the challenge of divided loyalties faced by members of a blended family in a time of crisis. ***Celtic Circle~for Better, for Worse*** examines how antagonistic members of a blended family channel their bitterness and grief.

In addition to her four novels, Ms. Schubert is a contributing author to the short story anthology, *Hauntings from the Snake River Plain*. All of her works are available as ebooks or paperbacks from Amazon.

Sherry continues to live and write on the family farm. For the record, she did shake the hand of President Kennedy, and she did play the guitar… badly.

Made in the USA
Charleston, SC
06 March 2014